The Assassin's Daughter

The Assassin's Daughter

An Akitada Novel

I. J. Parker

I · J · P
2015

Published 2015 by I.J.Parker and I-J-P Books
428 Cedar Lane, Virginia Beach VA 23452
http://www.ijparker.com
Cover design by I. J. Parker.
Cover image by Mizuno Toshikata
Back cover image: Hiroshige
Publisher's Note: This is a work of fiction. Names, characters, places, and incidents are a product of the author's imagination.

The Assassin's Daughter , 1ᵉ edition, 2015
ISBN-13:978-1514635599

Praise for I. J. Parker and the Akitada Series

"Elegant and entertaining . . . Parker has created a wonderful protagonist in Akitada. She puts us at ease in a Japan of one thousand years ago." *The Boston Globe*

"You couldn't ask for a more gracious introduction to the exotic world of Imperial Japan than the stately historical novels of I. J. Parker." *The New York Times*

"Akitada is as rich a character as Robert Van Gulik's intriguing detective, Judge Dee." *The Dallas Morning News*

"Readers will be enchanted by Akitada." *Publishers Weekly* Starred Review

"Terrifically imaginative" The *Wall Street Journal*

"A brisk and well-plotted mystery with a cast of regulars who become more fully developed with every episode." *Kirkus*

"More than just a mystery novel, (*THE CONVICT'S SWORD*) is a superb piece of literature set against the backdrop of 11th-century Kyoto." *The Japan Times*

"Parker's research is extensive and she makes great use of the complex manners and relationships of feudal Japan." *Globe and Mail*

"The fast-moving, surprising plot and colorful writing will enthrall even those unfamiliar with the exotic setting." *Publishers Weekly, Starred* Review

". . . the author possesses both intimate knowledge of the time period and a fertile imagination as well. Combine that with an intriguing mystery and a fast-moving plot, and you've got a historical crime novel that anyone can love." *Chicago Sun-Times*

"Parker's series deserves a wide readership." *Historical Novel Society*

"The historical research is impressive, the prose crisp, and Parker's ability to universalize the human condition makes for a satisfying tale." *Booklist*

"Parker masterfully blends action and detection while making the attitudes and customs of the period accessible." *Publishers Weekly* (starred review)

"Readers looking for historical mystery with a twist will find what they're after in Parker's latest Sugawara Akitada mystery . . . An intriguing glimpse into an ancient culture." *Booklist*

Characters

(Japanese family names precede proper names)

Sugawara Akitada - Governor of Mikawa
Yukiko - his wife
Fujiwara Kosehira - her father
Hatsuko - her mother
Arihito - her brother
Akiko - Akitada's sister
Kobe - Superintendent of Police
Genba - Akitada's retainer

The Case of the Assassin:

Prince Atsutada - the victim
Tanaka Tenji - his betto; the assassin
Mrs. Tanaka – Tanaka's wife
Masako - his daughter
Minamoto Yukihiro - Prince Atsutada's heir
Lady Otomo - an old matriarch
Maruko - the prince's housekeeper
Hideyo - her son
Yoshito - the prince's servant

I. J. Parker

The Case of the Merchant:

Nakai - wealthy silk merchant
Mrs. Nakai - his wife
Ujinobu - his assistant
Ichiro - the shop boy
Ingen - a monk physician
a pharmacist

1

The Swallows

Akitada looked up from his own mail at the wail of shock and pain in his wife's voice. She was chewing her pretty lower lip as she ran her eyes over the letter in her hand.

"What's the matter?" he asked.

"Oh, Akitada! I can't imagine how this could have happened. Oh . . . my father . . ." She choked. There were tears in her eyes.

Akitada felt his heart lurch. Something had happened to Kosehira. Had he died? Surely Kosehira was too young to die. They were about the same age. Kosehira was like a brother to Akitada—though now he was also his father-in-law, but that was another story. "Your father? Is he ill?"

"No, not ill. Though I think he must have gone mad. Oh, Akitada, he has quarreled with Arihito and will disinherit him. And Arihito's gone, no one knows where."

Well, it could not be very bad then. Akitada frowned. "Let me see the letter."

She handed it over obediently. It was from her mother, and Akitada had some trouble making out the feminine hand of Lady Hatsuko, all squiggly lines and trailing tails. She was mother to both Yukiko and the missing Arihito and Kosehira's principal wife. What he read did not make much more sense than what Yukiko had told him. Arihito, their oldest and the heir, had done something that had angered Kosehira to the point of telling him he would not inherit the considerable wealth his father controlled. Apparently Arihito had shouted back that his father could keep it and left the house. He had not returned for more than a week now, and nobody knew where he was. Yukiko's mother feared that he was distraught and might end his life.

Akitada returned the letter. "What could your brother have done to anger your father like this?"

"I don't know. It isn't like him. It isn't like father either. Something awful must have happened."

There was a hint of a wail there, and now Yukiko's tears overflowed. She flung herself into her husband's arms, scattering the papers he had been perusing. "Oh, Akitada, we must do something. We must find him. What if he does himself some harm?"

She was lovely even when in tears and her lips were moist and rosy. Akitada ignored the scattered official mail, now being crumpled under Yukiko's slender body and set about consoling her with a kiss. Her lips were soft and pliant, and deliciously both sweet and salty. His kiss led to another and his hand crept inside her gown while his other arm pulled her closer.

Alas, she pushed him away. "No," she cried, "I cannot make love when I'm thinking about Arihito lying dead somewhere. Or even just sick. Where would he go? He has no one."

Akitada cleared his throat and tried to banish the sudden heat desire had produced. "Nonsense," he said. "Arihito is a grown man. And he has plenty of money and friends. He's probably staying with one of them, hoping that his parents will worry and relent. Judging by the reactions, that's most likely. Your father will come round and forgive him, having been properly scared."

She jumped up, her cheeks rosy, though not with lust. Yukiko was angry. "In other words," she cried, "you will do nothing. Just as always! You never do anything. It's always your cursed work that is more important. Well, Akitada, I don't care anymore. My brother's in trouble and I shall go to him. I shall go alone if you cannot be bothered." She stamped her foot and ran inside, gowns fluttering.

They had been sitting in the sun on the veranda of Yukiko's pavilion. Her outburst had disturbed the pair of swallows that were nesting in the eaves. They were raising their young and had been greeted as an auspicious sign for the domestic happiness of the human inhabitants. Now both parents were outside the nest, fluttering and chirping in a panic.

3

That also might be an omen, Akitada thought glumly, shocked by his wife's words.

They had been in Mikawa for nearly three years now. Akitada was serving a four-year term as provincial governor. It had been a plum assignment: a peaceful province not too far from the capital and with a very good income. He owed the post to his marriage to Yukiko, eldest daughter of his best friend Fujiwara Kosehira, a man closely related to the chancellor and several ministers, not to mention one or two empresses.

But Yukiko, still only twenty-one years to his own forty-three, his pretty, lively, affectionate wife had become increasingly restive. She was bored. In the capital, she had had the company of his sister Akiko. The two of them had passed their days visiting. Here, Yukiko only had the children and her husband to converse with.

And apparently her husband was, in her eyes, a dry old stick who thought of nothing but his work.

The swallows settled down. Akitada gathered his rumpled papers and smoothed them out. Then he got up and walked through the garden to his study. There he laid his unread mail on the desk and went outside again to think about his problem.

He stopped next to his *koi* pond, installed by Yukiko as a surprise while he was away on the Ise assignment. The storm that devastated much of the Mikawa and Ise coasts had also ruined the pond, but that, along with other, greater damages, had long since been mended. It was a pretty pond, larger than the one at his own home in the capital, but then everything done by a

4

Fujiwara was larger than anything he or his family could ever have achieved.

He suppressed this twinge of bitterness quickly. Kosehira had always treated him as his friend and was closer to him than to any of the highly-placed men he associated with. And Yukiko loved him. Or at least she had loved him until now. The *koi* pond was an example of her affection.

He suddenly felt guilty for walking away from her when she was clearly distraught. She had no one here with whom she might take refuge in her tears and find comfort. She had a right to have him by her side now.

But then he remembered how she had repulsed him. And persistence on his part would surely have made things worse. It was hard to know what was expected of him.

He started pacing.

Those swallows. Raising a family under her eaves.

Yukiko had miscarried this past winter and had been as grief-stricken as if she had lost a living child. Akitada was guiltily aware that he had been relieved. He did not really desire more children. His two were enough for him. And he would never shed the fear of losing another wife to childbirth.

The gods knew he could handle the complicated and dangerous cases that fate had thrown at him, but he could not handle this relationship. Honesty suggested that he had also had grave problems with Tamako, his first wife, and she had been far more mature and self-possessed than Yukiko. He sighed and went to sit on the veranda steps. It had to be admitted, he was not cut out to be a husband.

Hanae, Tora's wife, interrupted him in his brooding thoughts. She called from the study, "Sir? Are you here?"

"I'm in the garden, Hanae."

She came to the veranda, and stood there, arms akimbo. Her posture was almost comical in someone so deceptively fragile and small, someone so pretty and graceful.

"Sir, your lady is packing. And she is crying. What have you done to her?"

Akitada stood up. "Nothing. She had a letter from her mother. Something about her brother having run away."

Hanae cocked her head. "No, sir. Her heart is broken. Only her husband could cause such grief. You'd best go to her."

He wanted to say, "Nonsense! Hearts aren't broken so easily." He wanted to blame this on a childish temper tantrum, or on the mysterious mood swings often exhibited by females, but in the end he thought of her being alone in her grief and walked back to his wife's pavilion.

She was in the middle of the room, kneeling before an open trunk. Gowns and skirts and undergarments lay all about her. She had stopped crying but gave a soft hiccup now and then as she rummaged among the clothes.

He turned and found Hanae on his heels, shook his head at her, and closed the door in her face.

Yukiko started up. "You! Go away! I never want to see you again. I divorce you."

"My love," he said reasonably, "you don't want to divorce me. Wives don't divorce their husbands."

"That is completely unfair." She hiccupped.

"Yes, I suppose it is." It occurred to him that it was not so unreasonable, as the present example seemed to prove. "Yukiko, I've come back to apologize."

She looked at him uncertainly. "You have? What do you mean?"

"I was wrong. You want to go see your family. I have no right to keep you from them."

"It's been almost three years." Another hiccup.

"Yes. It was very wrong of me not to think of that. And now you are worried about them."

She looked at him. "I can go?"

"We'll go together."

He saw hope light up her face, but she was not convinced yet. "How can you leave here? Won't you be blamed?"

"I will take care of some business with the central government. You can visit your parents and find out what is going on, and I'll have a look at our house and see how Genba has been handling things. Tora and Saburo can stay here and see to things." This last was perhaps the most worrisome aspect of the plan. Both of them had proved that they could get into all sorts of trouble in his absence.

Yukiko gave a cry of joy and flew into his arms. "Oh, I love you, Akitada. Please do not divorce me. No matter how angry you are."

7

2

An Unsuitable Match

The journey to the capital was unexpectedly enjoyable. Akitada, who had been feeling alternately put-upon and excessively forbearing for agreeing to his young wife's demands, had foreseen problems. Since he had to leave Tora and Saburo to look after the daily routine in the Mikawa tribunal and Hanae and the maids to look after the children, he and Yukiko traveled with only one armed servant and a pack horse.

But the weather was excellent, the roads were dry, the fields newly green with growing rice, the mountains blue in the distance, and Yukiko was a fine horsewoman and good company. Now that he had agreed to go and settle the family argument, she had readily admitted that perhaps Arihito was not homeless and starving somewhere after all. She enjoyed traveling with him in a way that surprised him. His first wife, Tamako, though also a good horsewoman, had never greeted every new day with such enthusiastic and energetic glee. Yukiko was convinced that it would bring ever more exciting sights and adventures. It made him realize how miserably bored she had been in Mikawa.

And so he felt guilty again, and also old. He had lost this relish for life and its surprises.

They reached the capital after dark. Being tired, they merely greeted Genba and his family. Mrs. Kuruda, Saburo's mother, a short, round, and meddlesome woman, immediately accused Akitada of preventing her son from visiting her.

This was particularly unfair since Akitada had urged such visits frequently. Saburo, secretary of the tribunal, had very capable clerks and an assistant secretary who had had better training than Saburo himself. He could have been spared easily, but he had always refused, claiming some urgent business. The truth was he had little love for his mother and still resented bitterly that she had sent him away to become a warrior monk when he was still a child. Besides, his own life had taken a happier turn lately. He now had a housekeeper. Sumiko was a widow with a twelve-year-old daughter. She had come to him after a former *sohei* had raped her daughter and Saburo had killed him. That had been over a year ago, and Akitada was not clear about their precise relationship, but certain signs suggested that it had taken a turn toward a permanent arrangement. Little wonder Saburo did not want to confront his mother with a wife who was a mere peasant of *emishi* descent.

Akitada escaped Mrs. Kuruda's questions by claiming Yukiko's need for rest.

∞

The next morning, Mrs. Kuruda lay in wait with their rice gruel. She barely took the time to wish them "good morning" and serve them before she started her interrogation.

"I noticed you taking such very good care of your lady last night," she said, eyeing Yukiko sharply. "May I assume that it is good news?"

This was a sore subject.

Yukiko snapped, "You may not. That is, if you are implying that I am with child."

Undeterred, Mrs. Kuruda pursued the subject. "Oh. What a pity! But you are still young. It will surely happen soon. I've heard of some methods that will bring about the happy condition. Allow me to share them with you."

Yukiko choked on her gruel and Akitada said, "Enough, Mrs. Kuruda. You mean well, but the topic is closed."

She was taken aback by his firmness. "Well, I thought you'd be the first to want to make your lady truly happy. There's no happiness greater than that of being a mother. Though your children don't always repay your love. Saburo's particularly difficult. I trust he is well?"

11

"He is quite well," Akitada said, wishing her gone. But she had a right to news of her son. "Saburo is the senior tribunal secretary, you know. That gives him a great deal of responsibility. He has nearly twenty clerks and scribes working under him."

Mrs. Kuruda's sallow face blushed with pleasure and she smiled. "I'm very happy to hear it. I always knew Saburo was brilliant and would make a name for himself. It is good that you appreciate him as he deserves."

"Oh, I do. I rely on both Tora and Saburo completely."

"Ah, Tora." Her tone was dismissive and she sniffed a little. "And how are he and his wife and son?"

"Also well, thank you."

"Does he still have those headaches?"

Akitada was puzzled. "Headaches? What headaches?"

"You didn't know? Oh, they were terrible. He could barely see. I happen to know because he asked me about some medicine that would help. I was very glad to make up something. Really, my lord, my greatest wish is to be of service to you and yours."

"Thank you. I suppose he must be better, because he didn't mention it to me."

Mrs. Kuruda became serious again. "I wish you would remind Saburo of his duty to his mother. He neither comes to see me nor writes. Is it too much to ask of one's only son to write an occasional letter? I have suffered silently all these months, not being one to complain. If it weren't for the fact that I'm needed here, desperately needed, I might add, I would accompany you and your lady back so I could be with my son."

Saburo would be in a fine pickle then, Akitada thought. Before he could find an answer to this, Yukiko put down her empty bowl and said, "But you *are* needed here, Mrs. Kuruda. What would we do without you? And even today, when we must rush away again to my parents, you brought us this delicious gruel so we could get away quickly."

Mrs. Kuruda took the hint. "I was glad to do it, Lady Yukiko. And now, if you'll excuse me, I'm much too busy to chat. I must see about the others and order food for your dinner tonight." She snatched up the empty bowls and bustled out.

Yukiko giggled.

Akitada smiled. "Thank you, my love. I thought she'd never leave."

∞

Yukiko's parents and siblings had returned to their mansion in the capital. Fujiwara Kosehira had completed his governorship of Omi Province a year ago and collected another rank promotion. He was now an imperial adviser of the fourth rank.

These new honors and responsibilities had not changed him much. When a servant had announced Akitada and Yukiko, he rushed out to greet them, his round face wreathed in smiles of joy.

"Akitada! Yukiko, my dearest girl!" He embraced them both. "What a joy! What a surprise! How I have missed you both! Come in, come in! Your mother will shed tears of joy to have her little girl back. She's always

13

been very emotional. Especially now . . ." He broke off to ask, "Have you eaten? We're still at our morning rice. Come, let's go to the others."

Akitada remembered the family gatherings very well from his visit to their villa in Otsu. Nothing had changed, with the possible exception of the absence of Arihito.

There was more excitement, and more embraces and questions, and Lady Hatsuko wept, as promised. They sat down, Yukiko beside her mother, and Akitada beside Kosehira.

When the chatter had died down, Yukiko said, "So what's all this about Arihito, Father?"

Kosehira reddened and looked at her mother. "You told her?"

Yukiko said, "Of course, she did, and we came right away. So, tell us. We are here to help, aren't we, Akitada?"

Akitada was not altogether certain what sort of help was required, but he nodded.

Kosehira exchanged another glance with his first lady. "Akitada and I shall retreat to my study and leave you ladies to gossip among yourselves."

Yukiko looked rebellious, but her mother put a hand on her arm, and Akitada followed Kosehira out.

Settled in Kosehira's comfortable study and furnished with cups of very good wine by a silent and attentive servant, they sipped, murmured, "Ah!" and then smiled at each other.

"Come, Kosehira, what's this really about?" Akitada asked. "Yukiko says you have disinherited Arihito. Can this be true?"

Kosehira sighed. "Not yet, but it may come to that. Arihito is being incredibly stubborn. I had no idea my son could be so lacking in respect for me and our ancestors. Is Yukiko angry with me?"

"She thinks you've gone mad," Akitada said dryly.

"Ah, those two have always been very close. Arihito moped about for months after she left with you. How are things between you, by the way?"

Akitada flushed a little. "None of your business."

Kosehira laughed, then became serious. "No, but I hope you'll tell me if there's something wrong. I've been feeling guilty about pushing you two together."

"Relax. All is well. Though she lost a child last winter and grieves sometimes."

Kosehira smiled. "I was sorry about that, but there are many more children in your future. I have a great longing to be a grandfather."

They both laughed, a little uneasily, given they were of an age. Akitada said, "Now stop getting off the subject and tell me about Arihito."

Kosehira plucked at the hem of his robe. "My son wants to marry. I don't approve of his choice."

It crossed Akitada's mind that a Fujiwara heir would be expected to marry a princess or at least the daughter of a prince and that Kosehira had forbidden a connection on a lower social scale. But that was unjust. After all, he had given his favorite daughter to Akitada who could never hope to rise very high in the administration. He asked, "Why not?"

Kosehira threw up his hands. "It's impossible. She's the only child of a notorious killer. The crime happened some fifteen years ago but it will never leave the memory of anyone who matters. You recall the murder of Prince Atsutada?"

"No. Fifteen years ago I was in Echigo, fighting a local warlord. What happened?"

"Prince Atsutada, a brother of Emperor Sanjo, was living a very retired life in the eastern hills. He had become a lay priest after the death of his last wife and practiced the life of a humble peasant. He kept a very small household and spent much time reading holy texts and meditating on life and death. Mind you, he was seventy, but he was still spry for his age." Kosehira paused here and pursed his lips. Well," he went on, "the farm was being run by a man called Tanaka, a very unpleasant brute. He lived in a house on the property with his wife and daughter. Apparently there was a quarrel between Atsutada and Tanaka, and Tanaka killed his master. It was a brutal murder. He bludgeoned the poor prince almost to pieces. So now do you understand?"

"Yes. Sorry, I'd completely forgotten, but you're right. I remember people still talking about it when I returned from the North Country. What happened to Tanaka?"

"Oh, he was tried, found guilty, and sent into exile. Only he never made it there. One of his guards killed him on the way. They gave out he'd died in an accident, but some of us knew that an order had been given."

Akitada reflected, not for the first time, on the peculiarities of a justice system that avoided at all cost the taking of a life and substituted exile in hopes it would produce the same result. In this case, someone, perhaps the emperor himself, had been outraged sufficiently not to wait for the mines or the fever swamps to do the job.

"Arihito's completely bewitched by the girl. She's a fox, no doubt, with a father like that." Koschira glared, clenching his hands. "The whole family is depraved, I expect."

"How did they meet?"

"She serves in the household of Lady Otomo. Arihito took her some documents from the tax office.."

"How did the daughter of a murderer get such a very respectable position?"

"Oh, her mother remarried, and the girl was adopted by her new husband. A clerk in the Mint Office. His name's Mori. Mori Yutaka. Very reliable man, I hear."

"Hmm. How old is the daughter, if this happened fifteen years ago?"

"Nineteen, I think."

"That means she was no more than a small child at the time. She could not possibly have been involved."

Koschira snorted. "Don't be a fool, Akitada. Blood will tell. I will not have it, not even if he takes her for a concubine. And he refuses that outright. He wants to make her his first lady. Can you imagine?"

A silence fell. Koschira's chin fell to his chest. "I've lost him, Akitada. May the gods help me, but I've lost my son and it grieves me terribly. Hatsuko thinks he'll kill himself. Maybe he's done so already."

Akitada leaned across and put his hand on Kosehira's clenched fist. "I don't think he would take his life, Kosehira. Arihito has too much sense to do that. We'll find him. Have you contacted all his friends?"

Kosehira shook his head. "No. It doesn't matter. He will be dead to me."

3

The Oak and the Bamboo

Akitada had known Superintendent Kobe almost as long as he had known Kosehira. They had crossed paths first when Akitada had become involved in the university murders. In the beginning there had been a great deal of hostility between them as Kobe had felt threatened by what he assumed was a young busybody who was trying to make him look incompetent. But gradually, very gradually, they had come to appreciate each other's strengths and had worked well together. Kobe had gone out of his way to protect Akitada and his family, and Akitada had used his influence to keep Kobe in his position.

So it was quite natural that he should pay Kobe a visit. He waited until late in the day and then called on Kobe at his home in the western city.

Kobe's life had changed dramatically four years earlier when the middle-aged Kobe had fallen deeply in love with a blind shampoo girl. His wives and grown children had opposed the liaison so angrily that Kobe had moved out of his family home and into a small, modest house in an unfashionable part of the capital. There he had been living very simply with his Sachi, letting his wives and children have all his property and part of his income.

It was ironic that Akitada should turn to Kobe when he was trying to help young Arihito who had also rejected his family for the woman he loved. But as yet Akitada did not know what was to become of this situation and only wanted to find out what had really happened fifteen years earlier.

Yukiko and her mother seemed to have some vague idea that he could somehow prove Tanaka's innocence and so make his daughter an eligible bride. He knew better. Arihito's beloved would never become a suitable wife for Kosehira's heir. Even if her father should turn out to be innocent, such a marriage would disqualify Arihito from any but the most insignificant positions in the government.

But Akitada looked forward to seeing Kobe again and the weather was still pleasant. Neither the summer rains nor the heat had arrived yet. Late cherry trees still flowered behind walls and fences, the air was perfumed by blossoming vines, and birds chirped everywhere. He had forgotten how beautiful the old city was. Even here, or perhaps especially here, where neglect and abandonment of large plots in favor of more fashionable residences in the eastern city or across the Kamo River had left large areas to the rampant growth of trees and shrubs, nature was determined to make a man glad to be alive.

Kobe's house was as he remembered it. Tucked away behind a tall fence of woven bamboo, lay a tiny house in its own garden. The property was small but very private, and the house was shaded by ancient trees. There was neither gatehouse nor gatekeeper. In fact, there was no way to announce himself. Akitada merely unlatched the small gate, walked in, and closed it behind him. He had hardly heard the latch fall back into place when a loud and angry barking made him turn quickly.

A huge shaggy dog came bounding toward him, claws clicking on the stones of the walk, eyes flashing and teeth bared.

Akitada backed against the gate and raised both arms to protect his throat. He was just in time, because the creature rose on its hind legs, both front paws on either side of his neck, and snarled into his face from slobbering jaws.

Shouts came from the house, a man's voice and a woman's. Akitada told the dog, "No! Get down! Bad dog!" or words to that effect. The dog's growling diminished somewhat, and the beast began to look uneasy. "Get down!" Akitada shouted into its face. This time the dog obeyed and sat down before him.

Akitada was quite pleased with himself, but Kobe's arrival might have had something to do with this docile behavior.

The superintendent was smiling. "It's you! What a surprise! Never mind Isamu. He doesn't bite."

"I think you should inform him of this," Akitada said, giving the dog a look and brushing slobber off his robe. The dog still watched him suspiciously, its nose twitching. Akitada hoped that the name really meant the animal was obedient. His own experience with Tora's dog Trouble had not convinced him that dogs could be civilized members of a household. He stepped cautiously around the animal and embraced Kobe.

Kobe had aged shockingly in the two years since he had last seen him. His hair was solidly gray now and his trimmed beard and mustache nearly white. He had also gained weight around the middle.

Kobe looked Akitada over also. "Marriage suits you," he said, slapping Akitada on the back with a laugh. "Your pretty lady has given you back your youth. Come in and meet Sachi. We're two lucky fellows, aren't we?"

Akitada agreed, though the bareness of Kobe's current home seemed to argue against this. The house could not have more than three rooms and a lean-to kitchen. The best room, where Sachi awaited them, was far from large and had bare floors, though everything was very clean.

Sachi, who must be nearly thirty years younger than Kobe, wore a plain blue cotton robe with a white sash about her slender middle. A shy smile hovered on her lips.

"Here's Akitada, my love," Kobe told her. "You remember? Lord Sugawara?"

"Oh!" Her smile widened and she knelt to bow. "Welcome, sir. We're very honored." She said softly, adding, "I'm so sorry about Isamu. Please forgive the rude welcome."

Akitada was not sure how he was to address her and avoided the problem altogether. "He's a very good watchdog and did me no harm. I'm happy to see you again and in such good looks."

She blushed and rose. "Thank you. Allow me to get some refreshments."

Sachi was blind, but she was very pretty and walked as gracefully as if she could see. Still, it was a very odd match. She probably knew this little house well enough to need no assistance. And perhaps the bareness of the room was due to her blindness. Akitada saw only some trunks for their clothing and a rack with Kobe's uniform, neatly smoothed and ready for the next day. There did not seem to be any servants.

Kobe brought cushions, three of them, placed them, and invited Akitada to sit. "She will be back in a moment. I hope you don't mind if she stays for a little. She has few visitors and I worry about her being lonely."

It was clear that Kobe was still deeply devoted to this young blind woman. It would not have occurred to Akitada to worry about either of his wives being entertained in his absence. He glanced around again and asked, "Are you happy here? Have you no regrets?"

Kobe smiled and shook his head. "No regrets, my friend. Only a great deal of thankfulness. How can she possibly love me, Akitada? I'm just a grumpy old man who knows little beyond giving orders to raw police recruits. And because of our situation, I can't even spoil her with fine things. We lead very quiet, simple lives here, but I've found a greater peace than I could ever have imagined."

"I'm very glad, and I'm sure she's as happy as you are."

"Well, that's what she says." Kobe chuckled. "So what brings you to me?"

"I see you get right to business as usual." Akitada chuckled. "I might just have wanted to check up on my old friend."

"Nonsense. As I recall, you also have little patience with social formalities. So tell me."

"I would have paid you a visit in any case, however, something has happened and it occurred to me that you might have some information. As you know, I married Kosehira's daughter."

Kobe nodded. "Young, beautiful and a Fujiwara heiress, no less. I was glad to hear it. And as there is also an age difference between you, it encouraged me to believe Sachi might not think me very tedious."

Sachi, who came back with a tray, overheard this. "Oh, never tedious, my dear. A little obstinate perhaps at times." She smiled at them, set down the tray, and served them wine and a plate of nuts and dried fruit.

"I can attest to the obstinacy," Akitada observed and watched with admiration as she poured the wine and placed the cups and the plate as perfectly as if she could see.

Kobe told her, "Akitada has some questions. If they don't involve a confidence, we'd like you to join us."

"I'd be very pleased to have your lady join us," Akitada said quickly. He had decided that Sachi had earned the title after sharing Kobe's life for four years.

She smiled again and found the cushion Kobe had placed by his side. There she knelt and turned her face toward Akitada. "You honor me, but I'm not his lady."

Kobe said firmly, "Hush, Sachi! She is my wife, Akitada. The only one who deserves the name. I have told her so many times, and I have made it official. I only wish we could have met in my youth."

She bowed her head and laid a hand on his. "My karma must be very good to have brought me to you."

Kobe snorted. "As a prisoner in my jail, accused of murdering a man. Where was your karma then?"

Akitada remembered the case as well as his shock at finding that the police superintendent had taken the blind woman as his lover after the case against her had been dismissed.

She said softly, "Sometimes we must walk through great suffering to reach our salvation."

Kobe, clearly moved by this, cleared his throat and said, "Enough chatter. Let's hear what Akitada has to tell us."

Akitada began, "Well, this happened some fifteen years ago. I was in Echigo, and very little that occurred here came to my attention. I do have a vague memory of someone murdering one of the princes, but I'm afraid that's all. As it turns out, that case has affected my new family after all these years, and so I have come to ask for information. Kobe, I believe you must have been one of the men who investigated the murder."

"I was." Kobe frowned. "The prince was Atsutada, though he had resigned any claim to the succession. He had the third rank, being of imperial blood. A nasty affair, as I recall. It was one of the first really big cases I was involved in. So what's your interest?"

"As it turns out the man who was found guilty had a daughter, a small child at the time. Now she is a young woman and, as fitful fate would have it, my young brother-in-law, Arihito, has fallen in love with her."

Sachi murmured "Oh! A love story."

Kobe snorted his derision. "Arihito? Isn't he Koschira's eldest?"

"Yes. Yukiko and Arihito have the same mother, Koschira's first lady. The parents are distraught over this."

Kobe cocked his head. "I don't see why. He can keep her as his mistress. She was a child and cannot be held responsible for the murder."

Akitada said, "My thought also, but it appears Arihito insists on a formal marriage."

Sachi breathed another "Oh!" and clasped her hands.

Her husband glanced at her with a smile. "Sachi is very fond of love stories. We've been reading *Genji* together. But Sachi, not even Genji would have been carried away to that extent. I recall distinctly that he submitted to marrying the chancellor's daughter even though he neither admired nor loved her."

Sachi murmured, "Yes, it was quite tragic. He suffered so, and that evil wife took her revenge for his dislike later by returning as a ghost and killing his Murasaki."

"Hmm," muttered Kobe, perhaps thinking about his own wives who bore him and Sachi a great deal of ill will. "Anyway, nothing the boy can do about it," he said firmly. "Can't say I blame his parents for refusing such a match. The girl's father was a depraved brute. Hard to imagine she'd turn the head of the son of our new counselor."

"Yes, it's strange. I don't suppose there was anything odd about the case?"

"Not at all. It was him all right. He had quarreled with his master, wanting more money. Being a gambler, he and his wife lived in near poverty. That night he was seen by a child coming from the place where the body was found. He had blood on his clothes and carried a bloody cudgel. And later we found gold in his place that he couldn't account for. But the most damning bit of evidence came from the chancellor's office. Tanaka was somehow involved with people who supported Crown Prince Atsuakira's forced resignation. The murdered man was Atsuakira's uncle and had bitterly opposed the chancellor in his plan."

Akitada took a sip of wine. "A political murder then. On top of a quarrel over money. It sounds like too much of a good thing," he said dryly.

"Believe me, no man was ever more clearly guilty." Kobe's eyes narrowed. "What are you suggesting? Surely you don't plan to dig up the whole mess in order to prove Tanaka innocent?"

Akitada raised both hands. "Not at all. But I have a wife who loves her brother. Arihito has disappeared, no one knows where to. I've promised to find him. At some point, I'd like to be able to explain to both of them that this has been a foolish dream."

Sachi gave a long sigh. "It would make a lovely tale," she murmured. "A handsome young nobleman head-over-heels in love with a poor girl condemned to live alone, scorned for something she didn't do. He risks everything, his birth, his family, and his wealth, to win her by proving her father innocent. "

"Sachi," said Kobe sternly, "you forget that this would place the blame for the man's death squarely on my shoulders."

Sachi's hand flew to her mouth. "Oh. Forgive me. It seems I'm also a very foolish dreamer."

There was no more to be said after this, and Akitada bade them good bye, promising to stop by again and inviting them both to his house.

4

A New Family

When Akitada returned from his visit with Kobe, Genba opened the gate for him. The big man was all smiles. "Lady Akiko's here, sir. It's just like old times. The ladies are together and said they were anxious to see you as soon as you got back. It's good to have you back, if only for a short visit."

Akitada patted Genba's shoulder. "Thanks, Genba. I've missed you, too. So things have been quiet here while we were gone?"

"Yes, sir. If it weren't for Ohiro and my little girl, I'd die of boredom."

"How is Tamiko? She must be getting big."

In answer, Genba turned and whistled. A moment later, a tiny girl appeared from behind the stables and ran to them. Her father, who seemed to have grown both taller and heavier as he aged, caught her and swung her up in his arms with a laugh. "Say hello to Lord Akitada, Tamiko."

Akitada saw a pretty face with huge eyes and a smile that put dimples in her cheeks. She must be four years old by now and had grown amazingly since the last time he had seen her.

The contrast between the little girl and her big, gray-haired father suggested that she was a grandchild rather than Genba's daughter, but Genba, a former wrestler, had married late. Ohiro, Tamiko's mother, had worked in a brothel and Genba had become involved in her master's murder. Akitada's retainers were prone to falling in love with women well beneath them, but the marriages had turned out well for Tora and Genba. And now Saburo was following their example, and Akitada's obligations increased as their families grew. But he would not have it any other way, and now he reached out to take Tamiko into his arms.

"Do you remember me?" he asked with a smile.

She stared back at him and shook her head.

"Say something," urged her proud father. "She speaks very well, sir. She's just shy."

Tamiko looked at her father. "I'm not shy." She turned back to Akitada. "Did you bring Yasuko?"

"I'm sorry. Not this time. She will want to know about you. What shall I tell her when I go back?"

"I can climb trees, and I can say the morning prayer, and I can make rice cakes, and I have a cat. Its name is Mi."

"A beautiful name for a beautiful cat, I'm sure, and you're very talented. Yasuko will be glad to hear it."

She grinned. "Yes. Shall I show you how I climb a tree?"

There were no trees about, and Genba took her back and put her down. "Later perhaps. His lordship must go see his sister now. Make your bow."

She did so very prettily. "Till later, Akitada," she said, and ran off.

Genba looked scandalized. "Sorry about that, sir."

Akitada laughed. "She's remarkable and very pretty."

Genba's smile returned. "Thank you, sir. She makes me very happy."

"Take good care of her."

Unnecessary advice, he thought, as he walked to the house. He had liked holding a small child again. His own children were too big for it and would not have tolerated being held in any case. Perhaps another child might not be a bad idea after all. He smiled at the thought.

He was still smiling when he walked in on his wife and sister. They were discussing clothes. Yukiko's trunk stood open, and some gowns hung on display on the stand.

Akiko ran to give him a hug. "Brother, I hate you," she cried, leaning back to look at him. "You don't write. You rarely visit. And you keep your wife in rags."

Akitada gave the clothes on the stand a startled glance. He thought what he saw there could not remotely resemble a rag. "Does she need clothes?" he asked guiltily. "I know nothing about such things."

Yukiko murmured, "Akiko exaggerates. "I have many new clothes at home. What I brought is only for a short visit."

Akiko frowned. "Short? We'll need time to shop. Those provincial shops are always dreadful. Besides, there's the matter of your brother." She turned to Akitada. "Come sit down, Akitada. I'm determined to enjoy your visit. Not only do you bring me Yukiko who is in dire need of new clothes, but I shall finally get a chance to help you with another case."

Akitada, his heart sinking, joined them. He would pay a hefty price, and not just for new outfits for his wife. "There is nothing to investigate, Akiko. Kobe assures me there's no chance that a mistake was made. He happens to have been in charge of the murder investigation at the time, and Kobe is nothing if not thorough."

"Pah!" Akiko waved that aside as casually as if it were a small gnat. "You forget how many times you have proved Kobe wrong. You'll see, it will be same this time."

"No," Akitada said sternly. "You will not bandy about suggestions that a mistake was made. I absolutely forbid it. It would further damage Kobe's reputation."

Akiko gave a ladylike snort.

Yukiko looked at her husband with reproachful eyes. "Surely we haven't come all this way for you to refuse your help us now?"

"Of course not. I shall set about finding your brother and then we'll see if we cannot talk some sense into him. And into your father, who is determined against him. Arihito must give up this ridiculous passion. Your father told me that the girl was adopted by a man called Mori. I'll start there. If Arihito hasn't moved in with her, she probably knows where he is."

Yukiko said doubtfully, "I don't know. You don't know Arihito. He's always been horridly stubborn. And so is my father."

Akiko laughed. "They are no match for my brother. But Akitada, it would not hurt to ask some questions about the old murder. Just out of interest. Yukiko and I will be paying visits later. I imagine members of the imperial family will be better informed about Prince Atsutada's enemies and their possible motives. We'll report what we find out."

Akitada knew that he could not stop Akiko once she was on a trail and while she gossiped with her high-born friends. He sighed. "Akiko, you mustn't mention that I am interested in any way. Can you remember that at least?"

"Of course. You know you can rely on my discretion. I'll make it sound perfectly natural. Everybody always talks about members of the imperial family."

And that was that.

∞

Mori Yutaka lived south of the market in a quiet, tree-lined street. The houses were modest but well-kept, each with its own small garden, each with a tall fence. Many of the fences were ingeniously woven of willow or bamboo and carefully tied with vines to make intricate patterns.

Akitada asked directions of a small urchin who led him to the right gate and even rattled the bamboo sticks that hung beside it to announce him. Akitada gave him a copper for his trouble, and he ran off happily.

The gate was answered by another boy, this one about ten years old. He looked at Akitada and said, "My father's not home yet."

"Perhaps your mother is available?"

His face darkened. "She doesn't live here anymore."

"I see. Well, is anybody home beside you?"

"The maid, but she's cooking dinner."

Thoroughly foiled, Akitada thanked him and left. But when he reached the end of the street, he saw a short man in the black gown and hat of a government clerk hurrying toward him. The neighborhood was one where many low-level government workers lived, and on an impulse he stopped the man.

"By any chance would your name be Mori?"

The short man halted, surprised, and took in Akitada's robe and his hat with the rank ribbon. He bowed quite deeply. "Yes, I am Mori, sir. How may I serve?"

"I just called at your house and your son mentioned that you had not returned yet. I would very much like to speak with you."

Another bow and an anxious expression. "Yes, of course. Just this way, sir." He gestured.

They walked back to the house in silence, Akitada just a step ahead. When they were almost there, Mori asked, "Are you from the palace, sir? Am I in some sort of trouble?"

Akitada gave him a reassuring smile. "Not at all. This is a private matter. I came about Arihito."

That stopped Mori altogether. "Arihito? A very nice young man. May I ask . . ."

Akitada said quite firmly, "Let's talk inside, if you don't mind."

The worry about being in some sort of trouble was symptomatic with the humble clerks who did all the real work in the administration. He had often wondered at it since it was their superiors whose assignments were in constant danger of ending abruptly. Perhaps the sense of insecurity transferred to their staff.

Mori's house was modest and somewhat unkempt. He led Akitada into the best room where the *tatami* mats were beginning to shred and a thick layer of dust lay on everything.

The boy who had answered the gate earlier was waiting there. Mori introduced him "My son Yoshimine. Yoshi, run and tell Haru to bring refreshments."

"Nothing for me," Akitada said quickly.

"No trouble, sir." Mori added under his breath, "I think," and placed two cushions after shaking the dust from them. "My house," he said, flushing painfully, "is not as it should be. I beg your forgiveness. Since my wife and my daughter have left, it's been a bachelor's place. My son and I are not good housekeepers and the cook . . ." He broke off as a very fat woman lumbered in, breathing heavily and staring at Akitada.

"Nothing's in the house but some stale *mochi*," she announced, and added accusingly, "You didn't give me money for the market."

Mori, said, "Oh, dear." He looked helplessly about the room as if fresh supplies were hiding somewhere among his books. "Yes. Quite right. Thank you, Haru." When she had lumbered back out, he started another string of apologies.

"Please," Akitada interrupted, "do not trouble yourself. I've just eaten and require nothing but a few moments of your time."

It was clear that Arihito was not here, but perhaps Mori knew where he was. And was the absent daughter by any chance the girl he had fallen for? If so, they were probably holed up somewhere together.

As they sat down, Mori said, "Young Lord Arihito is a most admirable young man. I hope he is well?"

"His parents don't know where he is. They are very concerned. I offered to find him. Some family matter they need to discuss. Arihito is the heir, you see."

Mori looked wary but nodded. "Yes. A very fortunate young man. I'm sorry, but I haven't seen him for some time."

"I understood that he had been courting your daughter recently?"

"Oh, yes. Masako. She's a lovely young woman. And kind. They are very much in love."

Under the circumstances, Akitada suspected that Mori had done his best to trap young Arihito into marriage. In a sharper tone, he asked, "Did I hear you correctly earlier? Both your wife and Masako have left you?"

Mori nodded sadly. "Yes. My wife, a blessed woman, has dedicated her life to the Buddha. That was many months. She now resides in a small nunnery attached to the Koryu temple just outside the city." He sighed deeply and glanced around the room again.

Akitada wondered what had made the widow of the prince's murderer first marry this man and then renounce the world to become a nun. Still, fifteen years was a long time, and lives changed. Mori, for all his ineffectiveness as a homeowner seemed to have stable employment. No doubt he had been a welcome change from the brutish Tanaka who had been a gambler. Perhaps she had waited only long enough for her daughter to find a place before resigning her responsibilities and seeking refuge in a nunnery.

But it was Masako who mattered. He asked, "And your daughter also left?"

A smile came to Mori's face. "Yes, Masako went to live in the household of Lady Otomo. It was very fortunate. Lady Otomo seems very fond of her and Masako has blossomed there. Positively blossomed!"

"Fortunate indeed," Akitada said dryly. "Do you see her often?"

He nodded eagerly. "She comes to visit her old father regularly. Truly, she's the best daughter a man could have." Mori smiled more widely.

"But I was told that she is not your daughter, that she is really the daughter of a man called Tanaka to whom your wife was married before."

The smile disappeared, and Mori flushed. "My poor wife has suffered much." He heaved a deep sigh. "We don't talk about the past. I'd hoped . . . I wished to give her a better life, a new family. But in the end, she left us to find peace. I think the past haunted her."

"I'm sorry," Akitada said, somewhat disconcerted by the grief in the other man's face and voice. "Your son is her son also?"

"Yes. A good boy, but he misses his mother." He paused. "I'm told that sometimes a nun can change her mind and return to her family. Do you think that is possible?"

"Perhaps. I don't know. But tell me, was Arihito aware of Masako's family background when he began his courtship?"

For the first time, Mori became angry. He drew himself up and spoke quite sharply. "This is Masako's home, and *we* are her family. I consider myself Masako's father. She was only four years old when she came to me. I adopted her and raised her as my own. She has never known any other father since that dreadful event."

Akitada apologized. "I'm sure you raised her as your own. Her love for you proves that."

Mori relaxed a little. "I should perhaps tell you that my wife has always said Masako's father was innocent of that dreadful charge. But in any case, it was Masako herself who told Arihito about him. I argued against it, but she insisted. After all, no one would have known.

She had my name. Now you can see the trouble it has caused. Arihito's family have turned against both of them. As far as I was concerned, no one was to know about that man. Masako grew up beautiful and kind and was always gentle, a young woman any man would wish for his daughter. Or his wife."

He had spoken proudly and with a tone of defiance in his voice. Akitada felt some grudging respect for him. He sighed. "Do you know where they are?"

Mori said stiffly, "I have no idea where Lord Arihito may be, but Masako is where she should be, with Lady Otomo."

Akitada thanked him and rose. On the way out, he said, "Forgive me for asking such questions. I had no intention of offending you or your family. Neither would I have reminded you of painful matters if I could have avoided it. I only wished to make sure the young man is safe. It seems I must keep looking."

Mori nodded. "I understand. His parents must be very worried."

5

An Old Crime

Akitada walked home, thinking about what he had learned from Mori. Against his better judgment—the man would surely do everything in his power to assure Masako married the Fujiwara heir—he was inclined to believe him. The man's love for his adopted daughter could not have been faked. And Mori had not struck him as a man who was a good liar. In fact, everything had shown him to be the kind of lower-level civil servant who prized his work and his family above status and wealth.

Or rather, he thought, such men never aspired to being more than they were because they accepted the distinctions of class and power as absolute. Mori had

41

only become agitated when Akitada had suggested his beloved daughter might have seduced Arihito into marrying her.

This nineteen-year-old, what sort of girl was she? Why had she told Arihito about her father when she could just as well have kept the matter to herself? Surely she was not proud of what the killer had done. It was very puzzling.

He promised himself a visit to Lady Otomo, whoever she was. The Otomo were old nobility, though no longer active in government. Presumably Masako was working there as a maid.

When he got to his house, the ladies had not yet returned from their visiting. Akitada hoped they were discreet. Akiko was mature enough to know what to say and what to keep to herself. Yukiko was another matter. His sister had been quite useful to him in the past. It was amazing how much information resided in the women's quarters, considering they hardly ever set foot in the world of men.

He greeted Genba and chatted with Ohiro, who blushed and bowed, and blushed some more when he complimented her on their little daughter. He had not been happy with Genba's choice for a wife, but she had become a quiet, proper housewife and mother no different from any of the respectable wives in the city. And she clearly made Genba happy. He was not nearly as fat as he used to be and while he was gray-haired by now, he looked healthy.

In his room, he changed into his comfortable old house robe, left behind when his new assignment seemed to warrant better clothes, and worked on some reports he intended to deliver to the palace. He looked forward to seeing old friends again: Fujiwara Kaneie, his former superior, the Minister of Justice, and Nakatoshi, who was now the head of the Ministry of Ceremonial.

Mrs. Kuruda interrupted him by peering into his room. "There you are! Nobody told me. Sometimes I wish I had eyes in the back of my head and ears everywhere. You should have sent for me, sir."

Dear gods, the woman was a trial! Sending for her was the last thing he had wanted to do. He frowned. "What is it, Mrs. Kuruda? I'm rather busy."

She took this as an invitation to come in. "You should have a secretary, sir. You should have brought Saburo. Then you wouldn't have to do all that writing yourself. Saburo writes a very fine hand. The monks taught him well. I saw to that."

"Yes, Mrs. Kuruda. We have been over all of that. Saburo is needed in Mikawa and I won't be staying long. Now what is on your mind?"

"Oh, nothing. All is in hand. Cook is preparing a good dinner. Will your sister be staying?"

"I doubt it. But it won't matter. I'm sure there is enough food."

"Certainly. I made sure of it. Is there anything else you wish? Some tea perhaps? I don't drink it myself. It causes flatulence. So embarrassing. But Ohiro says you are accustomed to it."

Did she mean he was accustomed to flatulence? "Thank you, Mrs. Kuruda. Nothing at the moment. And I usually make my own tea."

"Well . . ." She hesitated, and he bent over his papers again. A moment later, shuffling steps receded and the door closed. With a sigh of relief he returned to his report.

A short while after this, Genba brought Superintendent Kobe in. Akitada rose to greet him with an embrace, glad of this interruption. They could put their heads together about the Arihito problem, and Kobe might be able to answer some of the questions that troubled Akitada. He poured some wine and then went to the kitchen for something to go with it.

It appeared preparations for the evening rice were in full swing. Cook, red-faced and resentful hovered over the fire, while Mrs. Kuruda was cutting up things. A kitchen maid—since he had no recollection of such a servant, she might have been employed for their visit only—was scrubbing a kettle and staring at him wide-eyed.

Mrs. Kuruda put down her knife, an uncomfortably long one, and said rather sharply, "You have changed your mind about the tea?"

"No. Superintendent Kobe has come for a visit. We have wine, but I thought something . . ." His voice trailed off, seeing her frown. "Never mind. You're busy, I see. I'll get it myself." He looked around. A kitchen in the midst of food preparation was a confusing place.

Mrs. Kuruda asked, "Is he staying for the meal?"

"I don't know. Surely it isn't time yet."

She said darkly, "It's my experience that men will just go on and on talking and drinking. I shall need to know to adjust the servings."

The woman was beginning to irritate Akitada again. He said sharply, "I'll let you know. Now, how about a plate of pickles? Or some nuts?"

His tone produced service, though with a muttered comment he did not catch, and Akitada returned to his room.

Kobe said, "Forgive me for arriving unannounced, but I did some checking on that Tanaka case and thought you might like to know more."

"You know you're always welcome. And thank you for coming." Akitada poured the wine and told Kobe about his visit to Mori. "I'm intrigued by that family," he said. "Tanaka's wife remarried after Tanaka's death. The new husband, Mori, seems a most respectable man who adopted the little girl. They also have a son together, but then the wife decided to become a nun. Mori blames this on the crime, though apparently she has always insisted that Tanaka was innocent. You must have met her after the crime. How did she strike you?"

Kobe grimaced. "She would say so even if she washed the blood off his clothes for him after the deed. She struck me as a silly woman. Half the time, she was stone-faced; the other half, she railed against us, claiming we were persecuting them. Mind you, she was a good-looking woman back then. No idea why she became a nun, but given her unstable character, I can see why she couldn't play the respectable clerk's wife forever."

"Hmm." Akitada was inclined to agree that the killer's widow would deny his guilt regardless of what she knew at the time. "What exactly could she have known?" he asked Kobe.

"She said she'd gone to the village with her daughter to shop for their evening rice. When we asked her why she washed his clothes, she said they were stained. We found what looked like blood stains on his boots. He'd cleaned them, but the blood had seeped into the seams. Anyway, we asked if the stains could have been blood. She said very coolly, 'Yes.' So we asked him where he got the blood on his clothes, and he said he'd killed a rat that day. But of course he couldn't produce the rat. In the end, we assumed she knew very well what he'd done, but we couldn't shake her."

"Difficult."

"Not at all. We had enough. And more. By then the story had got out, and one day Konoe Ietada, who was the chancellor's secretary then, stood in my office and told me that Tanaka had come to him to offer his help in silencing the prince in exchange for a piece of land."

"You can't be serious! He went to Michinaga with an offer to kill Atsutada?"

Kobe chuckled. "No, no. Konoe thought Tanaka was offering to spy on the man and give them something they could use against him. In any case, Konoe says Michinaga refused the offer. But it gave us a motive. Of course we couldn't use it without involving Michinaga."

"It wasn't much of a motive when he was turned down. Any proof that he was?"

Kobe made a face. "Yes. I expect so. Michinaga was much too cautious. Still, a man like that might have hoped that the murder would produce the reward anyway and that the chancellor would protect him. You might say he struck out on both counts."

"How so?"

"In the first place, Michinaga would never have allied himself to such a man. And in the second, Michinaga made sure Tanaka would not live to tell his tale."

Akitada frowned. "His death at the hands of his guard was a miscarriage of justice as we practice it. Who is to say that his trial wasn't the same."

Kobe stared at him. "Are you suggesting I would have helped Michinaga to convict an innocent man?"

Akitada bit his tongue. "No. Not at all. You know how my mind works. I'm just eliminating possibilities. Given what you told me about Tanaka dying on the road on orders from above, it isn't so farfetched to suspect that the judge also had his orders."

"Trust me, the evidence convicted him. We found the gold."

"The gold?"

"Yes. Twenty pieces of gold. Under the quilts in an old trunk in Tanaka's room. After the servant told us that Tanaka had quarreled with the prince about money, we naturally questioned the source of that much gold."

"How did he explain it?"

Kobe grinned. "He had the nerve to claim Atsutada had given it to him to purchase seed rice. Only there was plenty of seed rice on that farm."

"How exactly was the murder discovered?"

"Well, it was summer, a little later than this; it was already hot. The prince was spending some nights in his summer house where there was a breeze. When he didn't return to the house the next morning, the woman he lived with sent her son to look for him. The boy was about five at the time. A peculiar child, though seeing such a sight might leave its mark even on a grown-up. He ran back to his mother, who went to look and started screaming for help. We were called in and found Atsutada in a pool of blood inside the summerhouse. The attack had been vicious. He had been beaten to death, and probably beaten even after death. It looked like something had done the job. There was blood everywhere, and bloody footprints leading away."

"I can see that the evidence must have made it look incontrovertible." Akitada pursed his lips.

"And I can see from your face that you take this to mean that Tanaka could not have done it. Too perfect? The fact that both he and his wife denied he did it becomes a good reason to start a new investigation?"

Akitada laughed a little uneasily. "You know me too well. You would think he'd have covered his tracks at least. Did anyone look for a dead rat?"

Kobe exploded. "No. Of course not. Really, Akitada! Do you ever think that you might be carrying your doubts too far? When do facts become something other for you?"

"You're right. I'm sorry. I'm sure I'm wasting time, but there is my wife, you see. And Kosehira."

Kobe calmed down immediately. "Yes. I can see that. Well, what else can I tell you?"

"Tell me about the people who were involved in one way or another."

"All right. Well, there was Tanaka, of course. Decent enough family, both parents dead and no siblings. He wasted a good inheritance with gambling. He was already pretty desperate for money when he married. She was the only daughter of a professor. He was very good-looking for all his brutish ways. Anyway, she married him after he found work running Atsutada's farm. Their little girl was very young when it happened. Nothing against the woman, except that she lied for her husband."

"A good marriage, do you think?"

Kobe grimaced. "Good enough. After all, she supported his story and was pretty stone-faced throughout."

"You mean she was loyal to him."

"Yes, though I think he beat her. But let me go on. There was another woman involved. Atsutada may have chosen a spiritual life after his wife's death, but he did not renounce the pleasures of the flesh altogether. He lived with a courtesan called Maruko. There was also a child, a small boy. No idea who fathered him, but Atsutada seems to have treated him like a son. As I said, the boy found the body. The only other person there at the time of the murder was Atsutada's manservant. He had been with Atsutada almost since the prince's birth. He was already elderly and had poor eyesight when I met him. Said he'd slept through the night and hadn't seen or heard anything."

"Did the courtesan's child inherit?"

"No. They got nothing. Atsutada had a grown son. He was in his early twenties then and lived elsewhere."

Voices sounded from the corridor and then the door opened. Yukiko peered in.

"Here he is, Akiko." She came in, looking rosy and happy. "Superintendent!" she cried. "How perfect! I'm so glad to see you."

Blushing, Kobe rose to bow. "Lady Yukiko! You are an enchanting sight for this old man." He caught sight of Akiko behind her. "And Lady Akiko, elegant as ever! It's a great pleasure to see you both."

Yukiko said brightly, "We won't stay. I know you have much to talk about, but since you're here, Superintendent, I must warn you that my father will pay you a visit. We stopped by to visit him and convinced him to look into that old murder."

Akitada saw Kobe stiffen. His jaw did not quite drop in shock at this news, but he clearly clenched his teeth.

Akiko, always the diplomat, said, "Yukiko and her family are terribly worried about Arihito. They want to know more about the young woman he is infatuated with."

Kobe relaxed a little. "I shall look forward to seeing your esteemed father, Lady Yukiko."

The ladies smiled, bowed, and left.

Akitada and Kobe sat back down, listening to the cheerful chatter receding outside.

"She's beautiful and full of spirit, your wife," Kobe said. "You're to be envied. So much youth and energy make me feel old."

Akitada, feeling suddenly every bit as old as Kobe, said, "Sachi is also young and pretty. You have no need to envy me."

"Ah, yes. But there is a difference."

Akitada knew this was so. Sachi was of a different class. Her manners would always be quiet and subservient to her husband, and the fact she was blind kept her from demanding entertainments and outings all the time. He suppressed a sigh.

6

An Awkward Meeting

Lord Kosehira did not relish his call on Superintendent Kobe. He liked and respected the man and was aware that his own, much higher rank and position would put Kobe on the defensive. He went therefore in his plainest gown and with only one attendant and he paid his visit to Kobe's office at the jail. He hoped that this way he would be seen as just another citizen who brought a problem to the police.

Of course, this was a vain hope. At least four police officers jumped to their feet when he entered and asked to see Kobe. One ran to announce him, another bowed and offered to take him, a third closed the door behind him and the fourth held open the door in front of him.

Kosehira nodded his thanks and walked into Kobe's office. There he found a different atmosphere. Papers and documents lay everywhere, and Kobe was bent over some letters with a brush in his hand.

This he laid down as he rose and bowed to Kosehira. "Lady Akiko, Akitada's sister, has warned me of your visit," he said in lieu of a welcome and without a smile. "How can I be of assistance?"

Kosehira stood, a little disconcerted by this reception, and said, "It's very good of you to see me. I came for information. It concerns my oldest son, Arihito. His mother and I are very . . . concerned."

Kobe relented a little. He gestured to some cushions. "Let's sit down while you tell me."

There was no offer of wine, though Kosehira could see a flask and some cups on one of the shelves. It was clear that Kobe expected to have his investigation challenged. He sighed.

"My son Arihito is my oldest," he said. "His mother and I are afraid he may have done himself some harm or intends to do so." He clenched his hands at the thought. "Or even forsake the world. He is my heir. A very good son until now. But it seems he's been bewitched by the most unsuitable female."

Kobe's expression did not change. "I'm very sorry to hear it. What is it that you want me to do? We can try to find him for you."

Kosehira shook his head. "Thank you, but no, you mustn't. He'd never forgive me if I set the police on him. I must hope that he'll come to his senses."

"Then is there some other way I can be useful?"

"I have forbidden a marriage and that is what caused my son to leave without so much as a goodbye. As a father, I'm burdened by guilt for having caused him to take some rash action. I came to have you assure me that I've not been wrong about my rejection of the young woman."

"Frankly, if I were in your shoes, I'd have acted the same way. There is no question about her father's guilt, and the case is notorious. Of course she was a mere child back then, but people have not forgotten and tend to assume that children follow in their parents' footsteps."

Kosehira heard this confirmation of his own feelings with dismay. It told him Yukiko's enthusiastic insistence that Akitada would prove Tanaka innocent and thus remove the obstacle to Arihito's happiness was doomed. Though, of course, as his daughter she should have known quite well that there remained any number of other objections to this young woman as a bride for his oldest son.

He sighed and asked, "Is there no possibility that the witnesses might have lied or been confused? One was a child, I think. Can we trust a child's word? Yukiko says Tanaka's wife was convinced of his innocence."

Kobe glowered. "I suppose Akitada put the notion in her head. We've discussed the case, since his lady was eager to . . . help her brother. The fact is that the girl's mother was uncooperative to the point of locking us out of their house. Her behavior was what I'd expect of a wife who knew her husband had killed someone. Furthermore, she washed his bloodstained clothing and cleaned his boots. I had a good mind to arrest her as an accessory."

"But in the end you didn't?"

"No. There was the child. What would have happened to her? They had no family. At least none that would acknowledge them."

Kosehira thought about this. It seemed inconceivable that this woman and her child had no one who would claim them. In his own world there were many people, high and low, to look after widows and orphans. He began to feel a stirring of pity for the situation the woman must have found herself in. He said, "I suppose it was good fortune that brought her another husband. I understand he's a most respectable man who adopted the child."

Kobe looked surprised. "I didn't know. You seem to be better informed than I. I'd say it was good fortune indeed. Tanaka was a brute who beat her."

Kosehira flinched. "That doesn't change the fact that she stood by him when he was accused. Apparently she really believed him innocent."

"I don't see how she could have known. She did know about the blood on his clothes, because she washed them. Isn't it more likely that he told her what he had done and that she helped him cover up the deed?"

A brief silence fell. Kosehira felt foolish to have suggested a miscarriage of justice. Kobe was a highly respected man. Akitada trusted him and had praised him often. Besides, did he really want Tanaka innocent? He sighed. "I expect you have children, Superintendent. I'm very fond of mine, and Arihito has always made me proud of him. He was a serious boy who worked hard at his studies and looked after his little brothers and sisters. I was content to have him step into my shoes when it was time for me to take the dark path. Now I not only have lost my heir, I have lost my son. How do I deal with that?"

Kobe was clearly taken aback by this baring of the soul by an imperial adviser. He muttered, "I'm very sorry, sir. What can I do?"

Kosehira looked at him and shook his head. "Nothing, Superintendent. Akitada has promised to look for Arihito. He's not with the young woman, and her adopted father hasn't seen him for several weeks. We'll find him. What happens then, I do not know."

"If I might suggest, sir, the fact that she has been adopted means that she bears a new name. Surely no one needs to know about her past."

"Since she told my son, she will tell others. It's not a matter that can be kept secret when she seems almost proud to claim Tanaka for her father. Besides, we shall always know. How can we invite her into our family when every time we look at her we think that she has a murderer's blood in her veins?"

∞

Akitada had returned early from the greater palace where he had delivered some documents and tried to look in on Nakatoshi. But Nakatoshi had not been in. An assistant told him that his superior had taken his family on a pilgrimage for a few days. Thus Akitada had returned home, thinking to spend a little time making music with Yukiko. Alas, this also was not possible. Genba informed him that Yukiko and Akitada's sister had left together for some shopping. The visit to the imperial ladies required preparations, it seemed.

At loose ends, Akitada had just made up his mind to return to the greater palace and look in on Fujiwara Kaneie when Kosehira arrived. Recognizing by his friend's long face that all was not well, he brought out some wine.

"What happened?" he asked.

Kosehira shook his head. "I made a mistake. I should've known Kobe would be no help. On top of that he is now angry. I wish to heaven, Akitada, men like that worried a little less about their face than about serving the people."

"I think you misjudged Kobe. Yes, he bristles a little when you imply that he didn't do his job, but that is because he takes that job very seriously. And knowing Kobe, I can assure you that he doesn't bear a grudge long. What did you say to him?"

"I was very careful, Akitada. I said I had come for more information about the people involved and when I saw that he was getting angry, I appealed to him as a father of youngsters."

"Oh. Well, he and his children aren't speaking to each other."

Kobe stared at this. "Not speaking? How extraordinary. Is it over that blind woman of his?"

Akitada nodded.

"But how can he bear it? I cannot imagine not speaking to my children. I love them all. It would kill me."

"I expect it isn't easy for him either."

"Hmm." Kobe sipped some wine and thought about it. "What shall we do then?" he finally asked.

Akitada told him what Mori had said and added, "I think we must speak to the young woman. She may know something."

Kosehira was on his feet. "Very well. I'm beginning to have a great curiosity to see the creature who turned my son against his parents. If I'm not mistaken, Lady Otomo still resides in their old residence. The family hung on to that even after they lost all influence at court. She must be in her eighties. A recluse, they say."

7

Living in the Past

It was getting dark as they walked together to Ejiri-koji, an old residential street, once having only four large mansions on it. But the land had been subdivided as the old families sold off parts of their estates or moved away altogether. The Otomo mansion still existed but had disappeared from sight behind huge trees. It had a high mud wall, much patched and reinforced with sections of fencing. The gatehouse was black with age, and the gates had been repaired so many times over the years that they presented a checkered appearance. No lights penetrated the thick mass of trees.

After some lengthy pounding, an old man carrying a lantern admitted them. He wore some sort of ancient livery that had faded unevenly to gray and was probably once blue. He hobbled ahead to announce them. They crossed an entrance courtyard that had long since become so overgrown with plants and trees that hardly any sky showed above them.

"Old Lady Otomo doesn't seem to keep horses or a carriage," Kosehira said, peering at tangled undergrowth. "I don't see any stables. Fallen on hard times, no doubt."

The house was very large and dark with age. Its bark roof was covered with moss and small ferns. They climbed wide stairs to the veranda cautiously; most of the steps were loose and the rest creaked disconcertingly. The railings and banisters were mostly gray, but bits of red lacquer still clung to them in places where they were protected from weather and use.

"How old do you suppose this is?" Akitada asked. He was himself the owner of a large house that had once seen better days.

"More than a hundred years," Kosehira said sourly. "A miracle it hasn't burned down or collapsed in all that time. Would've been better if it had."

"Have you ever been here?"

"No. And I'm glad. Frankly, the place looks haunted."

The servant having disappeared without holding the door open for them, Akitada took the carved handle and pulled. The door was heavy and opened on a wide, dark corridor. Up ahead, the faint light of the servant's lantern turned the corner and disappeared, leaving behind darkness. The air smelled musty, like old clothes and books.

"He must be deaf," Akitada said. "How long before he notices he's lost us?"

Kosehira was too impatient to wait. "Come on! Let's see what we'll find at the end of this dark tunnel." His anger seemed to have eased a little. Perhaps the great lord of the fourth rank was enjoying his adventure in this ancient and nearly derelict mansion.

They walked forward cautiously. The corridor had seemed wide and the floor smooth at their last glimpse of it, but there were strange rustlings and sudden currents of cold air. When they had almost reached the point where the light had disappeared, the servant returned, and they stopped in surprise.

By the trembling light of his lantern, they saw that the high walls of the corridor were covered with ancient weapons. All of these were old, some very old. Straight swords, the kind the Chinese produced centuries ago, their sheen dulled by rust, hung beside huge, red-lacquered bows that had long since straightened, their strings dangling broken. The leather quivers were stained with mold, their feathered arrows covered in cobwebs. There were many suits of armor laced with silks in all sorts of colors, and helmets, some encrusted with gold, and shields so old-fashioned that Akitada marveled at their strangeness. Among this large collection of forgotten military greatness hung banners of tattered silk, some still showing the Otomo family crest.

The servant cleared his throat and pointed ahead to the end of the side corridor.

Kosehira asked him in a raised voice, "Are you taking us to Lady Otomo, man? I have no desire to be left in the dark again. Where are the lights? Where are the servants?"

The man merely grunted and pointed ahead again.

There was nothing they could do but follow. Akitada gestured to the weapons "The Otomo must be proud of their military past."

"They're an ancient clan. A very long time ago they served the emperors as military commanders. The family fortunes were already in decline when the capital moved here."

They reached a half-closed door at the end of the corridor. Its surface was carved and gilded. The old servant opened this onto a large dim room with a curtained dais draped in faded hangings. Before this sat two women who seemed busy with some sort of needlework. A single flickering candle provided inadequate light. Near them were the sort of utensils commonly found in the quarters of highborn women: toiletry cases, writing boxes, a large mirror on its stand, a small brazier, and several large, ornate candle holders, though only one held the candle that lit the area. All around the small pool of golden light lay the darkness of the very large and high room. Rafters showed dimly above, and the shadows all around the walls hid unidentifiable objects.

Neither of the women was old enough to be Lady Otomo. One was middle-aged and had the broad face of the native people of Kyushu, many of whom had Korean blood. She was a servant by her simple gray clothes and her coiled hair. The other was much younger, dressed in a pale green silk gown and a small embroidered jacket, and wore her long hair loose. She was quite beautiful, with a slender neck, large luminous, expressive eyes, and a sweet smile.

Surely this was Masako. It was clear what had bewitched Arihito. Akitada had never shared Kosehira's belief that this girl had turned his son's head with some sort of magic or sorcery; her youth and beauty were quite powerful enough.

Before they could address the young woman, a cracked voice much like a raven's squawk came from the curtained dais. It demanded, "Who are you? And what do you want?"

Startled, Kosehira said, "What?"

The speaker was inside the curtained dais, an object of furniture more customary in the emperor's palace. She was sitting there in the half gloom behind the dusty silk curtains.

"Lady Otomo?" Akitada asked.

"Who wants to know?"

"I'm Sugawara. Sugawara Akitada."

"Hah. Knew your father. And the other one?"

Kosehira had lost his good humor. "Fujiwara Kosehira," he snapped. "And if you are Lady Otomo, you might come forth. I have business with you."

A harsh cackle was his answer. "A Fujiwara? Weaklings all. Don't know why His Majesty surrounds him-

self with you. Weakens the imperial line, all those Fujiwara women. We'll all be sorry."

Kosehira exchanged a look with Akitada. "The
woman must be mad," he said in an undertone. "Senili-
ty, I expect." He addressed the young woman, who had
risen and was bowing to him. "Are you Mori Masako?"

She smiled, a slightly tremulous smile. She was clearly nervous about this meeting. "Yes, my lord. I'm
Masako." She remembered Akitada and bowed to him
also. "And Lord Sugawara." She glanced toward the
curtained dais. No doubt, the exchange between
Kosehira and her mistress had upset her.

"Don't talk to him, girl," commanded the old one.
"Ignore him. Ignore them both. They'll leave soon
enough."

Outraged, Kosehira turned toward the dais. "How
dare you, madam? I'm counselor to His Majesty. I
would have thought that a member of one of the old
families would have a modicum of courtesy."

She cackled again. "Then you're wrong. The Otomo
did more for the emperor's ancestors than any of you
conniving pack of Fujiwara spawn ever did. I'm not
afraid of you or your powerful cousins."

"Some of whom are emperors," snapped Fujiwara,
having turned alarmingly red.

Akitada thought it time to intervene. "Lady Otomo,
please forgive our unconventional visit. My friend is
distraught because his oldest son has disappeared.
We've been calling on all of his friends with no results.
This young woman in your service may know some-

thing about him. We understand that Arihito has been courting her."

The old lady snorted. "Well, girl, do you know where he is?"

Masako blushed rosily and looked at Kosehira. "I'm very sorry, my lord," she said in her soft voice. "The last time I saw Arihito was two weeks ago. That day I told him that I cannot marry him. He didn't take it well. I haven't seen him since. I don't know where he is."

"You refused him? And he didn't take it well?" Kosehira stared at her. His already red face became an angry purple shade. "What have you done to my son, you hussy? His mother's afraid he'll harm himself."

Masako turned perfectly white. "Oh, you must be wrong. Surely Arihito would never do anything so desperate. He cares too much for his parents. I cannot believe it." Tears welled up in her eyes. "He just went away looking sad and—"

Lady Otomo interrupted, "Stop frightening the girl, Fujiwara. She's been silly enough to listen to the pretty speeches of a handsome fellow, but that's no reason to accuse her of things. In any case, I'm the one who put a stop to the affair. A Fujiwara isn't good enough for her."

Kosehira gasped. Akitada suppressed his amusement and said, "Then I take it that neither of you have any information of his whereabouts. Please forgive this visit." He bowed to Lady Otomo and separately to Masako and turned to go, taking the frozen Kosehira by the arm. When he was almost at the door, he paused to add, "We would be very grateful if you'd send us any news about him that may come your way. As my friend said, his parents and siblings are frantic with worry."

There was no answer to this, though a tearful Masako nodded.

Back outside on the silent street, Akitada released Koechira's arm. "A very pretty and well-behaved young woman," he said. "Mori must have done wonders for her."

Koechira exploded. "The old witch said my son wasn't good enough for the girl. Did you hear that? She's mad. I said she was mad, and so she is."

"Hmm. Yes. That was rather strange." Akitada smiled into the darkness. Old Lady Otomo had impressed him as unconventional, even rude, but he had not thought her mad or senile.

Koechira suddenly stopped and grasped his arm with a painful grip. "Akitada, tell me the truth, is Arihito likely to kill himself over a girl?"

"No, I don't think so. He's a sensible youngster." His reassurance sounded weak in the face of the anguish that had sounded in Koechira's voice. "And you heard what Masako said. She said he would never do something like that to his parents."

The grip relaxed. "She did say that. So you liked her?"

"Yes. A beautiful young woman who seems to have a good education and a good deal of character. The moment she realized that you objected to the marriage, she told him that she would not be his wife. If she were truly such a vixen as you seemed to think, she would surely not have done this."

"What about the old witch forbidding the match?"

"I doubt it. Mind you, she probably expressed her displeasure, but I don't believe Masako would be swayed by it.

"I don't know what to think. Or what to do? What can we do, Akitada?"

"Let's go together to talk to her adoptive father again tomorrow. Perhaps he knows something that may suggest a next step."

8

A Violent Incident

Kosehira arrived at Akitada's residence before dawn the next morning. He looked drawn and tense. Akitada, who had not yet eaten and was still in his house robe, asked, "Is anything the matter?"

"No. I couldn't sleep. That clerk, he'll be working during the day?"

"Yes. I expect so. Will you have some gruel with me?"

"If you insist on eating. We should go to the *Daidairi*. I can summon him to my office there."

"That will intimidate him."

"Good. I feel like using some of my power to get my son back."

Kosehira had clearly reached a point where his fears for Arihito outweighed all other considerations. Akitada went to the kitchen and a short while later they sat together sipping their rice gruel. Akitada had made some tea, but Kosehira rejected that. He hardly spoke and then only about trivial matters.

Given Kosehira's impatience, they arrived at the Greater Palace with the sunrise. Streams of clerks and officials in their black robes and hats entered by the great southern gate and dispersed between the halls of government.

Kosehira made for the imperial palace where he was recognized by the inner guards. They eyed Akitada suspiciously, but Kosehira simply said, "Lord Sugawara. We have business to discuss."

Kosehira's office was in the Kyosho-den, the home of the emperor's trusted advisors. Akitada recalled how, many years ago, on the occasion of the great smallpox epidemic that had taken his son's life, he had met Kosehira here. Neither of them had had any idea they would rise in the world until Kosehira would be one of the feared counselors and Akitada no longer in awe of such powerful men.

Kosehira nodded to two colleagues, but it was early and the building was empty except for servants. Kosehira called for a clerk and asked Akitada to make himself comfortable. Akitada looked around. The office was small for someone of such illustrious power and contained only a desk with writing implements, a second desk for a scribe, and some very handsome hanging calligraphy scrolls with sayings of wise men.

"Very tasteful," Akitada commented with a smile, but Kosehira was still morose.

The clerk arrived and was dispatched to bring Mori to them. Since neither knew exactly where Mori worked, they prepared themselves for a long wait.

Kosehira sighed. "How could Arihito just leave without saying anything?"

"Perhaps you used some words to him he could not forgive?"

"A son who cannot forgive his father's just reproof? I should hope Arihito was raised better than that."

"It is because he was raised better that I think you may have wounded him deeply. Without intending it, of course. Are you sure you didn't say something that made it impossible for him to contact you?"

Kosehira was silent. He frowned, thinking it over. "I don't remember what I said. He was stubborn and refused to acknowledge the impossibility of such a marriage. He kept asking me to meet her."

"Well, you've met her. What did you think?"

Kosehira fidgeted and looked around the room. "Young women all have smooth faces. You cannot tell from them what they might hide inside. This one's pretty enough to turn his head. But a man must look to his future. There are plenty of beautiful women to bed outside of marriage."

"I think neither you nor I are much of the bedding-outside type," Akitada said dryly.

That finally brought a smile to his friend's face. "And be sure you keep it that way," he said.

When the clerk returned with Mori, they saw that the man trembled with nervousness. He immediately fell to his knees and touched the floor with his head.

Akitada rose and went to him. "Thank you for coming, Mori," he said with a smile. Extending a hand to help him up. "Lord Kosehira was anxious to meet you and could not leave his office."

Mori stood and the clerk departed. Kosehira did not correct Akitada's words but gestured to a cushion. "Please be seated," he said. "I hope your superiors won't hold it against you that you've been summoned?"

Mori sat and hid his trembling hands in his sleeves. "I don't think so, my lord," he said. "But they were astonished and will ask questions."

Kosehira frowned, "Hmm. Well, we must find something to tell them." He glanced at Akitada, who merely looked vague, thinking that his friend might have considered this beforehand.

Mori waited tensely.

"Lord Sugawara is my friend and my son-in-law," Kosehira informed him. Mori glanced quickly at Akitada and nodded. "He has come to the capital to help me find my son. He called on you in your home recently. What he told me made me think that you might be of further assistance. Are you willing to help me?"

"Of course, your Excellency."

"We have spoken to your, umm, daughter at Lady Otomo's residence last evening. Your daughter says she told my son that she would not marry him. Is this true?"

Mori was beginning to shake again. "I believe so," he said in a low voice.

"Lady Otomo claimed she had forbidden the marriage."

This made Mori's lips twitch. "Perhaps she did, my lord, but it was my daughter who thought it best to break off the relationship."

"You surprise me. It wasn't you, then?"

"No. I could see they were very much in love. I felt that there was no obstacle, other than that of the great difference in rank and wealth, that would make a marriage impossible. Masako was raised carefully by her mother and me. She had excellent teachers and spent time in Lady Otomo's care where she learned to behave like a lady/"

Mori's tone had become almost defiant as he said this, and Akitada felt some admiration for the man. It must have taken great courage to speak this way to one of the first lords of the land.

Kosehira stared at him. "Hmm, what about her mother. What are her feelings in the matter, if she is aware of the situation?"

"My wife is aware. She has met your son and likes him very much. She is very eager for the young people to be happy together."

"No doubt." Kosehira compressed his lips. "How did you come to marry? You must have known about her past."

Mori clasped his hands in his lap. "I was a widower and all alone. She was similarly alone, but with a child. I fell in love. Perhaps her situation made me pity her and her child, but in the end it was for love that I made her my wife."

"But now she has left you."

Mori looked down at his clenched hands. "Yes," he said sadly. "It grieved me, but she said she could only find peace by forsaking the world. I could not stand in her way, though I miss her every day."

"Hmph." Kosehira fell silent. He looked irritated and unhappy.

It was an uncomfortable moment, and Akitada decided to carry on for him. "I assume your wife told you something about her marriage to Tanaka?"

Mori glanced at him and looked down at his hands again. "Very little, sir. I did not press her. I took it to have been an unhappy marriage."

"From all we've learned this Tanaka was abusive and a gambler who squandered his property. I wonder how they came to meet."

"Atsuko's father was a professor at the university. Her mother had died early. They had very little property and lived in seclusion. But her father started drinking, and eventually he lost his position. He managed to earn a bit by private tutoring, but then smallpox got him. Atsuko was alone and desperate. I think marriage must have seemed like an escape to her."

Akitada was reminded of his own courtship of Tamako, the only daughter of his professor at the university. The parallels were there, though Professor Hirata had not succumbed to wine. He sighed. "A very sad story. One never knows what life may bring. Instead of escaping from life with her father, she found herself married to a brutal husband who ended by becoming a notorious criminal."

Mori gave him a shy glance. "Her story nearly broke my heart. I've tried to make it up to her all these years, but some wounds go too deep to heal. She tried very hard, but in the end she only wished to seek peace in serving Buddha. That's why we wished our girl to have a happier life. Atsuko has always insisted that Masako's father was innocent. But it seems people's prejudice will blame this crime on the innocent."

It was dangerous remark and Mori realized too late what he had said. He immediately touched his head to the floor and said, "Forgive me, your Excellency. I didn't mean you or your family."

But Kosehira had had enough. He said coldly, "Thank you, Mori. You may leave."

Mori gave a little gasp, bowed again, then crept out of the room.

When the door had closed, Akitada said dryly, "He probably wishes now Masako and Arihito had never met."

"Prejudice indeed!" snapped Kosehira. "Who does he think he is? It's a very bad thing when people of his kind think we should be delighted to have their children marry ours. What is the world coming to?"

"I thought he was very properly subservient. It was only when it came to his wife and daughter that he turned into a bit of a tiger defending his own. It was rather admirable, you know."

"It was brazen of him to expect my son to marry the daughter of a brutal killer."

"Hmm. I think you need to get away from your worries for a little. The weather is fine. Let's ride out of the city and into the eastern hills. The prince's villa and farm are there. I'd like to see the scene of the crime and thought we might ask some questions of neighbors."

Kosehira muttered, "Good idea. My mind isn't on work today. I won't have any rest until Arihito's found. I'll make my excuses and we'll go."

∞

On this pleasant morning in early summer it was a pleasure to leave the capital behind with its miasma of cooking fires hanging low over the roofs and its streets crowded with traffic and the usual number of beggars and hawkers. Akitada rode his favorite horse again. The gray stallion Raiden had stayed behind in the capital when he had left for Mikawa. Man and horse enjoyed the outing equally.

The fields were under water and peasant families were out planting their rice plants. Birds circled overhead and rabbits darted across the narrow road, and deutzia bloomed everywhere.

Ahead lay the foothills, the deep green of pines brightened by fresh new leaves on other trees, and here and there blooming cherry trees looked like small white clouds floating across the hill side.

Prince Atsutada's farm was not far. The cultivated land was still fairly level, but his house was hidden in the woods above.

"I wonder who inherited all this," Akitada remarked.

Koshira looked around approvingly at the planted fields and the substantial looking farm buildings. "He had a son. Surely he owns all this now."

"His concubine still lives in the house. With her son. Perhaps Atsutada made provisions for them."

"What are you thinking? That maybe the woman decided to do away with him so her son could inherit? Surely that child was never acknowledged. The woman was a courtesan before she came to live with him."

"Men have been known to disinherit their older sons because they had a later child with a woman they were fond of."

For a moment, Koshira said nothing. Then he asked, "Do you think it was very wrong of me to threaten Arihito with disinheriting him?"

Akitada hesitated. "That was not what I had in mind. And I cannot speak to your decisions as a father. But I rather suspect that it wasn't the loss of his patrimony that drove Arihito away."

"No, it was that infernal girl. You're quite right. Arihito has never been greedy."

Akitada sighed. "We won't know what was in Arihito's mind until we find him and ask him. Don't blame yourself."

They passed the farm house and took the road to the private house beyond. This climbed steadily into the forest. Soon they came to an opening in the trees and saw a sizable building of age-darkened wood with moss growing on its bark-covered roof. A decrepit fence enclosed the grounds, but its gate stood open. They dismounted and tied up their horses.

"There doesn't seem to be anybody around. Let's go look for that summer house," Akitada said, pointing past the house at what must be the garden behind it.

Kosehira nodded and they walked through the gate, skirted the house, and found themselves in an overgrown garden where ancient azaleas still bloomed and perfumed the air. A small stream crossed the garden and disappeared under the bamboo fence. A very pretty curved bridge spanned it and a path led to a summer house. The bridge was old but well-built and the path was made of large stones sunk into the earth. The summer house also had survived the years, though here they saw missing roofing and broken floorboards inside. A small lizard was sunning itself on the threshold and darted away when they approached.

They climbed the steps to the veranda and stood in the doorway, looking at the small, bare room inside. The little house was open to the weather on four sides, though broken bamboo blinds hung crookedly in all the openings. The floor was covered with leaves and dirt.

Kosehira said, "I suppose he didn't expect the man to kill him or he'd never have spent the night in such a place."

"No, he didn't expect it. But perhaps he simply assumed that Tanaka would not dare raise a hand against him."

"Or that his woman might, for that matter."

"Ah, Maruko. So you think Tanaka might have been innocent after all?"

"I don't know what to think. It happened fifteen years ago. How can we possibly prove he didn't do it?"

"I have no idea. If you've seen enough, let's go meet this Maruko."

Just then they heard shouting and hurried toward the house. It was no longer deserted or silent. The shouts were coming from inside, and a red-coated constable lounged against the front stairs, chewing on a blade of grass while several more horses were tied up near theirs. The constable straightened up when he saw them. He eyed them suspiciously but came to attention and saluted when he took in their rank ribbons and recognized them as upper level officials.

Akitada returned the salute, having become accustomed to doing this as governor whenever he passed in or out the tribunal gates in Mikawa. "Is anything wrong, Constable?" he asked.

"Just a police matter, sir. Investigating an assault."

"You don't say." Akitada looked toward the house. "Doesn't Lady Maruko reside here?"

The constable suppressed a laugh. "No lady, sir, though she's called Maruko. Never been married, for all she has a son. It's the son we're arresting." This time the laugh slipped out.

"Hmm."

As the constable did not stop them, they walked unhindered into the house. The argument sounded acrimonious. The shrill voice of the woman held its own against the raised voices of several men.

Akitada glanced at Kosehira. "Are you sure you want to get involved? It may make trouble for you."

But Kosehira's expression was bright with interest. "Of course I want to see what's going on. Something has happened to people who may be involved in Arihito's disappearance."

The house was not only in poor repair, it was dirty and filled with the sort of debris other people throw away. In the corridor, ragged *tatami* mats were stacked on a dusty floor with broken book stands and a mutilated paper screen with paintings of birds and branches.

They followed the voices to a large room and found it occupied by five people. Three of these were red-coated constables, one of them a sergeant; the other two were an obese woman and a young man with spiky hair, a bloody bandage around his head, and chains around his wrists.

They all turned to stare at Akitada and Kosehira.

Kosehira snapped, "What's going on here?"

The sergeant stepped forward. "I'm Sergeant Joshu, Capital Police, investigating an assault, sir. May I ask what the gentlemen are doing here?"

Akitada said, "Sergeant, I'm Sugawara Akitada and this is Imperial Counselor Fujiwara. I know Superintendent Kobe very well. We are here on another matter."

The sergeant's eyes widened at the title. He saluted again and asked Kosehira. "Can I be of assistance, your Excellency?"

Kosehira nodded. "Perhaps. Who are these people?" He nodded toward the fat woman and the young man who glowered at all of them.

"The woman is called Maruko. She lives here with her son. That's her son with her. He's a known troublemaker and nearly beat a man to death last night. We came to arrest him."

The fat woman raised her shrill voice again, "It wasn't his fault. Look at him! He was attacked. Viciously attacked by a low peasant. Oh, if only his father were alive. He'd never permit this harassment from the police." She made an enormous effort and got to her feet with a lot of groaning and heavy breathing. Her son watched this without expression. Once she stood, swaying a little, they could see that her clothes, though heavily stained and wrinkled, were of good silk and had once been colorful. The outer robe was a deep green with a black embroidered border and other gowns in shades that had once been rose, blue, yellow, and white showed beneath. All of them seemed equally dirty, and since they did not quite meet in front because of her size, she had tied a wide sash around her middle that looked suspiciously like a priestly surplice.

Her face was painted carelessly, and her features nearly disappeared between her fat cheeks. Letting out another labored breath, she took a couple of steps toward Kosehira and made him a bow. "I'm Maruko, the widow of His Imperial Highness, Prince Atsutada. My poor husband was murdered fifteen years ago, leaving his wife and child to abject poverty and the indignities you observe. No one cares. No one comes here anymore. My honored husband must be a restless spirit, seeing how his family has been treated by those who owed him so much."

Kosehira looked as if he had just tasted a very repulsive morsel. He snapped, "In the first place, Atsutada was plain Minamoto by the time he died. He was a lay priest. Furthermore, he was not married, his wives having died before him, and lastly, he did not acknowledge any sons but his eldest."

She gave a little cry and swayed, reaching for his sleeve. "Prince Atsutada brought me here. We lived together for years before his untimely death. I was the only wife he had when he died. Is it our fault that a monster took his life before he could take care of us? Your Excellency, please help us."

Kosehira twitched his robe out of her fingers. Turning to the sergeant, he asked, "What exactly did her son do?"

Before the sergeant could speak, she cried "Hideyo is Prince Atsutada's son. Alas, it has done him more harm than good. They mock him wherever he goes, and sometimes he gets angry, especially when they also mock his father. This is what happened today. He defended his father when the bullies attacked him. The police listened to people's lies and came here. You can see for yourself how they treated him. They burst into our home to arrest him and knocked him about. It's a wonder they didn't kill him." She started to weep noisily.

The sergeant cleared his throat. He looked uneasy. "Her son's a drunkard and resisted arrest. That little cut on his head he got when we pulled him out of the woodshed by his feet. We arrested him for attacking a man in the village. The man is three times his age and frail, and he laid into him with a broom stick. The victim's unconscious and the doctor said he might not make it through the night. When he dies, this will be murder case."

"Lies, all lies," the woman shrieked. Her son's face took on a threatening expression. He clenched his fists as if he were prepared to fight again. Akitada decided he was an unpleasant looking individual for all that he was young and tall. His low forehead and small, deep-set eyes were bull like and brutish, and the broad chest and muscular arms made him a dangerous opponent.

The sergeant swallowed. "Seeing that you're friends of the superintendent's, we could, er, wait until we see what happens to old Oyoshi," he offered.

Akitada said, "No, thank you, Sergeant. I'm sure you know your business. By all means, go ahead and take him away. If he has done what he did, he should be in jail."

This produced a string of curses from Hideyo that made his mother's claim of his imperial blood laughable. For a moment it looked as though he would resist being taken away, but then he submitted. As the constables marched him out, he spat at Akitada.

His mother wailed and tried to stop the constables, but her size made her clumsy, and in the end she collapsed on the floor, calling on the Buddha to witness the injustice.

Akitada and Kosehira escaped.

9

The Faithful Servant

The encounter with Atsutada's concubine and her son had done nothing to solve their problem. Kosehira said the woman looked perfectly capable of murder, but he sounded discouraged and decided that he must return to work. As they rode back to the capital, Kosehira looked unhappy.

"What dreadful people!" he muttered. "I cannot imagine a person of imperial blood living with such a woman."

Akitada's mind had been on Yukiko. She had been so pleased to be back in the capital that he worried about taking her back to Mikawa in a few days. Now he thought about Kosehira's words for a moment. "I expect she was beautiful once," he said, "and, of course, much younger in those days. And he must have been about fifty. Older men often lose their heads over young women." Then he realized what he had said and bit his lip.

Fortunately, Kosehira had not noticed the parallel to Akitada's own marriage. He said, "Perhaps, but he was a lay priest. Presumably he had given up women."

"Lay priests have not yet renounced the world completely. In his case, it appears he had merely embraced a quiet and simple life. But I was a little surprised that he objected so violently to the crown prince's forced resignation."

"He never liked Michinaga. It was mutual. Michinaga's marriage politics had affected the imperial line again and again. Sitting out there in his country retreat, he probably dwelled on the subject constantly."

"Yes. I can see that. Do you think he fathered her son?"

"I have no idea, but if he did, it wouldn't make a difference. His first son was clearly the heir."

"Hmm. What sort of man is he?"

"Minamoto Yukihiro is about thirty-five years old now. Married with children and, surprisingly, coming up the rank ladder rather quickly. I say surprisingly, because Michinaga blocked his advancement because of his father's politics. He was dirt poor back in those days. Tried to scrape together a few coins by tutoring provincial youngsters who were hoping to make a name for themselves."

"So what changed all that?"

"No idea. Maybe Michinaga forgot about him after his father's death. I expect inheriting his father's land helped. Strange that he's letting that woman and her brute of a son live there."

"Perhaps his father had asked him to look after them."

"Perhaps."

Akitada asked, "If you could bring Arihito back to you, what sort of inducements would you offer him?"

"None!" Kosehira sounded angry, and Akitada fell silent again. After a time, Kosehira said in a broken voice, "What am I saying? I love him. I want him back at any cost. If there were only some way to make this girl more acceptable. Oh, Akitada, I'm at my wits' end. I'll never forgive myself if my son kills himself because of me."

"Then perhaps we should look a bit more closely into that murder. We have learned so far that some of the other people involved with Atsutada may have had motives as strong as Tanaka's. There is, as you pointed out, the woman Maruko, who was certainly conveniently close and may have quarreled with Atsutada. And then there is Atsutada's older son who ended up with his father's property. In fact, there may be people we haven't considered, men who served Michinaga."

Kosehira looked more hopeful. "If you can prove the girl's father innocent, that would help. Arihito would have to step aside for his brother, of course, but he won't mind that. He's never aspired to a great career. But won't Kobe be angry?"

"Kobe is a fair man. Very well. I think I'll have a talk with Atsutada's servant next. If he's still alive, that is."

∞

The servant Yoshito was still alive, though barely so. He was eighty-five years old and lived with his daughter-in-law in the village near Atsutada's house.

Akitada spent some time at home, hoping to see Yukiko, but she was out again with his sister. He ate his midday rice alone and then set out again to the eastern mountains.

By asking his way, he was directed to a small farm-house covered with thatch and surrounded by fields of growing rice. He saw a man and some half-grown youngsters tending to the fields, and outside the house a woman was washing clothes in a large tub. When he dismounted, she had just begun beating a new batch with a round stone. She stared at him in surprise, then dropped the clothes back in the tub and scrambled to her feet, wiping her wet hands on a dark gray cotton dress. She was gray-haired, but still sturdy and clear-eyed. Kneeling and bowing, she said, "Welcome, your honor."

"Thank you. I'm looking for a man called Yoshito who used to serve Lord Atsutada."

"My father-in-law. He's inside, but he doesn't always make good sense. The ghosts of the dead have taken his mind away, I think."

Disappointed by this, Akitada asked, "Do you know anything about his time with the late prince?"

"Very little sir. My husband died four years ago. He used to talk about it sometimes. How when His Highness still lived in the city, there'd been so many servants, more servants than people to look after." She chuckled. "He said some of the servants had servants themselves."

"It must have been quite a change for your father-in-law when the prince settled in the house in the forest."

"Oh, yes. But he said he was so honored to be chosen to come with him that he didn't mind all that work. He's always loved the prince more than his own family." She bit her lip and turned her head away. "Well, look where it got him. He's mine to look after now. And a cantankerous old devil he is."

"Could I see him?"

She sniffed. "He's not much to look at, but you're welcome." Tall for a woman and sturdy but slow in her steps, she walked ahead of him into her house.

It was like many homes of peasants: a single room under a steep roof where people slept, cooked, ate, and huddled together around a small sunken fire pit on cold days. The old man lay on some dirty quilts. He was on his back, staring up at the bare rafters above. In the dim light from the open doorway, Akitada saw that he was emaciated, shriveled, and almost as dark the aged timbers. Only the movement of the whites of his eyes showed that he had noticed their entrance.

The woman said, "Here's a fine lord come to see you, father. Be sure you talk nice to him and he may leave us a present. There's little enough to put in the pot for supper tonight." Turning to Akitada, she added, "He's not able to make his obeisance. I have to lift him to do his business." She grimaced.

The indignities of old age were terrible.

Akitada sat down beside the old man, putting aside worries about staining his robe on a floor that was hard-packed dirt covered with unidentifiable stains. A sour smell hung about the old man and mingled with other, more repulsive odors.

"You are Yoshito?" Akitada asked, hoping this poor relic of a once sturdy man was not deaf.

But Yoshito could hear quite well and he could speak. "I am," he said with a certain quiet dignity.

"My name is Sugawara. I came to ask you some questions about the murder of your master. Do you remember it?"

"Nothing wrong with his memory," interrupted the woman. "He's going on and on about those days. As if it would put food in the pot or take care of him now."

Akitada was beginning to feel a strong resentment toward her. He took a piece of silver from his sash and handed it to her. "Since he can hear me well enough and speak, I think you may return to your washing now," he said coldly.

She dropped the coin down the front of her dress. "Well, as I said, his mind isn't always right, but you can try." She turned and left with a sniff.

The old man tried to smile. It was a crooked smile because one side of his face was frozen, but his eyes were intelligent enough. "Ask away, your honor," he said hoarsely. "Never you mind her. She likes to make out I'm useless." He sighed and gave a small, rattling cough. "Which I am, but I still know what's what. I loved the master. He was a good man and a great no-bleman. You know that he might have been emperor?"

"I believe he was a younger son and resigned his rights to succession."

"That's so. But all the same, he might've been." The old man got a faraway look in his eyes. "I sometimes think how it would have been if he'd been emperor. I think about it when she tends to me."

Akitada nodded. "You would have had servants of your own."

The old man cackled. "So I would. He always liked me. He knew I'd be on his side, no matter what. But that devil came!" The old man's face contorted into a mask of hate. One of his hands clenched and pounded weakly on the floor he lay on. The other did not move.

The misery of living too long, thought Akitada. Parts of your body die before the rest. Unbidden came the thought of Yukiko having to tend to him when he had become a helpless wreck, a half-dead body clinging to life long after he should have relieved her of his disgusting presence. Would she become angry and resentful like this man's daughter-in-law?

"Do you remember much about what happened that day?" he asked.

"Like it was yesterday! Oh, my poor master! There was so much blood. The beast hit at his head and beat in his face. My poor master must've fought, but what good are hands against a brute with a cudgel. And the beast was big and young and very strong."

"Who all was there that night?"

"In the garden house? Only my master. He'd taken to sleeping there because it was cooler. It was summer then and the house got hot during the day. The garden house was open and there was a breeze, so that's where he had me make his bed every night. I'd put down the quilts and place his headrest just so, and then I'd hang the gauze curtains from a hook in the ceiling. That was to keep the mosquitoes off. It was all still that way when he was found." He heaved a deep sigh.

"I'm sorry to be bringing back those painful memories," Akitada said.

"I don't mind. I'm thinking about it all the time. You don't get a thing like that out of your mind ever." He lay, staring up into the roof, and told the story. Perhaps he had told it just like this many times before until people had become tired of it. "He sent me to bed. Always considerate, he was. I keep thinking I should've stayed with him. I could've put my head down on the veranda. The beast would've had to step on me to get in." He paused to cough and his chest rattled. "I woke up after they found him, the boy and then his mother. They made such a noise. I ran out and then to the garden house. He was lying there, on his back, in a pool of blood. There was blood everywhere. It had splattered all over the gauze curtains, and his candle had been knocked over and lay beside him. He was cold when I touched his hand." A tear formed in his eye and trickled down to his ear. "It was the child that found him and got his mother. And she made a horrible outcry. She wailed and wailed." The old man compressed his lips. "What could she know about losing him? She was only a woman from the quarter. She used to pretend she was his wife, but I knew better."

"So the child was not his?"

The old man's eyes swiveled to Akitada's face. "Never. She brought him after she moved in. Mind you, my master was good to the boy, which is more than I can say for his mother. She beat that child something terrible."

"But they are both still living in the house. Your master must've made some provisions for them."

"That was the young lord's doing. See, it never was in the will. Even if the woman kept shouting that they'd been man and wife and that he'd meant to make her boy his heir. She made a lot of trouble so Master Yukihiro let them have the house and some money until the boy was old enough to work. Though from all accounts he's a shiftless, lazy bum."

Yoshito closed his eyes and fell silent. He looked exhausted and heaved several deep rattling breaths. Akitada waited a little. He was afraid he might exhaust the man to the point of death. "I'm sorry, Yoshito, to have reminded you of such a terrible event," he said, laying his hand on the gnarled claw that kept kneading the quilt that covered him. "I take it you have no doubts that Tanaka was the one who did it?"

The old man opened his eyes wide and looked at him. "I knew it was him. And that boy got up for a pee and saw him coming from the garden with blood on his clothes. The police got the monster in the end." He paused to rest a little, then said, "He was mean, that Tanaka. Many times, he'd tell me he'd beat me if I told the master about his lazy ways. I was afraid and kept my mouth shut. Now I wish I hadn't." He started to cough up phlegm again and struggled for breath. Akitada tried to get up to call the daughter-in-law, but the claw like hand reached for his arm and kept him there.

When the coughing had subsided, Yoshito said, "The beast was always asking the master for more money. Telling lies about his kid being sick and needing to get a doctor and medicine. And my master paid. But after a while the master was getting wise to that devil. The day before he died, I heard them arguing. Can you believe it? That animal was shouting at the master. But it did him no good. No more money for Tanaka and his brood. The next day, the young master stopped by for a visit, and I told him about the way that animal had been shouting at the master. The young master thanked me. But it was too late. That night the beast killed him." He finished his story with a high wail that brought his daughter-in-law.

"Now behave yourself, Father," she said, shaking the frail shoulder of the weeping old man. "That's not the way to talk to the good people, and you always bragging about how proper all used to be when you served the old prince."

"Don't trouble him," Akitada said quickly. "We are done. It was very good of him to speak to me." He took a second piece of silver from his sash and passed it to her. "Here. That's for him. For medicine and whatever would give him pleasure."

"*Sake!*" croaked the old man, giving Akitada his lop-sided, toothless smile.

10

The Concubine

Yukiko returned home long after her husband. She was bright-eyed and excited and wore a new gown.

"Akitada," she cried, rushing into his study in a flutter of expensive silks and delicious scents, "you'll never guess whom we saw." She slid to a stop before his desk and sank into a billow of skirts, sleeves, and train.

Akitada reflected that most women would find formal court dress a hindrance to movement, but Yukiko did not let even the heaviest skirts and stiffest fabrics impede her impulsive ways. He had been waiting for her for hours and had finally eaten his evening rice alone. As a result, he was irritated.

"I cannot imagine. You'd better tell me," he said.

"Oh, come! Guess!" she teased. "You solve all sorts of mysteries. Surely you can solve mine. I'll give you a hint: it was the greatest honor!"

Akitada frowned. "I'm surprised that you're still so lively. It's late and I've had a long day, though not as long as yours. I hoped to find you home when I returned."

Her face fell. "I apologize, but when you're attending the empress, you cannot simply get up and say, 'Sorry, Your Majesty, I must go home now because my husband wishes me to serve him his evening rice.'"

He controlled his irritation and swallowed the lecture he had been about to deliver. "The empress?" he asked. "How very impressive. What did you think of her?"

She frowned. "You're mocking me. Why is it that you must always be so condescending? You'd think you'd be pleased that I am invited to the palace. Most men would welcome a wife's help in promoting their careers."

He bit his lip. "Forgive me. I'm tired. Please tell me about your day."

But he had made her angry. "I was just trying to help. You always shut me out. Akiko says you did the same with Tamako. And you refused your sister's help when she offered it."

Akitada felt a sudden, physical pain in the pit of his stomach. Tamako had complained of his treatment to Akiko? His sister was a busybody who kept putting her nose into his investigations and who became adamant when he would not comply with her demands. But

Tamako? She had been the soul of propriety at all times, the perfect wife. The only time she had argued with him had been on the occasion of their son's illness and death, and surely any mother could be excused for some irrational behavior at such a time. Had she really been resentful all these years?

Grief over her death welled up again.

Had she really thought him so neglectful, so uncaring, that she had turned to Akiko to ease her heart? The guilt was back, as fresh and strong as it had been when he found out she had died in childbirth while he served in faraway Kyushu.

He looked at Yukiko, beautiful, young, very much alive, and wished she were Tamako—calm, supportive Tamako, wise and patient with her busy husband.

The doubts returned. He had been afraid all along that Yukiko was too young for him. In the two years since they had become husband and wife, he had feared occasionally that he would have to pay a heavy price for his unseemly lust for her.

Yukiko was still angry. "Why are you just sitting there staring at me? That's what I meant: you refuse to treat me as someone worth talking to. I'm just your wife, a stupid, childish creature unworthy of serious regard. I'm only good enough to lie with you when you want to make the rain and the clouds."

Scandalized, he cried, "Yukiko! What a thing to say!"

"Well, it's the truth, isn't it? I suppose I'll have to settle for that, but Akitada, it's not what I had expected our life to be like."

Anger seized him again. "Being reprimanded by my wife for some imaginary offenses isn't exactly what I expected either," he snapped. "And what gave you the idea that Tamako had similar complaints? My first wife never questioned my behavior. It would not have occurred to her. But then, neither did she spend all her time gossiping with the wives of ministers or empresses. In any case, my relationship with my previous wife is not a suitable subject for you."

Yukiko paled. "Well, I'm not Tamako. Your sister said you made your first wife stay in her own quarters, and you never told her anything about your work. I'm not used to that. My father always spent time with his wives and with his children. Our world was his world."

"Since you have been visiting, you must be aware that his behavior is uncommon. Most men protect their wives and children from the more unpleasant realities. I'm very much afraid that I'm just a very ordinary sort of husband in that respect."

She looked deeply unhappy. Getting up, she made him a little bow. "Please forgive the interruption," she said in a dull voice. "Good night, husband." Her departure was everything he would have expected from Tamako. She even closed the door softly behind her.

He realized after a moment that her "good night" meant he was not welcome in her bed. He sat for a long time fretting over his marriage and thinking back to his life with Tamako, searching for incidents where he might have been the uncaring, unfeeling brute Yukiko had just made him out to be. His thoughts were dismal but inconclusive and eventually he made his bed in his study and went to sleep.

∞

The next morning he pondered how to mend things with Yukiko. It would not be easy. With Tamako, he would have gone to her and taken her into his arms, but Yukiko's accusation that he wanted nothing from her but her body had made that impossible.

He took a leisurely bath and dressed to go out. Then he walked the covered gallery to the north pavilion. A glance at the garden showed that it was as beautiful as ever. A yellow rose bush scented the air, and some late azaleas still bloomed.

He gave her door the merest tap and walked in.

Yukiko was not alone. His sister had already arrived. The two women looked at him and blushed, no doubt because they had been talking about him. He could well imagine the exchange and was angry again.

But anger would get him nowhere. He greeted both in his friendliest manner and said, "I had thought to pay Yukiko's father a visit. By any chance, would you ladies like to come along? We'll be talking about the Atsutada murder."

They accepted the invitation eagerly, and he congratulated himself on having bridged the awkwardness of last night's quarrel by proving them both wrong.

Kosehira also was in a better mood. He embraced his daughter and Akitada and bowed to Akiko. Then he took them on his veranda which overlooked a broad expanse of garden and a sizable lake and sent for food, wine, and fruit juice.

Yukiko informed her father immediately about having been admitted into the presence of Her Majesty, the empress. Her father expressed his pleasure but winked at Akitada. Akitada understood this to mean that Kosehira had been the one to arrange it. Yukiko and Akiko went into an enthusiastic description of what all the ladies wore.

Kosehira listened patiently, smiled, and said, "Akitada, this is going to cost you and Toshikage dearly. I expect a shopping trip is next on our ladies' agenda."

Akitada smiled, but his heart was growing heavy again. Akitada had always been poor, and in retrospect quite desperately poor, and he considered such spending frivolous. But he consoled himself that he could afford it these days and that their visit to the capital would be short. The distraction of pretty clothes would put Yukiko in a better mood and console her to the fact that they must soon return to Mikawa.

Kosehira told them of their visit to Atsutada's former home. The women were spellbound when he recounted the arrest of the loutish Hideyo and the fact that his mother claimed he was the prince's son.

Akiko said immediately, "But that means she had a much stronger motive to kill the prince than Tanaka. What sort of woman is she?"

Kosehira made a face. "Not the sort I'd want you two to know."

"Nonsense, Father," Yukiko said. "We are grown and married women. There's surely nothing that can shock us. And this is a matter of helping my brother. If we can clear Masako's father, he can take her to wife."

Koschira said dubiously, "She will not be a suitable match even then. If you had seen the place and the people, you'd know that none of my sons should choose such a connection."

His daughter was unconvinced. "From what you said, Masako has behaved very well. And if it bothers you that much, you can always find him a first lady whose birth is noble enough to stop any snide remarks."

Koschira glanced at Akitada and smiled a little. "She has worked it all out, it seems. Well, if we can indeed prove that Tanaka didn't do it, perhaps something can be arranged."

Yukiko gave a cry of joy and went to embrace her father. "We'll do it," she assured him. "You and Akitada and Akiko and I. You'll deal with the crime and the police, and we'll get all the gossip about Prince Atsutada's enemies."

Akitada was not hopeful. He doubted Kobe could have overlooked the obvious at the time, and it was now fifteen years later. People's memories were not the same. The crime was old. And perhaps worst of all, it would set them all against Kobe as they destroyed his reputation.

But he said nothing about this. Instead he shared what he had learned from the servant Yoshito. He stressed the old man's virulent hatred for Tanaka after all these years. "His description of Tanaka's character and his belief that he was the killer could well have been influenced by animosity," he concluded.

"There!" said Akiko. "That old man doesn't sound very stable. And his daughter-in-law doesn't seem to take him seriously either. Some people start imagining things when they get old and sick."

Yukiko agreed. She added, "Akitada, I wish you would start looking for ways to prove Tanaka innocent instead of talking to people who hated him enough to believe anything of him."

"I don't arrange the truth to suit my wishes, Yukiko. And neither should you or you'll pervert justice. All you can do is to gather the facts and interpret them."

This clearly did not please his wife, but fortunately there was an interruption at this point. A servant came to tell Kosehira that a woman was anxious to speak to him, claiming that he knew her."

Kosehira rose with a sigh. "I cannot imagine what a woman would want with me. She must be the wife of one of my tenants."

The servant said, "She says her name is Maruko."

"Oh, do bring her in," Yukiko cried, clapping her hands.

Her father looked mildly shocked. "I told you, she is not the sort of person you should know."

Yukiko turned to Akitada. "Please make my father understand that I'm now a married woman and that my husband should be the one to make such decisions."

Akitada was appalled and looked helplessly at Kosehira. He also felt that the former courtesan was someone neither Yukiko nor Akiko should meet. He said, "It is very unsuitable, Yukiko. Your father and I have met her. She is . . . a very uncouth character. I think your father and I should speak to her. We will return to tell you what she had to say."

Yukiko's eyes widened and her face grew white and bitter. "I see. It seems both fathers and husbands prefer their women to be children forever. Do not expect me to become your obedient slave, Akitada. I have a mind of my own and shall use it."

Akiko gave a little sniff, but wisely said nothing.

When they had left the room together, Kosehira said, "I'm sorry, Akitada. I'm afraid she's become used to having her way. But she'll forgive us. Yukiko is the most affectionate girl. You'll see, she'll come to you all softness and love and you'll make up again. I've always thought patching up these small quarrels with one of my wives was most delicious." He slapped Akitada's shoulder and chuckled.

Akitada was too dismayed to answer. Yukiko's behavior shocked and puzzled him. Something had happened to their relationship that could not be fixed so easily. He suspected that that her discontent with him had started gradually some time ago. Perhaps the move to Mikawa had had something to do with it. What shamed him more than anything, though, was that she had spoken to him in this manner in front of her father and his sister.

The woman Maruko stood waiting. She was looking around Kosehira's elegant reception room with wide eyes, turning a little this way and that. When they entered, she started, then got laboriously on her knees and bowed.

"Your Excellency," she cried, knocking her forehead against the floor boards several times. "I came to ask your help for my child, my innocent son, now languishing in prison where they beat him and starve him until he confesses to anything. I'm a mother, sir, who will do anything to save her child. Please help me. They say you're a great man, a man who speaks to the emperor. You can make the police do whatever you want. For the sake of my late husband, who was my son's father, for the sake of the Buddha I beg your assistance."

Kosehira regarded the fat figure in her dirty silks with distaste. "I have no power over the police," he said coldly. "You've wasted your time by coming here."

She sat back on her feet. Tears had left black streaks under her eyes where the heavy *kohl* that outlined them had run. Her eyes went quickly from Kosehira to Akitada. "You, sir, you were at my house when they took my child away. Have pity. My son's not well. He says things he doesn't mean. It's not his fault. He lost his good sense when he saw his father lying there in a pool of blood and the killer threatened to kill him also. It was enough to make any child go mad, and Hideyo was only five yours old."

"Your son actually saw Tanaka after the murder?" Akitada asked, suddenly interested.

"So he did. And Tanaka had blood all over him. He grabbed my boy and shook him and said, 'I'll kill you, too, if you tell anyone you saw me'. Hideyo still wakes up screaming. The ghosts of his father and his father's killer come back to haunt him every night."

Kosehira looked at Akitada. "Well, it explains why the police didn't look any further."

Akitada nodded. He was not altogether convinced by the woman's story. She did not strike him as very trustworthy, and she wanted their sympathy and help for her son. But there was no point in saying so in her presence. He asked her, "How did you come to live at the former prince's house and why are you still there?"

She gave him a sharp, unfriendly look. "Fifteen, twenty years ago I was beautiful. I could have had any man. But the prince fell in love with me and I with him. He used to send for me all the time. Then, after the child was born, he brought us to his home. He made a will before he died. It left the land and most of his money to me and Hideyo. But they told me the will wasn't legal. So after he was gone, everything went to his first son. But he is a good man. Seeing his father's intentions, he let us stay in the house and he sends us a little rice—a very little rice—every quarter. It isn't just, but what could I do?"

Kosehira cleared his throat. "Thank you for coming. I can make no promises, but Lord Sugawara and I will try to do what we can for your son."

She bowed, knocking her head on the floor, and cried, "May Amida bless you, your Excellency!"

11

Shadows of the Past

After the woman Maruko had left, Koschira and Akitada looked at each other.

"Will you really help her son?" Akitada asked.

"If he's Atsutada's son, someone should look after his interests. We can't have members of the imperial family treated like common hoodlums."

Akitada stared at this. "Oh, come! Why not, if they are common hoodlums? You heard the sergeant say he beat a man near to death. That means it could be a murder case."

Kosehira nodded. "Yes. It's nasty. Well, there may well be nothing I can do. Or want to do. But if she's telling the truth and the young man is who she says he is—and there seems to be some reason to think so—then he has been treated abominably and that may well be responsible for his present actions."

Akitada digested this. "Yes, I see your point. The fact that Atsutada's legitimate heir allowed them to stay in the house suggests that his father did want some provision for them. And considering that he grew up in poverty, reared by this woman who apparently beat him when he was child and later filled his head with tales of his having imperial blood, does suggest extenuating circumstances."

"Precisely," Kosehira said with a smirk. "Let's go back to the ladies and satisfy their curiosity.

The ladies still glared. They had clearly decided to make a common front against male dominance.

Akiko demanded, "Well? Are you any wiser and will you share your wisdom with us?"

Akitada said in a reasonable tone, "Akiko, that is quite unfair. We were simply saving you from witnessing an unpleasant and upsetting encounter. As for wisdom, we are as much in the dark as before. This woman, who used to be a prostitute, claims her son is Atsutada's and that he should be protected from arrest and punishment after having nearly killed a man in a fight. You see, it's a common and ugly tale about people we would prefer you not to come in contact with."

"I wish men wouldn't always try to protect us," Yukiko countered. "Frankly, I think the common people are much luckier. Their daughters and wives aren't kept locked away behind walls and blinds until they are barely aware there's sunlight in the world."

Akitada was offended by this charge. Yukiko had had an amazing amount of freedom since their marriage. Here in the capital, she was forever going out with Akiko or visiting her family, and in Mikawa, she had a lovely garden and his company if she wished to go beyond. But he said nothing. There was no point in making things worse. He would guard his tongue with her and wait for her normal cheerfulness to return. So he sat silently, listening to Kosehira report what Maruko had said.

"But don't you see?" Akiko said when he was done. "It means that she has a strong motive to kill the prince herself. What if he refused to acknowledge them? Maybe there was a quarrel and he told her to take her child and leave his house. She thought she'd gain his property by killing him and claiming Tanaka had done it. Maybe she knew that Tanaka was angry about being refused money, and it gave her the idea."

"It was the servant who told me about Tanaka wanting more money," Akitada pointed out.

"That proved they'd discussed money. It doesn't prove Tanaka killed the prince."

Akitada sighed. "There was other evidence. The blood on Tanaka's clothes, the fact that Tanaka had been desperate for money yet twenty pieces of gold were found hidden in his house, and the child seeing him that night coming from the garden house."

"Oh," Yukiko cried, "You don't want to help us. You don't care about Arihito, or my parents, or me." She burst into tears.

Akiko put an arm around her, gave Akitada a reproachful look, and said, "It's what he has to do. Don't forget that your husband spent most of his adult life in the Ministry of Justice, weighing the pros and cons of opposing factions."

Yukiko dabbed at her eyes, sniffed, and nodded. "I'm sorry, Akitada. I didn't mean it. I'm just a little overwrought lately. I think Akiko and I will go home. They were supposed to deliver some silks."

They rose, made pretty bows to Akitada and Kosehira, and departed.

As soon as the door had closed behind them, Kosehira poked Akitada with his elbow. "'A little over-wrought lately'? Gets tearful over every little thing? Are congratulations in order?"

Akitada shook his head regretfully. "Sorry, but I doubt it. At least she hasn't told me."

"Well, but it might be so, right? Sometimes the ladies like to wait to be sure."

Akitada considered the possibility and found that, on the whole, it would be a good thing. A child would fill Yukiko's life. It had become abundantly clear that he could not.

"You'll be the first to know if that's the case," he said lightly. "To return to the subject of Atsutada's family, I think I'll have another talk with Kobe. Do you want to come?"

"Sorry, I'm due at a council meeting today. I'll try to ask some questions there."

∞

Akitada did not feel like going home for his midday meal. Instead he walked into town and ate in one of the restaurants in the eastern market. He recalled it well from previous visits and was pleased that little had changed. The food, some fresh fish and assorted vegetables, was as good as always, and as the restaurant overlooked the market, he could confirm that all was well in the city, for there seemed to be more stands than ever and people thronged among them, intent on buying goods. It was perhaps a sign of his having entered the ranks of governors that he paid more attention these days to the general welfare of the people, his eyes always observing human behavior and gauging the contentment or discontent of the population.

After his meal, he returned to the northern section of the city and sought out Kobe in his police headquarters.

The superintendent did not seem to be very busy—was this, too, a sign of the well-being of the capital?—and was happy to receive him.

"Are you and your lady enjoying your visit to the capital?" he asked with a smile, as he poured them some wine.

"Yukiko is shopping and visiting," Akitada said with a sigh, and I'm still trying to help Kosehira."

The first part of this received a chuckle from Kobe. He sobered quickly, however, and said, "Yes, I hear you've been asking questions. Have you found any answers?"

"Not really. Just more questions. The rumor that the murder may have been political keeps surfacing. Atsutada apparently protested too strongly against Michinaga's efforts to replace the appointed crown prince. One of Michinaga's secretaries suggested Tanaka may have killed Atsutada in hopes of a reward from the chancellor."

"Yes. Rumors fly and it's true that there was a good deal of popular opposition at the time. We had a hard time stopping crowds from marching into the *Daidairi* to protest. Apparently this gave Tanaka the idea to speak to the secretary. Of course he was turned down. A thoroughly reprehensible character, our Tanaka."

Akitada said, "But isn't it equally possible that this may have given someone in Michinaga's faction the idea to use someone else to kill Atsutada?"

Kobe frowned. "Highly unlikely. Really, Akitada, as a rule the guilty person is the one against whom there is a preponderance of evidence. Let me remind you that Tanaka had lost heavily at gambling and owed money to some very dangerous characters; that he argued with the prince about his pay and that twenty pieces of gold were found in his home after the murder. In addition, he was seen coming from the garden house by the boy who noticed blood on his clothes and his wife had washed those clothes before we could collect them. What else do you need? Why go looking for mysterious assassins hired by our late chancellor?"

"I know, I know. But still I wonder. It was all so . . . convenient for everybody."

"Including me?"

"No. I never doubted that you were very thorough and kept an open mind. But still I have more questions. What for example about the woman he was living with? I've met her, and frankly I wouldn't put murder past her."

"Ah, yes. One of my sergeants reported that you and Kosehira were looking around the murder scene when he was there to arrest her son. Seems the charming young man nearly beat a man to death. Since the victim apparently also did some damage, we had to let him go. Of course, if the other man dies, we know where to find him. He's known to us from previous violent acts, but I'm afraid we cannot pin Atsutada's murder on him. He was a mere five years old at the time. As for his mother, she was very upset by the murder. I doubt it was out of fondness for the late prince though. Whatever their relationship was, she was about to lose a comfortable home for herself and her child. I was a little surprised to hear Atsutada's son let them stay on. He claimed his father had taken them in out of charity and he wished to honor his father's memory. She wasn't particularly grateful, as I recall. Said she was the prince's widow and the boy was his. Nobody believed her. She was past her prime for her trade by then—the successful whores were less than twenty years old—and she had a child to support. Anyway, I regret to disappoint you. It wasn't her either."

Akitada heard the anger in his friend's response. "Kobe," he said, "Bear with me. It's not that I disbelieve you. I'd just like to find out whatever there is to know about the people around the victim. What do you know about his son?"

"You don't give up easily, do you? Minamoto Yukihiro is a junior secretary in the Ministry of the Treasury. He is widely respected. He is married and said to be well-to-do."

"Wasn't he in dire straits before his father died?"

"He was struggling. No doubt the father's politics kept him from succeeding in spite of a good university career and his, somewhat diluted, imperial blood. Father and son were not on speaking terms, by the way."

"You surprise me. Someone—I think it was Atsutada's servant—mentioned that the son had visited his father before the murder."

Kobe snorted. "So now you think the man was killed by his own son?"

Akitada flushed. "Not really. Oh, well, I give up. So Tanaka did it, and his wife tried to cover up for him by washing his bloody clothes?"

"She did. A strange woman, if you ask me. Maybe they were in it together. I thought about that, but she really didn't show much emotion when we arrested him, and there was some evidence that he'd been beating her."

"Why would a woman marry a man like that, or stay with him?"

"You know, for someone who's dealt with crimes for so many years and administered justice during two postings as governor you are strangely uninformed about what goes on in some families."

Akitada chuckled. "You're right. Only, I met their daughter and it seemed inconceivable to me that she could be the child of such parents."

"Well, perhaps I've exaggerated. I was frustrated by the fact that she wouldn't talk to us. She comes from a decent family. Her father taught at the university."

"Yes. I heard about that. Tamako's father also was a professor. And you remind me. She, too, was left destitute by Hirata's death, though she had made up her mind to become a nun rather than marry me." They both chuckled. "So Tanaka's wife just made a bad choice?"

"Well, Tanaka was quite handsome in those days. Who knows why women do what they do. For that matter, her father was very different from Professor Hirata. He was a drunkard who lost his position. I have a vague memory that there was some scandal that cost a young man his life. I think the young man's family blamed him."

Akitada pondered all of this. He asked, "Would it bother you if I had a talk with the girl's mother? I think Kosehira's weakening a little in the matter of a marriage between the two."

Kobe spread his hands, "By all means. Talk to whomever you want. It won't change the case, but I would be the last man to stand in the way of two lovers."

∞

The Koryu temple was a small one by most standards. Like Prince Atsutada's retreat, it lay in the eastern foothill, but more to the south. Akitada's journey there involved another pleasant ride, though a much longer one. He only glanced at the temple, the usual walled enclosure with a number of halls and a small pagoda rising within, and asked directions to the convent.

This was even smaller, another enclosure behind closed gates guarded by a sharp-featured nun who peered from a small window and informed him that no visitors were allowed since the inhabitants had chosen to leave the world behind.

Akitada told her that he wished to see the lady abbess on a legal case affecting one of her nuns, and she reluctantly told him to wait, slamming the shutter closed.

Akitada waited for a long time. Eventually, half of the gate opened. The sharp-faced nun stood there, scrawny in her gray robe and sour of expression. "Leave your horse outside!"

Akitada dismounted and tied up his horse, worrying about thieves. The horse was Raiden, his favorite, a present he had brought back from Echigo. No longer young, it had become a friend and had remained in the capital because Akitada worried the journey to Mikawa would be too much for it.

The nun slammed the gate shut, in much the same way she had closed the shutter before. She seemed to be angry at the world outside their convent.

"Follow me!" she said and marched off past a hall and a reliquary to a small building toward the back of the enclosure. There she stopped and pointed. "She's inside." And with that she turned and went back.

Akitada walked up the few steps and knocked softly. The door was opened by an elderly nun, indistinguishable from the gatekeeper nun except by her greater age and the fact that she smiled at Akitada.

"Come in and sit down," she said. "I'm the abbess. I'm afraid I don't know who you are or why you've come."

Akitada introduced himself, thinking that the hostile gatekeeper must be a trial to her abbess.

"I've come to speak to the nun who was previously the wife of Mori Yutaka. He told me that she is here."

"Ah, Nyodai. Yes, she is here, but I'm afraid she may not want to see you. May I tell her what it is about?"

She was everything the other nun had not been, but she exerted the same care to protect her nuns against unwelcome visitors from the outside. Akitada explained about Arihito having disappeared and his connection with the Mori family.

The abbess looked concerned. "Yes, I recall the young man very well. He came to visit with young Masako. And you say he has disappeared? They are such a nice couple and Nyodai was so eager to see them married. What very bad news! Let me send for her."

She went to the door and called to someone, giving instructions to the unseen nun. Then she returned to her seat. Akitada assumed that he would have to conduct his conversation in her presence. Perhaps this was another sign of the care the mother abbess took of her flock.

He did not have long to wait before the door opened again and another slender gray figure slipped in. The nun Nyodai bowed reverently to the abbess and took the offered seat, giving Akitada only the briefest glance before turning her eyes to the abbess.

"Lord Sugawara is here on behalf of Arihito," the abbess told her.

Nyodai's large, deep-set eyes now met Akitada's and she made him a bow. He could see remnants of past beauty in her face, but she was much too pale and thin and some deep lines marred what must once have been a resemblance to her daughter. Her hair was gray and cut short, and the general impression was of a uniform colorlessness. She said nothing and waited for him to speak.

"Forgive me for calling on you and troubling the peace you have sought here," Akitada began.

The abbess interrupted him, "He has come because Arihito has disappeared, causing great worry to his parents."

"Oh!" Nyodai frowned. "Has something happened to him?" she asked Akitada.

"We hope not, but we must try to learn where he might have gone. Since he was courting your daughter, and you have met both of them, I thought you might have some information."

She looked thoughtful but shook her head. "I don't think so. Masako came alone last time. She said their plans had changed. I was very sorry to hear it. They were made for each other and so much in love. I don't understand it."

Akitada seized the opening. "It appears that Arihito's father objected to the marriage. His opposition has to do with Masako's father."

She flushed and cried, "Masako's father did not kill the prince. You must make him believe this. Has he met my daughter?" Akitada nodded. "Then he should have known. Anyone who sees Masako knows her goodness."

"Your daughter is charming, but I'm afraid it isn't that simple. Could you help me understand? Could you tell me about your first husband?"

Her eyes flicked away from his. "I want to forget. The past is the past. It's gone. Why bring it up over and over again? What happened then is like clouds blown away by the wind. The two young people met each other now, many years later. Their love shone from their eyes like the radiant sun in a cloudless sky. That is all that matters."

The poetry of her words almost took his breath away. How could this woman have been the wife of a worthless and brutal man? But he remembered that she was a professor's daughter and would have been given a good education. He studied again the lines in her pale face and realized that she must have suffered much.

He sighed. "It matters because Masako herself broke the engagement and that sent Arihito away. If we could find him, perhaps we could talk to him and find some way to make the young people accept what cannot be changed."

Her hands, so far hidden in her long sleeves, emerged with her prayer beads. She started counting them as her lips moved in prayer and tears slid down her pale face unchecked.

The abbess, who had been quiet throughout, made an impatient move. Before she could interfere, Akitada urged again, "Please help me understand! I want to help."

Nyodai looked up at him with her tear-filled eyes. "Masako's father was a good man. He was kind and brave and would not have hurt anyone. He was no murderer. You must believe me." She gave a small sob, then rose and ran out, leaving the door ajar.

The abbess sighed. "There you have it. It must suffice. I'll not have Nyodai so troubled again. She has come here to heal, to forget the past."

Akitada bowed. "I understand. Yet, her second husband, Mori, is a good man. From all I have learned, a much better man than Tanaka. She stayed with Tanaka, yet she left Mori to seek refuge here. It doesn't make sense."

"I have met Mr. Mori and I feel for him. He clearly cares greatly for her. But it is his belief and mine that she suffers from something that happened in the past. I do not understand it either, but we must let her find peace. She was getting better and so happy for her daughter until just recently. Now the dreams are back and she weeps all the time. So, you see, I will not change my mind."

There was nothing else to be said. Akitada bowed his head and departed without protest.

12

Old Friends

It was a strange feeling. He was no closer to the truth, but Masako's mother had somehow convinced him that he must prove Tanaka innocent. She had been so firm, so utterly convinced. And yet, everything people had told him contradicted her.

He walked away from the convent, weighing his options. He could not return to Kobe with his new-found conviction. Kobe was already angry at him. No wonder, really. If either Kobe or Kosehira had questioned his own decision so persistently, he would not only have been angry but considered them no longer friends.

There was also no point in returning to the place of the crime. The woman Maruko had nothing to add.

That really left only the victim himself. Atsutada had been murdered by someone. If not Tanaka, there were others. No man reached Atsutada's age without making enemies. And in his case it could be assumed that supporters of Michinaga and his candidate for crown prince were the most likely suspects. There were still a few hours of daylight, and he decided to pay some long overdue visits in the *Daidairi*

Very little had changed in the Ministry of Justice, and yet everything was different. The halls rising on three sides of a bare, gravel-covered courtyard were just as always, and the inside of the main hall looked just the same. But there were new faces peering from doorways and nobody recognized him. An unfamiliar servant popped up beside him, asking if he could direct the gentleman. A clerk passed them staring curiously. And when Akitada asked, somewhat anxiously, for Fujiwara Kaneie, he was told that his former superior, the Minister of Justice, now served in the prime minister's office. He had been promoted to counselor and held the same rank as Kosehira but served in a different sphere.

Somewhat diffidently, and feeling quite estranged in the world that had formerly been his, Akitada made his way to the prime minister's office and was shortly shown into a large room where Kaneie, reassuringly unchanged from his former cheerful self, came to embrace him.

"My dear Akitada," he said, "I have missed you terribly. Have you been to the old ministry?" When Akitada nodded, he said, "I couldn't manage without you and they fired me."

Shocked and puzzled, Akitada looked around the fine room with its elegant furnishings, and asked, "What? I was told you were promoted. Was there some mistake?"

Kaneie laughed. "Not at all. They didn't know what to do with me so they put me here and told me not to meddle in affairs." His face fell. "To tell you the truth, Akitada, it was pretty humiliating though they cushioned the blow with the rank promotion and some very productive rice fields to increase my salary."

"I don't know whether to congratulate you or commiserate."

"Neither, my dear Akitada. But you see, I did miss you. Still do. You're in Mikawa for another year or more?"

"Yes. And I'm very sorry, sir."

"Don't be formal. Call me Kaneie. You've made astonishing progress yourself. How's the family?"

"Thriving. The children are in Mikawa, but Yukiko is here with me. It's only a short visit to present some reports and look into an unfortunate romance between my young brother-in-law and an unsuitable woman." He thought of Masako as he had seen her in Lady Otomo's house and amended, "Or rather, a young woman thought to be unsuitable by the young man's father. Kosehira told his oldest son he would disinherit him if he married her, and Arihito promptly left the family and hasn't been seen since."

"Ah, are you playing go-between, then. How very romantic! I suppose the lovely young maiden you married has softened your dry, official heart." Kaneie laughed uproariously and patted him on the shoulder. Come sit down. Perhaps you will share a meal with me before you leave again?"

Such an invitation was an unexpected honor. Akitada was not sure whether it was due to his new stature since marrying Kosehira's daughter or to Kaneie's fondness for him. But he was moved and accepted gratefully.

They chatted for a while about changes in the government and conditions in Mikawa. Eventually, Kaneie's curiosity veered again to Arihito's dilemma, and Akitada asked, "Did you know Prince Atsutada personally?"

"Met him once or twice. Mind you, I was young then, and he seemed to me an older man. A very grumpy older man. He hated Michinaga, who was a cousin of my father's. I expect your friend Kosehira must have felt much the same about him. Kosehira's the son of one of Michinaga's sons. We made a solid front against Atsutada and his supporters."

Akitada raised his brows. "So he had supporters?"

"Oh, yes. Well, you know as well as I the rewards bestowed on a chosen crown prince's staff. And when he duly becomes emperor, there will be even more tangible honors. The opposite is also true. When Atsuyasu was passed over, there were many people who were very angry because their careers were suddenly gone. Mind you, Atsutada had no expectations. He objected on principle and out of affection for Atsuyasu. But, of course, he became the spokesman for the discontented."

"Is it possible that someone removed him to stop his opposition?"

Kaneie looked astonished. "You mean someone who was supporting Michinaga's choice?"

"Yes. I think it was generally known that Michinaga had forced Atsuyasu to resign in favor of Prince Atsunaga."

"I doubt Michinaga would have permitted or encouraged such a thing. He may have been a bit high-handed in forcing people to resign, but he certainly would stop short of murder. In such matters he was very careful indeed. Now that you mention it, I recall that Atsutada's killer tried to get a reward for what he did. Michinaga was outraged. I understand he saw to it that the man didn't survive the journey to the mines." Kaneie pursed his lips. "It was much the best thing. Such a horrible crime against a person of imperial blood. And of a man who had employed him."

"This is much the same story I was told. One cannot help wondering, though, if Tanaka died to keep him from talking."

Kaneie raised his brows. "That too, I would think. Very embarrassing for the chancellor to have a killer claim a reward from him."

Akitada agreed. He thought privately that this did not make it impossible that someone else had acted on instructions. But it was not a subject he could discuss with one of Michinaga's close relatives. Instead he asked if anything was known about Atsutada's marital affairs.

Kaneie knew little. He did confirm that the prince has lost his wives and several children before retiring to his retreat. "He didn't get along with his son," Kaneie said. "The son blamed him for destroying the family's future. He was young and angry then. Later, he settled down, made a good marriage, and is doing well now. It happens frequently like that. Even Michinaga had trouble with his sons."

"Could he have been angry enough to kill his father?"

This thought shocked Kaneie to the core. "A son kill his own father? He would never do such a thing."

"Come, Kaneie, you served long enough in the Ministry of Justice to have come across several such cases," Akitada said with a smile.

"Yes, but not among the good people. For the gods' sake, Akitada, the young man has imperial blood in him."

"Well, for all that Atsutada had imperial blood, he seems to have lived with a common prostitute and may have fathered her child."

"That's altogether different," Kaneie said a little stiffly. "He was, by all accounts, eccentric."

At this point, Akitada changed the subject and they parted amicably a short while later.

∞

Nakatoshi, now returned from his pilgrimage, was still working in the Ministry of Ceremonial. He, too, was delighted to see Akitada, and he, too, extended a dinner invitation to Akitada. Akitada suddenly felt overwhelmed by these new social obligations when he had planned to return to Mikawa within a week. But since he had not made any progress in his endeavors, he accepted with pleasure. They settled down to a chat that was quite similar to the one he had had with Kaneie and similarly led into the matter of Prince Atsutada's murder.

Nakatoshi said immediately, "But that was almost before my time. I was still a very junior clerk in the Ministry of Justice. In those days, I'm very much afraid my mind was on other things. I was courting my first wife." He smiled reminiscently.

Akitada thought that he, too, had only just been married, and now here they were, both somewhat risen in the world, both with the first gray in their hair, both sufficiently disillusioned so that they could look back at that time as a happier one. He said, "I was in Echigo then. Do you recall anything? It was quite a scandal."

"Oh, yes. So it was. I remember people being very upset. We all liked Atsutada, who was by way of being something of a saint in popular opinion. Popular affection had turned away from Michinaga after he forced the crown prince's resignation. Did you know that he first declared him a retired emperor and then gave him his daughter for a wife?"

"Can this be done?"

"Apparently Michinaga could do it. It assured his daughter imperial status and was supposed to console the crown prince for losing the succession. He was a sly old devil, our chancellor."

"Yes, well, I'm beginning to understand Atsutada's opposition, but from what I was told, he was hardly a saint. He lived openly with a prostitute while claiming to be a lay priest. Kaneie called him an eccentric."

Nakatoshi chuckled. "I tend to think all saints are eccentrics. They certainly don't behave the way the rest of us do. But in this case, my understanding is that he took in a lot of poor people and gave them work or shelter. This woman must have been one of them."

"Hmm. There was a child. She claims he fathered it. And his legitimate heir allowed them to stay on in his house. Why would he do so if her claims were false?"

"I have no idea, Akitada. You'll have to ask him."

"Yes, I think I must. The whole story is confusing. And not only about those who have died, but the characters who are still with us also seem very strange." He told Nakatoshi about Tanaka's wife who had remarried and then left her second husband, who apparently loved her devotedly, to become a nun. "She insists Tanaka did not murder the prince. This in spite of the fact that the man beat and abused her. When I pressed her about her life with Tanaka, she simply said she didn't want to talk about it."

Nakatoshi listened with great interest and agreed it was very odd.

"And then there is old Lady Otomo. For no reason that I can see she took Tanaka's daughter into her service. I met the girl. She is very lovely, well-behaved, and lady-like, and treated more like a companion than a maid by the old woman. None of it makes sense. People simply don't act the way you expect them to."

"Ah, but Lady Otomo is another eccentric, you see," Nakatoshi said with a chuckle. "She's not expected to behave normally."

"Do you know anything about her?"

"Just more gossip. Her husband died early while he served as governor in some province. It seems he was attacked and killed by bandits. They had one son and a daughter. The daughter died during childbirth, I believe. By then people were muttering about there being a curse on the Otomos. She ignored them and devoted herself to raising her son to resurrect the family's wealth and influence. He completed his studies at the university with honors and received an appointment in one of the ministries. Alas, during one of the smallpox epidemics he died.. After that, she kept to that tomb of a house, served only by a handful of servants who had been with her most of her life. You say she employed the murderer's daughter? I'm a little surprised, but I suppose she needs more help these days. She must be at least seventy years old."

"I wouldn't know. She stayed hidden inside a curtained dais the whole time I was there. She insulted Koschira to his face, and his whole family with him." Akitada chuckled at the memory. "And she told him that she had forbidden a marriage between Masako and Koschira's son. He was speechless."

Nakatoshi laughed. "I can well imagine. He's imperial counselor these days, isn't he?" Akitada nodded. "Yes, that seems to fit what people have been saying about her. She doesn't care whom she insults."

He turned the conversation to other oddities among the good people, all of them very entertaining but not helpful to Arihito's future. After a while, Akitada made his goodbyes, promised a visit before he returned to Mikawa, and went home.

13

The Heir

Somewhat to his surprise, Akitada found that his wife had returned hours ago and without his sister. It was Mrs. Kuruda who informed him.

"Came home early, your lady," she informed him. "Lady Akiko just dropped her off at the gate. If you'll take my advice, you need to speak to both of them. Gallivanting about in town and visiting every single day since you arrived. It's not what was considered proper in my day."

Akitada tended to agree, but this did not stop him from being outraged by this criticism of his wife and sister. He snapped, "I won't need your advice, Mrs. Kuruda. The ladies in my family do not behave improperly, and I'll thank you not to say such things about them here or elsewhere."

She gulped, then bowed. "I beg your pardon," she said in an affronted tone. "I thought it my duty as an older person to make sure all is as you expect it in this house. But if you do not wish me to inform you in the future, I shall not do so."

"Thank you."

Akitada walked past her and went to his study. He was again in a bad mood and did not want to see Yukiko because he thought he would end up reprimanding her and make things worse between them.

In the fading light, he read his mail. There was nothing from Mikawa yet, and he was mildly uneasy. He also worried again that he had disappointed Yasuko and Yoshi. His daughter was now twelve and beginning to take on the shape and demeanor of a woman. He was out of his depth when it came to girls and hoped that Hanae would help her through the adjustments. Yoshi was almost ten. He had not complained at all about being left behind. Tora and his son Yuki, who was four years older than Yoshi, were his daily companions and there was no lack of activities that thrilled a boy. Their various excursions hunting, fishing, and exploring interesting places made Mikawa a young boy's paradise where the capital would have put great constraints on him.

He smiled a little, remembering his family and suddenly wished himself back with them.

At this point, his door opened and Yukiko drifted in on soft feet. She looked pale and strained but utterly lovely in a pale green gown with a red embroidered jacket. No doubt more new purchases, he thought, and reminded himself to look over his accounts. Beyond that thought, he steeled himself for another attack.

"Forgive me for troubling you," she said softly. "I came to apologize."

Pleasantly surprised and relieved, he rose to go to her.

She had tears in her eyes. "I was wrong to speak to you in that way. I'm very sorry. I have been . . . I haven't been myself lately."

She looked so contrite and so lovely that Akitada took her into his arms. "Never mind, my love. Are you ill?" He held her away a little to look at her. She blushed and buried her face against his chest.

"Not ill. No," she murmured into his robe.

"Then what is wrong?" His right hand stroked her silky hair while his left held her closer. He felt a sharp surge of desire, and murmured, "I love you, Yukiko. Never forget that. Whatever may happen, I shall never stop loving you."

She trembled a little in his arms. "I love you also, husband. I came to tell you that I think I'm expecting a child again."

Joy filled him and love, and he kissed her tenderly, murmuring endearments.

The letters on his desk forgotten, he took her in his arms and carried her to her room.

Later, when they lay side by side, smiling at each other, he said, "You have made me happy. I never thought I could be happy again, and perhaps I never was this happy before."

She touched his face. "I may not be able to have this child either, Akitada. After losing the first, I've been afraid that I cannot carry a child to birth. I've been afraid that I will be a big disappointment to you."

"And I've been afraid to lose you," he said. "You see, my love, I am content to have you even if we have no children together. It is you I need. I have Yasuko and Yoshi and am content. I love you as you are."

She crept into his arms again. "'A love that grows and swells beyond concealment like a young bamboo in a grassy field,'" she quoted with a soft laugh.

"A love," he responded, "that is as strong and lasting in its color as the needles of the pines in our garden." His heart was full. They fell asleep in each other's arms, their evening rice forgotten.

∞

The next morning they shared their morning gruel like two young lovers, saying little but speaking with their eyes. For Akitada, all his past doubts and self-recriminations had fallen away. He allowed himself to enjoy life in the moment. It did not matter that he was old enough to be her father, or that she sometimes thought him dull, or that she sought society's approval where he disdained it. He drank in her beauty with his eyes and lost himself in the thought of her lovemaking and that she had conceived his child.

For the first time he hated leaving her company, and this time she did not reproach him. He bathed, had himself shaved, then spent some time over his accounts.

The expenditures were shocking to a man who had been poor all his life and only yesterday he would have called his wife to order, but today he reminded himself that he must learn to adjust to a new life, just as she would adjust to the demands of his career. It appeared that most of the charges were from a silk shop owned by a man called Nakai. Apparently, he specialized in rare silks and brocades. He sighed a little. Part of the blame must go to Akiko who spent lavishly herself. Her husband, Toshikage, was wealthier than Akitada and had always given her free rein.

Putting domestic matters from his mind, he thought instead of the Tanaka case. He had postponed too long speaking with Atsutada's son. In his mind, this man, Minamoto Yukihiro, was a possible suspect in his father's murder. Minamoto was the name bestowed on the prince's descendants when he resigned all claims to the succession and agreed to become a commoner. It had been clear from what he had gleaned in various conversations, most recently with Nakatoshi, that the son had had cause to blame the father for his difficulties, and that most likely the father's death and his inheritance had changed his misfortunes quite amazingly. This suggested the two most common motives for murder: greed and revenge. Besides, the man had acted very uncharacteristically in allowing his father's protégée and her son to remain in the house all these years.

Minamoto Yukihiro was dutifully at work in his office at the Ministry of the Treasury. He received Akitada courteously, though he was clearly puzzled by the visit.

He was a few years younger than Akitada and a handsome man with an intelligent face and a rather stiff manner. "Lord Sugawara? What gives me the honor of your visit?"

"The honor is all mine," Akitada said smoothly. "I had long hoped to make your acquaintance. Somehow we must have missed each other in all those years."

If anything, this increased Minamoto's stiff manner. "Please be seated and allow me to send for some wine." Without waiting for an answer, he clapped his hands and told the prompt servant what he wanted.

Akitada sat down and they looked at each other for a moment. Neither seemed to know how to start. Minamoto was the first to speak.

"I believe I heard that you work in the Ministry of Justice?"

"I used to, for many years. At the moment, I'm governor of Mikawa. On a brief visit to the capital."

This made Akitada's visit seem even odder, and Minamoto stared at him blankly. "I see," he said.

The wine arrived and was poured and served. The servant departed. Akitada decided to relieve Minamoto of his puzzlement. "I came in hopes of getting some information about your honorable father's death," he said. "Some questions have arisen as to the circumstances."

The other man raised his brows. "I recall now that you are the Sugawara who solved some very famous murder cases. Are you applying your expertise to the murder of my father?"

Akitada did not know how to respond to this direct question and took a sip of his wine. As it was very good, he complimented his host. Then he said, "I am sure that Superintendent Kobe did a very thorough investigation at the time, but a relative has expressed an interest in knowing the details."

Minamoto frowned. "I cannot imagine why that should bring you to me," he said coldly. "I wasn't there. I know nothing about it."

"But I understood that you paid your father a visit shortly before his death. A visit that must have been unusual, since you had been estranged from him for a number of years."

Angry color rose in Minamoto's face. "What are you implying?" he asked sharply. "That I killed my own father? How dare you make such an accusation? Get out of my office! I shall lodge a complaint against you!"

Ouch! Akitada had only himself to blame for not having approached the matter more cautiously.

Or was the reaction perhaps due to a guilty conscience?

"Please calm down, sir. Nothing of the sort crossed my mind," Akitada said. "I had simply wondered if your father had expected some attack and asked to see you for that reason. And even if that wasn't the case, I thought he might have mentioned something that would explain what happened later that night."

"Oh." Minamoto still frowned as he considered Akitada's words and his own response. "No. It was nothing of the sort. I had heard that he was not in good health and decided to check on him. As it was, I'm very glad I did. It gave us a chance to patch things up."

This, Akitada thought, was a lie. It was too convenient, too proper, too unlikely. But he merely nodded. "A happy memory. And a great consolation, I should think."

"Oh, yes. Though his death was a terrible shock. Very painful under the circumstances."

"Did you know or meet Tanaka?"

"Not until the trial. I knew he was my father's *betto*. We had spoken about him that day. My father disliked him very much and didn't trust him. He said the man drank and gambled and kept his wife and child half-starved, but that he had run out of patience with giving him money every time he asked for it. Alas, his decision cost him his life."

"Why didn't he simply dismiss him?"

"He felt pity for the man's wife and child. My father was forever taking in beggars. The woman who lived in his house also had a child. He took them in when he heard that she worked as a prostitute to earn money. Frankly, I was rather shocked. It led us to quarrel."

"Ah, Maruko. I was surprised to hear that you allowed them to stay in the house. And you even let them have a rice allowance every year."

Minamoto flushed. "My father had asked me to look after them if anything happened to him. I promised. Of course, I didn't expect it so soon. He wasn't really ill. The rumors had exaggerated his condition."

"People tend make their stories more dramatic. He did have complaints, though?"

"Yes. He had pain in his back. He said sometimes, especially in cold weather, they got very bad. But when I saw him, he was quite well."

"I'm very glad to hear it

A brief silence fell. Akitada finished his wine and prepared to depart when Minamoto returned to the beginning of their conversation.

"May I ask now who the family member is who wished clarification?"

Akitada would have preferred to keep the information from Minamoto, but he complied. "My young brother-in-law wishes to marry Tanaka's daughter. She is a grown woman now. It's not surprising that she should wonder about her father's crime."

The other man relaxed. "Ah. Yes. I suppose it must be very unpleasant for her. I'm afraid I know nothing in his defense."

Akitada thanked him for his time and took his leave.

14

A Son Returns

The sun was high when Akitada left the Ministry of the Treasury. He decided that he should report to Kobe what he had learned so far before walking home for his midday meal. Leaving the greater palace enclosure by the Joto-mon, he walked across to police headquarters.

Kobe greeted him with a broad smile. "I was just thinking of you. Sachi has been saying I should bring you with me for a meal next time I see you. Is today a good day?"

Akitada hesitated—he seemed to have more social engagements lately than he could well accommodate— but then accepted with thanks.

143

Kobe rubbed his hands. "Excellent. We live very quietly, you know. Hardly anyone ever calls at the house. This will be pleasant indeed. Sachi is very fond of you." He laughed a little. "I might even be jealous if I didn't know her better."

"I hope you know me better, too," Akitada said with a smile, "though I grant you Sachi is lovely enough to turn any man's head."

"Yes, she is, isn't she? Akitada, she has made me so happy. It was all worth it. Giving up my properties, I mean. She manages on very little, and we have each other."

Akitada, still filled with the warm thoughts of his night with Yukiko, said, "Indeed. You are to be congratulated. I've always believed that there is little connection between wealth and happiness."

"Well," Kobe said, nodding, "and what news are you bringing me?"

For a moment, Akitada was tempted to tell him of Yukiko's pregnancy, but he had not yet told Kosehira and besides his own good news might remind Kobe that Sachi had not given him a child yet. He started into his report about the Tanaka case instead. Halfway through his meeting with Kaneie establishing the fact that Atsutada had had many political enemies who might well have acted for their own personal reasons and not because Michinaga had asked them to, he realized that Kobe's expression had become grave. He trailed to a stop.

"So you are still determined to prove me wrong," Kobe growled.

Suppressing a sigh of irritation, Akitada said, "Not at all. I thought you wanted to hear what I have learned. What you make of it is up to you."

There was a brief silence. Kobe visibly readjusted his expression and attitude. "Go ahead then. Just as long as you don't expect me to reopen the case."

"I wouldn't dream of it. In any case, as I said, Kaneie, who is related to the ruling Fujiwara clique stressed the point that Atsutada had lots of enemies that were not in the pay of Michinaga whom he considers above reproach. The implication was that the prince was an unpleasant character. Against this you may hold the views of my friend Nakatoshi, who is not related or obligated to Michinaga's crowd. He says that Atsutada was considered a saint by the people." He paused, waiting for comment, but Kobe said nothing. "Well, my last interview was with the man's son. Now this was very interesting. Minamoto Yukihiro confirmed the saintly nature of his father by telling me that he had been in the habit of taking in people who needed help. Tanaka himself had been such a man, down on his luck and with a wife and young child to feed. But Tanaka turned out to be a gambler who kept demanding money all the time. Apparently the only reason Atsutada kept him on was because he felt sorry for his wife and child. Maruko and her son were also charity cases. The son continued the father's provisions for them to honor his memory. You may or may not want to believe this."

Kobe grimaced. "You *have* been busy. Why was the son particularly interesting? I take it you didn't believe him."

"Well, it all sounded very filial. The story is that father and son had a falling-out because the son blamed the father for having ruined his prospects in the world. These prospects changed dramatically after the father's death. The son claims he visited his father on the day before he was murdered because he was concerned about his health. He said they made up their quarrel before he left. I have a suspicious mind, as you know, and it struck me that he would say this now even if the opposite had been the case."

"And by the opposite you man that father and son had a quarrel and the son returned later to kill his father out of spite and because he needed the property?"

"It sounds more plausible than what he told me."

"Only one thing wrong. You have no proof for either of your options. Whereas I have plenty of proof that Tanaka killed him."

Akitada sighed. "I just wanted to know what you thought, that's all."

"Not much. You're wasting your time and mine."

Offended, Akitada rose. "Forgive me. I just remembered. Yukiko will be expecting me today." He did not think so, but continuing the fruitless and hostile discussion with Kobe over the midday meal had lost its appeal. "We'll share a meal another day."

Kobe nodded, saying nothing. He did not bother to get up.

∞

Akitada walked home depressed by the breach between Kobe and himself. He did not know how to mend it and thought again that they must find Arihito. It might not be possible to clear Masako's father. In that case, Kosehira must resolve the situation with his son.

He returned home not so much because he really expected Yukiko to be there, but rather because he had lied to Kobe and had a vague notion that he was now obligated to follow through.

When he reached his street, he was surprised to see Genba busy with a bucket of water and a rough twig brush working on some writing on his gate.

Genba saw him coming and stopped. "Sorry, sir. I would've been done in a moment. No idea it was there until the young gentleman knocked and told me."

Akitada blinked at the message, apparently brushed on in haste with some sort of black ink. The characters were poorly formed, but the words were clear enough: "Kill Sugawara!"

He was stunned into speechlessness, and Genba said again, "I'm sorry, sir. I don't know when it happened. I don't suppose you noticed when you left this morning?"

"I don't think so, but I didn't really look. Just get it off before too many people see it and wonder what I've been up to."

What he had been up to hardly accounted for such hatred. It was senseless. Shaking his head, Akitada stood at the gate.

Genba took up his brush again and sloshed more water on the words. Whatever the person had used seemed to be hard to get off. He said, "I'm afraid the young gentleman saw it. I'm sure your lady heard about it, too."

"What young gentleman?"

"He said he was your lady's brother, sir."

"And you let him in on his word?" Akitada demanded. "After you saw that message? Where is he?"

Genba paled. "With your lady, I think. He looked perfectly proper, sir. Mrs. Kuruda took him in. Did you expect trouble?"

Akitada bit his lip, sorry he had snapped at Genba. "Never mind. It's probably all right. Just get that writing off the gate." But he hurried inside, suddenly uneasy about Yukiko.

He need not have worried. Mrs. Kuruda, with her eagle eyes and catlike curiosity, was waiting for him. "Good," she said. "You're home. I'll tell cook you'll be three for the midday rice. I suppose you've heard."

"Genba said my wife's brother stopped by. Which one is it, do you know?"

She knew. "Why, the one everybody's been looking for like a lost treasure. I could've told you he'd turn up."

Arihito!

Ignoring Mrs. Kuruda, Akitada hurried to his wife's pavilion.

They sat beside each other, and so Akitada could see the resemblance between them clearly for the first time. They looked serious, but Yukiko's face lit up when he came in.

"Oh, Akitada! You've come home. Look who showed up at long last. I've been giving him a lecture about the way he treated our parents."

Arihito flushed and got to his feet. As he came toward Akitada, he hesitated a moment, perhaps wondering if he should make him a formal bow. Apparently he decided their relationship was more personal and embraced Akitada. "I'm very sorry," he said, sounding contrite. "I was sure Father had not only disinherited me but also disowned me. It was very painful and I went away to think what to do next. I'm glad I was wrong. It's been terrible to be all alone in a world where nobody cares and you don't have a home to go to."

"Serves you right," said his sister. "What a foolish fellow you are. Don't you know we all love you? Yes, Father, too. He blamed himself and suffered the pains of hell."

Arihito hung his head. "I'm sorry," he murmured again. "Do you think I should go to see them?"

"Of course," said Akitada, sitting down and waving Arihito back to his seat, "but we'll send a message first. Yukiko, you had better write a note to your parents. Tell them to come. I think the meeting will be easier if we are all together here."

Yukiko jumped up and got her small desk and her writing box.

Arihito shot Akitada a grateful glance. "Thank you, Brother."

Family bonds being thus reestablished, Akitada asked, "Where have you been?"

"In Hikone. A friend of mine is a monk in one of the temples there. I needed a place to think."

"You didn't intend to take the tonsure, I hope," his sister said, looking up from her letter.

Arihito gave her a smile. "I was thinking about it, but I found their life didn't suit me. My mind was on Masako instead of Amida."

"Well," she said, "I'm glad this Masako at least kept you from making a bad mistake."

"I wish you could meet her, Little Sister."

"Akitada met her. He says she's beautiful."

Arihito turned to Akitada, his face filled with love. "Yes. She is most beautiful, but there is more. Such goodness and love shine from her eyes that looking at her is almost like . . . like . . ." Words failed him.

Akitada smiled. "I think even your father was impressed, and he had made up his mind to dislike her."

"So Father went to see her. That's good. That's very good. Maybe there's hope after all. Mind you, if she would have me I would have married her even after Father disowned me. Alas, she said it was impossible unless Father approved.." Arihito heaved a sigh. "Do you really think there's some hope?"

Before Akitada could answer, Yukiko cried, "Of course there is. Akitada will prove Masako's father innocent and then Father will allow the marriage." She waved the note about to make the ink dry faster, then called for a servant.

Her maid appeared for the note and instructions, and Yukiko came to join them.

"I'm afraid it's not easy to prove Tanaka innocent, Yukiko," Akitada said. "The evidence is very solid. I've talked about alternatives with Superintendent Kobe, but he is getting very short with me. I'm afraid suspicions won't do. We need proof."

Arihito said, "Please tell me what you have discovered so far," and Akitada took him through all the conversations he and Kosehira had contrived with the people who had known the prince and Tanaka. When he was done, he said, "So you see that we have been unable to discover any solid facts that would prove Tanaka innocent and another man guilty."

Arihito's eyes were shining. "But that doesn't matter," he said excitedly. "They will be found. I'm back now and I'll take a hand in this. Between us, we'll surely find the guilty man."

Yukiko clapped her hands. "Exactly! And Akiko and I shall go and ask more questions at court. There are people who will know. And even if they won't talk, we'll know where to send you and Akitada to probe further."

Her cheeks were rosy with enthusiasm and she regarded both her brother and her husband with such loving joy that Akitada did not have the heart to contradict her. It struck him once again how beautiful she was and how warm and tender she could be, this young wife of his and, with good fortune, soon-to-be mother of his child. He wanted to have her to himself, but here was Arihito and a moment later Mrs. Kuruda, eyes bright with curiosity, showed in Kosehira.

Kosehira saw only his son. "Arihito!" he cried, opening his arms wide, "where have you been?"

Arihito jumped to his feet and went to be embraced. When they parted, both had tears in their eyes. Arihito muttered, "Sorry, Father. I thought you didn't want to look at me and went away."

"Nonsense. You should know me better. How could you think such a thing, my son?"

"I . . . thought I had disappointed you so greatly that you disowned me."

"Disowned you? Are you mad? Did I say so?"

"Not exactly. But Father, I was so upset at the time that I may have heard things. That's why I decided to come back. When I heard Akitada was in the capital, I thought to ask his advice."

Akitada cleared his throat. "Come, Kosehira, sit down and have a cup of wine and you can clear matters up between you."

15

Joy and Sadness

Father and son made up their disagreements and Akitada's wife informed them of the expected happy event. The result was a celebration. Good fortune had returned to them. They went to Kosehira's house to share the joyous news with the rest of the family and shared an impromptu feast. Akitada once again watched the easy way in which this family shared their lives. It had never been thus for Akitada and still was not, and he worried that the fault might be with him.

Yukiko wanted to stay with her mother, but the men eventually returned to Akitada's study where wine and some light refreshments awaited them. Mrs. Kuruda knew what was going on. Akitada suspected she listened at doors.

It was here that Arihito made the first suggestion that perhaps not all was well. He mentioned the writing on Akitada's gate.

"I didn't want to say anything to Yukiko," he told Akitada. "Now I'm glad I didn't. She told me she lost your last child. She mustn't be upset by something that is probably of no importance."

Akitada shook his head in puzzlement. "I cannot imagine why this should have happened. I'm not aware of having angered anyone lately." This was not altogether true. He had angered Kobe, but Kobe was hardly the sort who would come at night to paint hate messages on Akitada's gate. Kosehira's suggestion that Akitada should call in the police for protection seemed exaggerated. He protested, "It's surely just a prank. A juvenile prank."

But the feeling of happiness had dissipated for Akitada. It was not just the message at the gate. Both the memory of his conversation with Kobe and Yukiko's pregnancy had raised new worries. She had not said anything, but Akitada realized belatedly that she could not travel back with him on horseback. In fact, she should not have come this way. But a carriage or litter had been out of the question because that form of travel was much too slow. It was also too slow to return this way. Akitada was needed in Mikawa and could not spend three additional weeks on the road. Yukiko would have to remain here in the capital or travel separately.

Kosehira mentioned this fact directly. "It's a good thing you found out about the expected child while you're here. Now Yukiko's mother can look after her properly while you're at your post."

This sounded as though Akitada could not be trusted to look after his wife. He bit his lip and considered the point. The prospect of returning to Mikawa alone was dismal. They would be separated. The situation was no different from when he was serving in Kyushu when Tamako had died in childbirth. Panic flared up and he clenched his fists. "No! I will not leave Yukiko behind. Not again. Not ever again. I'll arrange comfortable travel for her. Tora and Saburo can come to fetch her with a carriage and a litter. They'll bring her maid, and I'll meet them halfway."

As expected, Kosehira objected vociferously. "You can't be serious. She'll be on the road for weeks. There are bandits everywhere. You cannot expose her to that or the discomforts of inns and monasteries for overnight accommodations. No, Akitada, she should be with her family at this time. Unlike Tamako, Yukiko has family. She'll be looked after with the utmost care, I promise you."

Akitada looked from Kosehira to Arihito and saw the concern in their eyes. "I'll think about it," he muttered weakly.

The message on his gate worried him less, but Kosehira was outraged by it and returned to the topic. "It isn't safe in your house as long as this villain is loose. You must call the police right away. Someone may have seen something. Are you sure you have no idea who is after you this time?"

"This time" referred to the many attacks Akitada had suffered from assorted enemies. Some of these had tended toward ruining his career and depriving him of his livelihood. Attacks against his person and his family usually came from some criminal who had felt threatened by him. He thought back over his recent activities and his most recent cases.

"The only people who would have sufficient cause to kill me or harm my family are either dead or in jail or exile," he said.

The memory of Ise and the abduction of the shrine virgin raised more depressing thoughts. The good had died along with the villains. But before that had been the serial killer Hatta, Hatta had been a madman who had sought out and killed all those he held responsible for his father's death. Akitada had caught up with him in Otsu. He had lost track of the man later because he had fallen in love with Yukiko and married her. "I don't suppose Hatta could have escaped again," he said doubtfully.

"Hatta's dead," Kosehira said. "I heard while I was still at my post as governor there. But think! There must be something else. When you were in Naniwa, someone sent his warriors to attack your home. They killed old Seimei, I recall. And before that vandals set your house on fire."

Akitada nodded. "You're right. I've made an astonishing number of people angry. But the Naniwa case involved pirates, and that has been settled, and the young arsonists were all caught. Besides, I doubt they would have hidden their grudge for years and only now come forth to deliver a threat. Though this smacks of the same type of mentality. Someone young, or at least someone simple. But I cannot imagine who that could be."

Koschira clapped his hands. "I've got it. What about that fellow they arrested at Atsutada's house? He seemed to have taken a dislike to you. Though why he would do so now escapes me."

"I had nothing to do with his arrest. He's the one who got the constables after him when he beat up another man and put him at death's door."

"If this man is in jail, it couldn't have been him," Arihito pointed out.

Akitada disabused him. "They had to release him. The victim is improving and witnesses confirmed that the fight was mutual." Akitada made a face. "Just another drunken brawl. Given what we know of him, I wonder how he could claim imperial blood."

Koschira chuckled. "You surprise me. Usually you regard people of your class as far more prone to malfeasance than ordinary people."

"Yes, but this was mere thoughtless violence."

"Just the type to write threats on your gate," Arihito commented. "In any case, I think I'll have a look at some of the people you and Father talked to. There must be something somewhere we can use to throw doubt on Tanaka's guilt."

∞

Father and son left soon after. Akitada sat for a while, worrying about Yukiko. Slowly he came around to considering the fact that she would be safest if she stayed. She would have the best of care from her doting parents, and he would not be quite as far away as he had been in Kyushu. In any case, he could make every effort to return when it was time for the child to be born.

The idea of welcoming another child pleased him. He loved his children, had always adored them, though he had never had enough time to spend with them. Gradually he had lost his touch until he no longer knew how to talk and play with children, and he now felt that was a great loss. Tora had always had that skill and still had it. This new child would be his chance to learn again. And it would bring him and Yukiko closer together again.

Having somewhat settled his assorted concerns in his mind, he became restless. After some thought, he decided to return to the place where the late prince had lived and died. Surely there were still people there who knew him and who also knew the people he had lived with.

Genba saddled his horse, and Akitada set off into the western mountains again. It had turned cloudy and a slight wind had sprung up. Before he reached the foothills, the first drops began to spatter in the dust of the road.

He reached the small village where the prince's old servant lived with his daughter-in-law and took shelter in its small wine shop. The wine was atrocious, raw, grainy, and of a potency that burned his throat and stomach, but it left behind a welcome warmth. The day had turned chilly outside, and Akitada's moist clothes made him shiver.

Only the owner of the place, an elderly man with a forbidding scowl, was working. The other customers were two old peasants who were throwing dice in a corner. For a while nothing much happened. The owner sat beside his barrels and earthenware containers and stared out through the open doorway at the rain.

Akitada said, "A summer shower. I expect it'll stop soon."

"I wouldn't count on it, sir," the man by the barrels said.

"Have you been here long?"

"What's long? I've been here since the time the river flooded. It rained for ten days then."

Akitada, not having been in the area at the time, could make nothing of this, but one of the gamblers said, "Terrible, that was. Washing away people downstream. Fast. They never found 'em. I bet they swam all the way to the sea." He laughed in a heartless way.

His companion added, "Took away part of a temple, statues and all. I guess they were traveling with Buddha himself."

Both laughed at this. The wine shop owner looked bored.

Akitada suppressed another shiver and bravely swallowed more wine. "I hear someone nearly got killed here the other day."

His host finally paid attention. "Who's spreading tales about my place?" he asked belligerently.

"Nobody to my knowledge. I was there when the constables arrested one of the men. They said he'd nearly killed the other one. He looked big and strong and mean."

One of the peasants cackled. "He's mean all right, is our Hideyo."

The other grinned and added "For all that he's a mama's boy."

The wine shop owner gave them a look and said, "Hideyo's not all there." He placed a fist to his head, then opened it. "Pah! Crazy. Mostly he's all right, but when someone says something against his mother he turns into a tiger."

The cackling peasant laughed again. "Makes it hard not to offend him. Old Maruko's a mess and a half."

His companion corrected him. "She's at least two messes, Takeo. Have you seen her lately? That woman can eat!"

"Good thing Hideyo's not here," their host said. "Best watch out. The constables let him go."

The peasants stared. "How could they?" one asked. "After what he did to old Fumio? He'll never work again. The bastard broke his arm."

"And knocked out his teeth," the other added, then asked Akitada, "You won't tell Hideyo what we said, will you?"

Akitada reassured them.

Their host grumbled, "I can't afford to have the constables arresting my best customers. He'll be here later."

The peasants looked at each other and decided to go home.

Akitada asked the host, "Hideyo's a regular here?"

"Just about every day. He likes his wine and he likes the dice."

"I wonder where he gets the money."

"Oh, his mother keeps him in funds. She dotes on him. Mind you, Hideyo doesn't fight very often. Most of the time he's quiet as a dove. But when he's got one of his bad days, then you've got to watch out. Mostly his mother keeps him home then. People say he's possessed by an evil spirit."

Akitada was not convinced that this was so, but such erratic behavior was not satisfactorily explained by simple madness. In any case, it made Hideyo a dangerous man to be around. Perhaps he should reconsider the significance of the message written on his gate.

Thanking his host, Akitada paid.

Outside the rain had stopped. The air was cool and fresh and perfumed with the scent of the pines that covered the hills above the village. The sun had come out, and the world glistened as if it were new. A cat walked gingerly across the muddy road, lifting its feet delicately, and Akitada's horse raised his head and shook rainwater from its mane and tail, the drops shimmering for a moment before they fell.

It was not far to the farmhouse. When he arrived, Yoshito's daughter-in-law greeted him with the news that he was better. She passed on this information sullenly, and Akitada began to suspect that she had been hoping for the old man's death. The thought filled him with sadness. What must it be like to live your life in the faithful service of others and end up being a burden to your family who pray to be rid of your failing body?

He followed her into the main room and found Yoshito looking at him with bright eyes. Akitada smiled and knelt beside him. "I see you're feeling better today, Yoshito. Do you remember me?"

"Yes," Yoshito croaked. "You were here before asking about my master."

"Do you mind telling me a little more about him?"

"Do I mind? No, sir. He was a saint, my master. Always good to me and to other people. Too good, to some, in my view." He heaved a rattling breath but did not cough.

"Some people didn't deserve his goodness, you mean?"

He nodded. "That female! She kept pushing her son at him. It was disgusting. Little snot-nosed kid used to chase the chickens and kick the dog." He heaved another breath and rested a little. "Came to no good, I hear," he summed up.

"I've met Hideyo. He was involved in a fight at the wine shop. Apparently his opponent was badly hurt. They said he drinks and gambles."

The old man nodded several times. "Him! His mother tried to pretend he was the master's, the dirty bitch. Not true. She was a streetwalker got knocked up and was starving with her brat when the master offered them a place to stay for a while. She never left, more's the pity. He was too good!" The old man closed his eyes and tears began to trickle down the wrinkled cheeks.

Akitada reached for a tissue in his sash and dabbed them away.

"Thank you, sir." The old man's clawlike hand reached for Akitada's and squeezed it. "Your kindness to the weak is like his. You'll understand how I loved him. How I miss him. But soon, very soon —" He stopped with a smile. His breath began to rattle in his chest again.

Akitada was greatly moved by the old servant's love for his dead master, but almost everything he said made Tanaka's guilt more certain and more heinous. He sat quietly, waiting for the old man to start speaking again.

The old man's features had taken on a definition that was more pronounced when he closed his eyes. With a shiver Akitada saw the outlines of the skull, as if the living flesh were being absorbed into the skeleton. For a moment he thought Yoshito had stopped breathing, but then the eyes opened again.

"His son," he said, "his real son, is like his father. A good man. He let'em stay for his father's sake." A couple of rattling breaths. "And he gave me what his father wanted me to have. A good man." He stopped, his eyes fixed on Akitada's face, perhaps waiting for his agreement.

"I heard that the son was poor until the father died and that he is now a wealthy man and very successful."

Yoshito nodded. "The gods reward goodness. He came to his father that day to tell him he loved him. My master was very happy." He gasped and went rigid. His face contorted. He screamed, "Until that cursed Tanaka came . . . came that night . . . came like a wolf or a hungry bear. . . he . . . he . . . Amida!" He choked and reared up, hands scrabbling at the air as if they wanted to catch a breath, and then he fell back, his eyes closed and his chin slack."

Shocked, Akitada felt for a pulse. The daughter-in-law, alerted by the old man's shouts, came in.

"I'm very sorry," Akitada said to her. "He was quite calm until just a moment ago."

"He's dead?" She came to bend over Yoshito and nodded. "It's talking about the murder. That always upsets him. Oh, well, I'll go get the monks." She eyed Akitada, who was getting to his feet. "Did he tell you what you wanted to hear?"

Akitada felt that he had just been accused of bringing on the death with his visit. "I just let him talk. He was very sure that Tanaka killed his master."

She nodded, looking down at the frail body in its blankets. "Funerals cost a lot of money," she muttered.

Disgusted, Akitada reached into his sash and gave her some silver, then walked out of the house.

On the way home, he thought of old Seimei who had died in his arms, another faithful servant. Seimei would have summed up the events of this day with one of his sayings: "Good fortune and bad fortune are like the strands in a rope."

16

Arihito's Tale

The next day the skies cleared outside as well as in Akitada's marriage. Yukiko was quietly happy and affectionate. Somewhat to Akitada's surprise, she left the decision of where she was to await the birth of their child entirely up to him. Perversely this had the effect of his trying to accommodate her wishes entirely. In the end, he postponed a decision.

Yukiko showed him her purchases. She was having some new gowns made but also planned to do some stitching herself. He was moved that she seemed to care for his approval and complimented her choices.

"The merchant," she said, "is an elderly man, very proper and with such a love for fine silks and their weaves and patterns and colors that it's a joy to listen to him."

Akitada thought the man was also clearly a good businessman but did not say so. "Where is his shop?" he asked, thinking he might have occasion to buy her a present in the future.

"On the corner of Rokujo and Omiya. His name is Nakai. But he isn't at all well. And his young wife doesn't seem to care." She frowned. "She's much younger and very friendly with men. It must bother him."

Not for the first time, Akitada considered the fact that women seemed to take a much greater interest in other women and their relationships than men did. This also he did not mention. They parted on friendlier terms than they had for a long time in the past months.

Akitada, who was becoming restless about returning to his duties in Mikawa, planned to concentrate on solving the mystery of Prince Atsutada's murder as quickly as possible. Their investigations so far had only suggested two possible suspects, Maruko and Minamoto Yukihiro, the prince's son.

It was the latter who interested Akitada most, partially because of his unexpected visit to his father on the day of the murder, and partially because of his astonishing financial success after the father's death.

But he did not know how to explain a second visit for more probing questions. As it turned out, he was spared this, because his young brother-in-law arrived for a visit. He announced he had information to share and Akitada sent for Yukiko.

They sat near the open doors to the garden where birds chattered and bees buzzed, and rain drops still glistened on the leaves. Arihito looked excited.

"I've been to see the son," he announced. "My money is on him. You should see the house he lives in!" He paused for effect.

Akitada, who had visited the man in his office, became interested, and Yukiko, all smiles and happiness, clapped her hands. "Go on," she cried. "Tell!"

"You first." Arihito looked at Akitada.

"I don't have much to report. I went to see the old servant again, hoping for some memory he hadn't mentioned. He was very feeble the first time I talked to him. This time, he seemed more alert, but . . ."

"He died," supplied Arihito.

Akitada was astonished. "How did you know?"

"Atsutada's son mentioned it, making a point about what a devoted servant the old fellow had been and how he was paying for a fine funeral. What did the old man tell you?"

"Nothing we didn't know. That the prince was a saint and that he took in Maruko and her son out of charity. That Maruko tried her best to make the prince fond of the child. That the prince's real son visited the day of the murder, and that he, too, was a good man like his father."

Arihito grimaced. "Old people get confused. They see people in their past in a much better light. I think the servant was fond of his master and over the years he turned him into a saint and his son, too. I didn't find Minamoto Yukihiro at all saintly."

"How did you manage to talk to him? He seemed very reserved when I met him."

Arihito grinned. "He wouldn't have talked to me if he'd known who I was and what I wanted."

His sister laughed. "Clever Arihito. What did you tell him?"

"I said I was writing a paper on the descendants of Emperor Sanjo and their achievements. And as I'd been told that his father had been Prince Atsutada and that he was known as the saintly prince, I was making a special point of him. You should have seen his face. He practically adopted me then and there."

Yukiko clapped her hands. "And that meant you could ask absolutely anything about Atsutada's household and his friends and enemies."

Akitada asked, "Did you introduce yourself as your father's son?"

"Of course not. Father wouldn't have liked it. And neither would you, I expect."

"Perhaps not, but this may be worse. Who did you pretend to be?"

"Kiyowara Ishiro. He was a fellow student when I was at the university. He was very studious." Arihito grinned. "Just the kind of dry old stick who'd think of doing something useless like writing a history of men who didn't become emperors."

"My impression of Minamoto Yukihiro was that he was quite intelligent. Are you sure he didn't become suspicious?"

"Absolutely. He loved the attention he was getting. And you should've seen the style in which he lives. Every bit the great court noble for all that he only holds the sixth rank."

Since Arihito had not yet achieved this, Akitada cleared his throat pointedly.

His young brother-in-law caught his meaning instantly. "Rank doesn't matter to me, but it does to some people."

"True enough. But go on."

"Well, first off, he occupies a large house in the best part of town. Secondly, he employs a major domo and a large staff, all dressed in matching outfits. Thirdly, the room where he received me contained costly furnishings and his house robe was of the best silk. The man must have a large income. If all you told us is true, he was barely scraping along before his father died. So I decided to find out more about his inheritance." Arihito paused for approval.

He got it from Yukiko. "Oh, this is exciting. Go on, my clever brother! I wish I could have been there."

Akitada said nothing, and Arihito continued. "As I said, he was so pleased at the attention he was getting that he started telling me all sorts of things about his father's life. And he got to the murder right away to make the point what a great pity it had been for such a good and wise man to be killed like that. I asked him if he'd been close to his father and you'll never guess what he said. He admitted that they had not seen each other for some years, but he claimed they had made up all their differences the very day before Tanaka killed him. Can you believe it? He was there on the day of the murder."

Akitada nodded. "So I've been told. It doesn't prove he killed his father."

Yukiko said, "I thought you didn't believe in coincidence, Akitada. Surely this is too much of a coincidence."

"I grant you, it's an odd coincidence, but it could have happened. I must remind both of you that the police had very substantial evidence that Tanaka did it. Unless you can provide the same for Atsutada's son, we don't have much of a case."

Yukiko looked exasperated. "Don't you want us to find the killer?"

It was a difficult question to answer. Did he want to prove Kobe wrong and ruin his old friend's career to help Yukiko's brother win the young woman he had fallen in love with. Of course not. Young, love was a fleeting thing. For men like Kobe the loss of his reputation and income could be fatal. He tried to frame an answer, but his hesitation had already told Yukiko the answer. She turned away abruptly, clenching her hands.

An awkward silence fell.

Akitada said, "I will support you if you can convince me that a mistake has been made." He could see from Yukiko's stiff posture that this had not been good enough, that he was still seen as a traitor to her cause and her family.

Arihito, considerably subdued by this exchange and the chilly atmosphere, said, "I thought it significant, because Atsutada's son had needed money until he inherited his father's wealth. We have only his word for it that they put away their differences. It's equally possible that they quarreled again and the son went away angry. Suppose he brooded about it and decided to go back. Maybe just to argue his side again, but Atsutada made him so angry that he killed him."

Akitada was impressed by Arihito's explanation. He nodded. "It could have happened that way. But we need some sort of proof. What you have given me is a motive."

"And I will find the proof," Arihito said confidently. "He said I could come back any time I wished if I had more questions. And he served me some of the best wine I've ever tasted, so I'll probably take him up on it."

"Has it occurred to you that going to a man's house and drinking his wine while attempting to prove he killed his own father might not be entirely proper? The murder of one's own parent is, after all, the most serious crime a man can commit."

Arihito and Yukiko exchanged glances. She said, "Well, since my husband has no better suggestion, perhaps you and I will think of another plan."

And with these simple words, she had effectively cut him off from the family endeavor. He was no longer one of them. Akitada was appalled that the happiness he had so briefly recaptured should have melted away as quickly as a snowflake in the sun.

He changed the subject. "Have you been to see Masako since you've been back?"

Arihito's face contracted. "She will not see me."

Akitada raised his brows. "Have you tried?"

"Of course. Nothing has changed. Perhaps it's all over anyway. Perhaps I'm just playing useless, hopeless games."

"Oh, Arihito," cried his sister, "don't talk like that. We will find a way."

He put his head in his hands, and Akitada was afraid that he would weep. "Arihito," he said, "All isn't lost. If she loves you, she'll be your wife anyway. Give her time."

"No," mumbled Arihito, "no. She won't. She won't as long as my father objects to the marriage."

"But your father may come around."

Arihito raised his head and looked at him bleakly, but with dry eyes. "She knows that he'll always hold her birth against her. No. I have lost her . . . and yet . . . I cannot lose her. Dear heavens, Akitada, what shall I do?"

The pain in his voice and face was palpable, and Akitada laid an arm around his shoulder. "Let me try one more thing," he said. "I'm not at all sure what role the woman Maruko played in all of this. But I'd advise against seeing Minamoto Yukihiro again. If he discovers your little impersonation, he may complain to your father."

Arihito thought about it and nodded. "Better not. Thanks. Well, could we . . . I mean you and I . . . visit Atsutada's place to see how his son might have done it?"

The proposition was singularly unappealing, but Akitada glanced at his wife's set face and nodded. "If you wish."

Arihito brightened. "I'd like to check the house and garden to see where Minamoto could have hidden to wait until dark when his father would be alone in the garden house."

"Tomorrow then."

His brother-in-law's face fell. "We could go now."

"I'm sorry, Arihito, but I have some work to do and I'm to visit a friend tonight."

Arihito left and Yukiko accompanied him from the room. Akitada wanted to go after her, but her set expression discouraged him. He waited for her to return, but she did not.

17

Mother and Son

Akitada's visit to Nakatoshi's house was his first. Since it was only two miles from his own and it was a beautiful evening, he decided to walk. This gave him time to do some more brooding about his damaged relationship with Yukiko. It seemed to him that Arihito's romance with Masako had come between them. He was resentful that this should be so, since he felt that their marriage should be of greater importance to Yukiko. Indeed, by law, she had become his, and her first duty was obedience and loyalty to him. But what their ancestors, and indeed the wise Kung-fu-tse, had thought of proper relations between husband and wife hardly applied to reality. His resentment was thus directed at Yukiko as well as at her brother who had involved them in his troubles.

But such thoughts put him in a bad mood that was greatly at odds with the scented night on the shaded streets of noblemen's houses. He passed the Otomo house, and wondered briefly again how Masako had come to be employed by old Lady Otomo. He thought of his own good fortune, come to him finally after all these years by marrying Kosehira's daughter. Surely there was hope for them. He had fallen in love, was still in love, with a beautiful and charming young woman who was going to give him a child. That must outweigh everything else. Tomorrow he would make peace, and after that he would do his best to treat her with the love and patience she deserved.

Having thus calmed his anger, he arrived at a substantial compound of buildings and was pleased to find it belonged to Nakatoshi. His friend received him with great pleasure and showed off his new garden with pride. They walked along the winding paths while Nakatoshi explained the origin and care of his favorite plants and Akitada thought of Tamako again. Yukiko was satisfied with telling gardeners to make things pleasant, but she left the details up to them. Seeing his friend's delight in his plants and listening to his plans for future improvements he felt envious. He had little to come home to except his flute. Perhaps he should take up gardening.

Eventually they went inside where servants had laid out a fanciful meal but left them alone to serve themselves. Nakatoshi apologized for this, adding, "I thought we could talk without interruptions."

Akitada agreed and found he had rarely had a more enjoyable meal, both for the quality of the food and for the conversation.

Eventually the talk turned to the murder of Atsutada.

"I checked on Atsutada's will," Nakatoshi said. "It left his property to his son Yukihiro, though there were some sizable bequests."

"You say 'his son Yukihiro'. Were there other sons, or daughters for that matter?"

"No. It was a recent will. It's my understanding that Atsutada lost his wife and all but the eldest son to an epidemic."

"Yes. I heard the same. I wondered about the child of the woman who lived in his house."

"The child got nothing. But he left her fifty pieces of gold and the same to his servant."

"What about the property?"

"That went to his son along with everything else."

"I see. It has been suggested that this inheritance was the foundation of Yukihiro's present wealth."

Nakatoshi chuckled. "A motive for murder?"

"Yes. Is it likely, though?"

"Probably not. Even given the fact that they were apparently not on speaking terms for a long time. Besides, I don't think the farm, the house, and the city property amounted to much when compared to his current status."

"He inherited the city property? I thought he bought it more recently."

"No. It's in the will. Really, Akitada, the will seemed very ordinary to me. Anything of real value went to his only son."

"Well, if we eliminate Minamoto Yukihiro, that leaves me with no one but the courtesan and her son. The son is the murderous type, but, alas, he was a mere five years old then."

Nakatoshi grinned. "Sorry!"

∞

Akitada had enjoyed the dinner with Nakatoshi so much that he promised himself that he would make a point of entertaining his friends more frequently at his home when he had completed his governorship in Mikawa.

The next morning he set out in a hopeful mood on another visit to Atsutada's former home. Arihito had sent word that he would be detained, and Akitada was alone, but he wore his sword and was glad of it when he arrived and found Hideyo occupied with splitting firewood with an axe.

Hideyo froze when he recognized him. The piece of wood he had been working on tumbled off the bottom step of the house, and Hideyo's hand clenched around the handle. Akitada dismounted without taking his eyes off the big man.

"I see they let you go," he said conversationally. "I hope the arrest taught you a lesson."

Hideyo gave a low growl and started toward him.

Akitada put his hand on his sword hilt, and warned him, "I have a sword, and I know how to use it. Put that axe down."

The sound of his voice brought Maruko out on the veranda. "You again," she said. "You're not welcome; for all that you're one of the good people. You got my son arrested. We don't need your kind who torment poor folk, persecute poor widows, and throw orphans in jail."

Hideyo had stopped just below his mother. "Let him try, Mother," he said. "I'll show him. I'm not afraid of his sword. Those officials don't know how to use them. They just wear them to show who they are."

Akitada eyed him with distaste. "You would soon find out otherwise," he said. "Your axe won't do you much good against a sword." He drew it and held it up for them both to see its length and the wickedly shining blade.

She spoke first. "Leave him alone, Hideyo!" And to Akitada, "What do you want this time?"

"I want you to tell me what happened the night of the murder. I'll pay for your time." He held up a gold coin in his left hand.

She narrowed her eyes to see it. "I'll want two of those."

Hideyo looked up at her. "You're never going to tell him things?" he protested.

"Shut up. Take his horse and get back to your chores," she snapped.

Turning the gray stallion over to Hideyo, who clearly intended him no good—even if he was not the one who had written "Kill Sugawara" on his gate—was completely unpalatable. When Hideyo approached with an evil grin on his face, Akitada said in a dangerously low voice, "If you hurt this horse, I'll either kill you myself or see to it that the constables arrest you again and use the bamboo whips on your back."

Hideyo scowled, but after a moment, he nodded and led Akitada's horse away. Akitada climbed the steps to the veranda, and told Maruko, "I'd like you to tell me all you remember of the day before the murder, of that night, and of the next morning. I know it was a long time ago, but I think you would not easily forget."

She gave a snort. "It's like it was yesterday. You don't forget the worst time of your life."

"Well, then, where were you and your child during that time?"

"Here," she said, pointing to the house behind her. "The prince played with Hideyo. They were very close. You could see how much the prince loved the boy. Then his son came. I didn't know him, because he'd never come before. He stared at me and Hideyo. He didn't like what he saw, but he said nothing in my hearing. They went into the garden together. I don't know what they talked about there." She paused. "Is that what you want to know?"

"Yes. You're doing very well. What happened next?"

"His son came back and left. The prince stayed in the garden house. I took him his evening rice and spread out his bedding. He liked to sleep there on hot nights." She blushed a little and cleared her throat. "He was writing something, so I left and went to bed myself. I don't know what happened in the night, but Hideyo saw something. He crawled in bed with me, crying. I thought he'd been dreaming and told him to be quiet." She stopped and sighed.

"What do you think he saw? And when was that?"

"I think he saw Tanaka coming from the murder. He saw the blood on him and the club in his hand. That's what I told the police. I think Tanaka threatened to kill him, too."

"Did Hideyo tell you right away that he saw Tanaka coming from the murder?"

"No. Hideyo doesn't like to talk about it. What he saw made him what he is now. I think it's what Tanaka did to him."

"If Hideyo didn't tell you, how do you know that he saw the murderer?"

"He talks in his dreams."

Akitada digested this and found it was unreliable evidence. Still, something had happened to the boy that night. He asked Maruko, "And the next morning, Hideyo went to the garden house and found the prince dead?"

She nodded. "I was in the kitchen, starting the fire under the rice pot. He screamed and screamed. I ran out and he came to me, shouting, 'Blood! Blood!' I went to look and found the prince. It was terrible. And Hideyo crawled into a trunk and wouldn't come out. He was never the same again. I had a terrible time with him all those years. You saw what he is. Can't work and can't get along with people. It wasn't just the prince's life that Tanaka took. He ruined ours, too."

"I'm very sorry for your troubles. I think you expected to be taken care off in the prince's will?"

"Of course, I did. He'd told me again and again he'd take care of us. Hideyo's his son as much as Lord Minamoto is. That will was a big shock."

"Hmm. But Lord Minamoto does look after both of you, doesn't he?"

Her face set. "That's only as it should be and it's little enough. We have a roof and enough to eat, that's all. He owed us."

Akitada refrained from pointing out that this was a great deal more than many other people had, more than she would have had before Atsutada took them in. He did not believe Hideyo was the prince's son. His features and size were completely unlike Yukihiro's. Hideyo was big, with clumsy arms and legs, and his face was square, with a beetling brow, a broad nose, and fleshy lips. Minamoto was short, small-boned, and had a pale, slender face.

He considered the possibility that the murder had been committed by Yukihiro and that Maruko or Hideyo knew something incriminating so that he had bought their silence by paying for their support all these years. He liked the idea but found no support for it in anything he had learned so far.

"Would you walk with me to the garden house and show me what you found?" he asked her.

She nodded but was unenthusiastic. Descending the stairs, they walked into the overgrown garden, along the path, and over the bridge to the small building in the clearing. Maruko moved slowly and gasped for breath as she lumbered along. When she saw the garden house, she stopped.

"It's ruined," she said in a tone of surprise. "It was very nice back then. Look at it! The roof's about gone."

"You haven't been here in a while?"

"Not in a long time. Couldn't bear thinking about it."

"Perhaps your son can mend the roof and the floor."

She gave a bitter laugh. "Hideyo? You won't catch him anywhere near the place. He thinks Tanaka's ghost's still lying in wait for him."

They stood looking at the derelict little house. It must have been pretty once when all the cedar shingles were still in place and the railing was painted red. Small traces of the paint still showed here and there. All around trees and shrubs formed an enclosure. Some of the azaleas had late blooms, though the shrubs themselves had long since lost their tidy clipped shapes and now sprawled everywhere. Next to the eaves was an old cherry tree, half dead now, its limbs reaching through the broken roof.

"Did the prince usually bring money here?" Akitada asked.

She gave him a strange look. "Sometimes."

"Tanaka is said to have stolen twenty gold coins after the murder. I've wondered why the prince would have this much money here."

"It was meant for my housekeeping. The police never returned it."

Akitada raised his brows at this. "Did they keep it?"

"No. His oldest son got it. It was very unfair."

"But why had he not given it to you in the main house?"

She flushed and looked coy. "I think he expected me to come later and get it, but I was tired that night and went to bed early."

"Then it wasn't intended for Tanaka? Money to buy seed rice?"

"No. It was mine."

Akitada sighed. He had tried and again learned nothing helpful. Instead every word had pointed ever more surely at Tanaka being the killer. "Why do you think Tanaka visited the prince that night?"

"To get money from him, of course. He was forever doing that and the prince was getting fed up with him."

Akitada turned to go back. When they reached the house again, Akitada gave her the promised coin and said, "Thank you, Maruko. It was kind of you to go up there with me."

She mellowed considerably. "Thank you, my Lord," she said with a little bow.

On an impulse, Akitada asked, "Why does your son hate me so?"

She glanced in the direction of the stable. "Hideyo doesn't know what he's doing. There's no harm in him, but sometimes the evil dreams get hold of him and he can't help himself. I'll talk to him."

Akitada collected his horse, thanking Hideyo and getting a curse for his troubles. He rode away to the sound of Maruko "talking" to her son.

18

The Silk Merchant
and his Wife

On his return to the city, Akitada felt some gratitude for his own children. Yasuko and Yoshi
made him proud almost every day. He
thought of how obedient they were, and how affectionate to a father who was mostly too busy to spend time
with them. He thought of the impromptu concerts they
had had in Mikawa with Yukiko and Yasuko. He had
left his flute there and missed it.

And now Yukiko was carrying another child, a child
for them to raise together. He felt quietly thankful for
all of that and decided to buy a gift for his young wife
and gifts for the children, too. The children were easily
accommodated. It was time Yoshi had a decent sword,
and this he bought from a shop that specialized in such

weapons for boys. For Yasuko he found two very pretty painted fans. She had exhibited signs of taking an interest in fashion lately.

Yukiko was not so easily pleased. She had always had enough money to buy what she wished, though she had shown remarkable restraint until his sister Akiko took her in hand. In the end the only thing that came to his mind was more silk. She loved pretty fabrics and he knew the name of the shop where she had placed her orders. He would go and add something special to that order.

The Nakai shop was not far from the Eastern Market. It occurred to him that Yukiko might have revealed its exact location with just such a purpose in mind. He entered the large shop with a smile on his face, thinking about this. On the raised sections on either side of the stone corridor, mats were spread and customers perched on the edge while shop assistants waited on them. The walls on both sides were covered with shelves, and on these shelves rested multi-colored lengths of silk and brocade of the size to make a full kimono-style robe, but folded into neat packages. As he knew from Yukiko, the shop also offered the services of a seamstress, and a number of items Yukiko had ordered were to be sewn up here.

There were three women and a man shopping at the moment. The women occupied the right side where a very handsome and well-dressed young man and an older saleswoman were waiting on them. Akitada joined the male customer on the opposite side and was greeted by a young woman of extraordinary plainness. She had, however, a cheerful and polite manner. He explained who he was and about Yukiko's prior order. When he got that far, another woman suddenly appeared beside his shop girl. She was a little older but less than thirty years, very handsome, and dressed in a fine green silk dress with an embroidered Chinese jacket in a pale golden color over it. Her hair, which must be long, was coiled elaborately at her neck. She told the girl to go and help the other customer and introduced herself as Mrs. Nakai, proprietress of the shop.

Akitada, who knew that it was the husband who owned the business, assumed that she merely wished to impress him with special attention. He explained again about Yukiko's order and said that he wished to add a special present.

"A very fortunate, lady," she remarked, smiling. "I recall the ladies very well. Both will look ravishing in their selections."

At this point they were joined by an elderly man in a sober dark blue robe made of ramie rather than silk, who bowed and introduced himself as Nakai. Akitada's first impression was that he must be dreadfully ill, too ill to be waiting on his customers. His was so pale his skin looked almost yellow, his hands trembled, and he walked shakily as if the floor under his white-stockinged feet were shaking and undulating. His wife, all concern, asked him if he should be up, adding unnecessarily to Akitada that her husband was not well. The difference in their ages struck Akitada painfully. Nakai was old enough to be her father rather than her husband. He knew to his own embarrassment that such marriages were not uncommon, yet surely most people thought it as unsuitable as he did.

Mr. Nakai explained that he had overheard Lord Sugawara's words and wanted to be of assistance since he had had the pleasure of assisting the ladies when they had made their selection.

They eyed each other, two older husbands with young wives. Nakai must have been surprised to find that Yukiko's husband was far from youthful.

Akitada politely assured him that his wife had mentioned the merchant's poor health and that he had no wish to keep him on his feet when he was ill. Nakai claimed he felt quite well enough and it gave him great pleasure to wait on his lordship.

A lively discussion ensued about special gauzes and Chinese embroidered jackets—Mrs. Nakai demonstrated her own beautiful garment—but they finally settled on a formal train suitable for attendance at court.

Mrs. Nakai sent the plain girl, who had since finished with the other gentleman, to bring silks and embroideries and to show Akitada sketches of designs for ornamentation. In the midst of this pleasant occupation, a monk came into the shop. He carried the sort of basket that doctors used. Seeing him, Mr. Nakai grimaced, excused himself, and took him to the back of the house.

Akitada asked his wife if her husband's illness was serious.

"It worries me, Your Excellency. How very kind of you and your lady to concern yourselves about the illness of a mere merchant. I'm afraid my honored husband is getting much worse. Lately, he has been bringing up blood, if you'll forgive my mentioning such a thing."

"I'm well used to blood," Akitada said dryly. "What brought on the disease?"

"I'm not sure. He's far too fond of puffer fish, but he won't admit to having eaten it."

Akitada was very much aware of the dangers of the poisonous little fish that was so delicious if prepared properly but deadly if the poisonous part of its gut had not been removed carefully by the cook. Years ago, an imperial prince in exile for starting a rebellion against the emperor had faked his own death from eating contaminated puffer fish in order to escape the prison island and lead another uprising.

This memory made him think again of the murder of Atsutada. The appointment of crown princes invariably stirred up factions displeased with the choice. Sometimes a prince who had been passed over objected violently, but mostly such uprisings were the work of highly-placed and ambitious men who had seen their hopes for preferment dashed. And that fact had made Atsutada a loud voice against passing over the proper crown prince in order to place another on the throne and a danger to many people. Alas, it was now fifteen years later, and he saw no way of exploring such a scenario that must have been highly secretive even back then.

He turned his attention back to the choice of a gift and eventually decided that the design should be of cherry blossoms against a sky blue background, and that swallows should be flying amongst the branches and blossoms. It was after all still early summer, he thought, and some cherry trees still bloomed. Besides, this was for Yukiko who was young enough for such a display. The swallows would be a secret message between them, reminding her of the swallows under the eaves in Mikawa, omens of a happy marriage.

Mrs. Nakai was delighted with his choice. Not only did she think such a design quite wonderful, but the work entailed would bring in a pretty income. She immediately called, "Ujinobu!" and her male assistant responded, bringing a variety of blue silks and a collection of embroidery silks. As Akitada chose a heavy silk in a soft and lustrous shade of blue, he noticed that the young assistant stood quite close to Mrs. Nakai and at one point touched the nape of her neck familiarly.

He wished very much that he had not seen it and wondered at this caress. It reminded him again of the dangers of older men marrying young wives. Not wishing to see more, he turned away to study the embroidery silks. A moment later, the monk-physician returned from seeing his patient.

Paying no attention to Akitada, he addressed Mrs. Nakai quite bluntly. "This cannot go on," he said in a harsh voice. "If you don't follow my instructions about the gruel he is to eat and if you don't stop making him take this medicine, he'll be dead within the week."

Mrs. Nakai gasped, apologized to Akitada, then walked out of the shop with the monk. Akitada could see them talking or arguing outside. Eventually she returned and went to the back of the house, while the monk walked away.

Akitada looked at the handsome assistant and remarked, "It sounds very serious and must be a worry to you."

The young man looked surprised. "A worry to me? Not really. The shop isn't so busy that we cannot manage quite well."

It was heartless as well as thoughtless. Either Nakai had been treating his assistant badly, or this Ujinobu was only concerned about how his master's death would affect him and expected to reap welcome rewards.

As it turned out, Ujinobu had a skill that was valuable to the business. He was a talented artist and would be the one designing Yukiko's train for her. Watching him sketch the design, Akitada forgave him his remark, especially as, on second thought, it might only have referred to illness and not death.

He saw with amazement as the young man sketched flowering branches and fluttering birds on sheets of rice paper, his brush flying as he explained colors and details. When Akitada had approved a particular sketch, he promised to have a detailed color version ready the next day, when partial payment was customary upon approval.

He never saw either Nakai or his wife again and left, bowed out with smiles by Ujinobu.

Walking homeward, his satisfaction of having selected a particularly beautiful present for Yukiko gradually changed to some unease about the scenes he had observed. The merchant's illness was merely a sad fact of all human lives, but Akitada had been very troubled by the intimacy between the sick man's young wife and his handsome assistant. It was quite easy to see how this story would end: the silk merchant would die, and his young widow would take the handsome and talented assistant for her next husband. It was convenient, made good business sense, and pleased both widow and assistant.

But it troubled him nevertheless.

What he found when he got home drove such idle thoughts from his mind. He had smelled the smoke from a good distance and wondered where the fire was. Then he turned the corner and saw. His gate stood wide open, and people were running in and out with fire buckets. An acrid smell of burning hung in the air.

Hurrying now, Akitada dodged between them and paused in the courtyard, staring at the charred remnants of his stables. Genba saw him and limped over. He was covered with soot and blood, and his face looked grim.

"What happened? Are you hurt?" Akitada gasped.

"I'm all right." Genba wiped a weary hand over his face. "I sent for you, sir, but the boy couldn't find you. Some bastard set fire the stable. It started in the hay, and the stable went up in flames. I was at the market, but the boy saw the fellow that did it."

"How did he get in?"

"The boy let him in. Stupid and disobedient. I'll whip him later."

Akitada sighed. "We'll rebuild."

"That's not all, sir." Genba's head sank. "Raiden's dead."

"What?" Akitada's stomach clenched. "He died in the fire?"

"Not exactly, sir. He panicked, and the boy was useless. The horse broke his leg trying to get out. I had to kill him. I hated to do it, but . . ." Genba looked up, tears in his eyes. "He was like my brother, sir."

Akitada nodded. "I know, Genba. You did right." Grief for the beautiful gray seized him and twisted his stomach. "Where is he?"

"I'll show you."

As they walked around the burned stable, Akitada asked, "The other horses?"

"They are fine. Docile creatures, they waited to be taken out."

The other horses had been taken away to be stabled with neighbors. Raiden lay in a patch of grass near the fence between stable and garden. Even in death and at his great age, he was a beautiful horse, finely made, with slender legs and a graceful neck. The elegant head lay relaxed, its large dark eyes now dull and sightless. Genba had cut his throat with a sword. The broken leg was his right front one, the bones splintered, and the hoof lying at an odd angle.

"He fought to get out," Genba said.

"He was always a brave horse." Akitada's voice was thick with sadness. He knelt beside Raiden and stroked the soft muzzle. It was still warm.

The gray had been a gift from the lord of Takata in gratitude for Akitada's help in the killing of the man who had usurped his patrimony. They had both been young then, Akitada and Raiden. When Akitada had been sent to Mikawa, he had regretfully left the aging horse behind because the journey would have been too hard for him. The irony of his death now struck him painfully.

He was truly like a god. "Raiden" was the name of the god of thunder. It had seemed right for the young gray stallion those many years ago.

19

Complaints

Kobe had finally confided the reason for his depression to Sachi when he found her weeping because she thought his love for her had caused new repercussions. He had never been able to reassure her completely that she was his whole happiness and that nothing mattered as long as he had her by his side. She knew what he had given up, and it weighed heavily on her mind in spite of his love for her.

"No, no," he said, holding her close. "It's that infernal Akitada. We're not speaking. I've finally had it with him."

"But he is your best friend," she protested. "You said so yourself. Many times. And he has come to see you, see us both. What can have happened?"

He told her.

197

She argued that he had been too rash and should not have assumed that Akitada would do anything to harm him.

He responded by pointing out to her what was sure to happen if word got out that the famous Akitada thought Tanaka had been an innocent man who had been tormented by Kobe into a confession and summarily murdered by his guards on his way into exile.

"I'll lose my post," he said, his voice heavy, "and then we shall starve because I've given everything else to my wives and children. Now do you see?"

She was silent for a moment. Then she said sadly, "And that is because of me. You must go back to your family if that happens."

And that tore it. Kobe released her, shouted, "Never! I'd rather die," and stormed out of their small house.

On the way to work, his resentment for Akitada grew quite out of proportion. He was short with his officers and scribes, and spend his time at his desk glowering into the distance. Into this mood, a young constable, looking very nervous, admitted a visitor.

The visitor's name was Minamoto Yukihiro. He was very well dressed, and his rank ribbon indicated that he outranked Kobe. Kobe got to his feet, bowing and rearranging his mood to meet the situation.

"What can I do for you, Lord Yukihiro?" he asked, after inviting him to sit and offering wine which was declined.

"I came to make a complaint. A criminal has bluffed his way into my residence, talked to my servants, asked questions, and made accusations. I want him arrested."

Kobe raised his brows. "A thief? Has anything been stolen?"

Minamoto said irritably, "Nothing yet. But it's clear he has something in mind. He probably works with a gang."

"What does this fellow look like?"

"He's young and dresses well, but of course these days that means nothing. Only the other day, a shop assistant in the city waited on me, and he wore a silk robe. I ask you, what is the world coming to? It's time we started enforcing the laws." He gave Kobe an angry look.

"Do you mean the law about gangs of thieves or the laws about what people are allowed to wear?"

"Both, of course. If you ask me, when the common people try to dress like the aristocracy, they do so because they have criminal tendencies. And given the cost of silk these days, they've probably stolen it someplace."

Kobe decided he did not much like Minamoto. But people like him could be dangerous. If they felt that their rank and background had not won them special consideration, they were likely to complain to government officials higher up. So he nodded, smiled, and said, "So this person who invaded your residence was young and dressed like a nobleman? When was this and what exactly did he do?"

"Yesterday. He questioned my servants first, then confronted me. Can you imagine? He walks right in and starts asking his questions. I must say the criminals are getting more brazen every day. Only last week some of them entered the Gwako-shi, the paintings bureau in the *Daidairi*. They destroyed several masterpieces being worked on for His Majesty and for the crown prince. In the *Daidairi*! Where are the police when crime even enters the Great Government Enclosure?"

Kobe said mildly, "The police have no authority in the *Daidairi*. It is under the protection of the imperial guard. We work on crimes committed in the capital."

Being corrected did not please Lord Yukihiro. He snapped, "Well, then. Start investigating my complaint."

Kobe nodded and pulled some paper toward him. He rubbed ink and remarked, "I need some particulars, and then I assure you we will look thoroughly into the matter."

"I don't have much time. I'm expected in the palace."

"Just a few brief questions." Kobe dipped his brush into the ink and asked, "Where is your residence?" He elicited this information as well as the names of Lord Yukihiro's servants who had spoken with the alleged thief. Then he asked, "What sorts of questions did this person ask you and why did you speak to him?"

"Things that are none of his business," snapped Minamoto, looking slightly uneasy.

"Did you tell him so and send him away?"

Lord Yukihiro bit his lip. "He pretended to be a graduate student at the university working on an essay."

"I see. What sort of topic?"

"About my father." Seeing Kobe's blank expression, he added irritably, "My father was Prince Atsutada."

Kobe compressed his lips. "I see. About how old was this . . . student?"

"Maybe twenty. He looked like he might be a student, and he sounded convincing."

"Maybe he really was a student," Kobe offered, not believing this for a moment.

"Nonsense! Haven't you been listening? He merely pretended to be a student. Gave his name as Takeda Masamune. Something like that. It was a barefaced lie."

"How do you know?"

"I didn't know. Not until after he left. I thought of something I forgot to tell him and stopped by the university. They told me they had no such student there and had not had anyone from the Takeda clan in a decade."

"Ah! But he wanted to know about your father? What sorts of things?"

Lord Yukihiro reddened slightly. "He asked about a disagreement we had and how it had come about that I went to see him just before his death. Outrageous!"

"This doesn't sound much like someone planning to rob you."

"Don't forget, he'd already questioned my servants."

"Ah, yes. You did mention it. What questions were these exactly? Did he ask where the valuables were being kept, for example?"

"He asked them questions about my income. That's the same thing. And how many servants there are, how many horses, and how long I'd been living in the house.

Where I'd lived before. Who had been with me the longest among my servants and what properties I own elsewhere."

Kobe had stopped writing and stared at his visitor as he explained the suspicious visitor's behavior. "Those are very peculiar questions for a thief to be asking. I've never heard of a thief who goes to the house of his intended victim in broad daylight to interrogate him and his servants. Are you quite sure this person was a criminal?"

"Of course! Look, I don't have time to start explaining it all again. I have to go. Send one of your brighter officers to speak to my people and then search for this individual." He got up without bowing and walked out.

Kobe pushed the paper aside and washed out his brush. Muttering angrily, he got up himself and went to tell the sergeant in the front room that he had business to take care of and would be back later.

∞

Akitada and Genba stood on the veranda, surveying the damage.

"It's bound to be the same villain," Genba said. "He started with defacing our gate and progressed to setting fire to the stable."

"Perhaps. Actually, I suppose it's highly likely. The boy's description leaves a lot to be imagined, but I think I recognized the villain."

Genba was astonished. "Really? Who is it?"

"Some lout by the name of Hideyo. He's connected with the case I'm working on. I angered him, and from all accounts he's not normal like most people. He has a violent streak."

Genba said sadly, "There was a time when you'd take me into your confidence, sir. Along with Tora and Saburo."

"I'm sorry, Genba. The household and my work have both changed over the year and somehow you took over the running of the property. You've always had my entire trust, you know that."

"I know, sir. Pay no attention. What will you do about this Hideyo?"

"I suppose I'll have to report it to the police now," Akitada said. The thought was unpleasant. After his quarrel with Kobe he did not feel like going to him for help in this situation. Changing the subject, he said, "Genba, I have no secrets from you. I'm sorry I did not keep you informed. This probably would not have happened if you had known about this case." He gave Genba a brief outline of the old murder case and their investigations so far and was nearly done when the decision of whether to report to the police was taken out of his hands.

Superintendent Kobe walked in through the still open gate and stopped to stare at the burned-out ruin of the stable.

20

Kobe's Ultimatum

A kitada went to greet the superintendent. "How did you hear so quickly?" he asked after returning the small bow Kobe made him.

No friendly smile or expression of sympathy showed on Kobe's face. "I didn't hear. I came on another matter. What happened?"

"It appears that I have attracted the ill will of the young man who was recently released by your constables," Akitada said, adding somewhat pointedly, "This seems to prove he is too violent to be trusted running about loose."

"Not my constables, sir." Kobe snapped. "The village is outside the capital."

Stung by being addressed formally by the man he had counted his friend for so many years, Akitada returned an equally blunt comment, "That may be so, but I assume they report to you. It was you who informed me that there was no reason to hold the man. Perhaps you believed him to be of princely blood and therefore above the law?"

"Are you accusing me of unfair practices?"

"Not at all, Superintendent. It just occurred to me that you might have thought the son of an imperial prince could not possibly commit illegal acts."

"How dare you?"

Akitada stared at Kobe. But the blackened beams of the stable and the memory of his dead stallion interposed themselves. He bit his lip. A quarrel would get him nowhere. He needed protection for his wife and his people, and those he would certainly not get by insulting Kobe. "I'm sorry," he said. "I just lost my favorite horse and am concerned about the safety of my wife who expects a child and mustn't be upset if she isn't to lose it again."

This took Kobe's breath away. "Oh," he said, adding awkwardly, "Yes, of course. Best wishes."

Akitada nodded his thanks.

"The horse? It wasn't that gray, was it?"

"It was. Raiden broke a foreleg trying to break through the wall. Genba had to cut his throat."

"Dear gods! I'm very sorry."

"I do need your help with Hideyo. Having made things worse by talking to his mother, I have no idea how to handle him."

"Can we go inside?"

"Yes, of course. Forgive me. I just got home and am not myself yet."

Kobe said nothing as they went to Akitada's study. There he sat down and asked, "How do you know it was this Hideyo who set fire to your stable?"

Akitada outlined his previous meetings with the young man, ending with, "Besides, the boy saw him."

Kobe, whose face had become progressively darker, asked, "He saw him setting the fire?"

"Well, no. He let him in because he claimed to be a hired workman. Later he saw smoke coming from the roof of the stable."

"This boy recognized Hideyo?"

"No. He'd never met him. He described him. Young, big, flashy clothes, and spiky hair."

Kobe shook his head. "They all look like that these days."

Akitada snapped, "I saw him close up. He cursed me." Controlling his temper with an effort, he said more calmly. "I talked to his mother. She says he's troubled by dreams and not himself sometimes. He lashes out when he thinks people make fun of him. The dreams go back to the night of the murder. And I also talked to the man who owns the wine shop where Hideyo nearly killed a man. He didn't want to say too much. It seems Hideyo is a very good customer. But he also says that Hideyo has bad days when people stay out of his way. In think it's time he's put behind bars."

Kobe sighed. "We have no proof he did anything to you. And the man he knocked out is recovering and doesn't want him arrested. My hands are tied."

Akitada told himself he should not have expected help from Kobe. He was silent for some long moments, then said slowly, "I see."

Kobe flushed. "I told you there was no point to raking up that old case, but you didn't want to listen. Now look what you've caused. And all because some spoiled youngster insists on marrying a murderer's daughter."

Not bothering to reply, Akitada was about to rise and show Kobe out when he remembered something. "You didn't come because of the fire, you said?" he asked.

Kobe was still flushed with anger. "Oh, I almost forgot. That spoiled youngster had the gall to go to Minamoto Yukihiro's residence to question his servants, and then asked to see Yukihiro himself. He pretended that he was a student at the university and planned to write a paper on his father. Then he started asking all sorts of questions about the quarrel between Yukihiro and his father and what they talked about on that last visit before the prince was murdered. He also wanted to know how the son became so wealthy and why he allowed Maruko and Hideyo to stay in that house, paying her an annual rice stipend."

Akitada winced. "If you want me to say that that was very foolish, I will. I hope you don't think I sent him."

"These days I don't know what you may do."

Akitada bit his lip. "Why did Yukihiro answer such questions if he suspected Arihito's purpose?"

"I take it that came later, when he thought about it and remembered your visit. At the time, he was flattered by the attention and looked forward to having his father remembered and himself mentioned. I think he's vain."

Frowning, Akitada said, "I don't recall saying anything to the man that would make him suspicious of Arihito."

Kobe threw up his hands. "What does it matter? His lordship came to me to complain. He expects me to stop people meddling in his affairs, and he wants me to arrest the man who lied to him."

"That will never happen if Kosehira has anything to say about it. Does Yukihiro know who Arihito is? Did you tell him?"

"No, I didn't tell him. And again you accuse me of protecting the powerful. I suppose you think I'm hard pressed to decide between his lordship Yukihiro and his lordship Kosehira?"

Akitada almost smiled. "Surely Kosehira wins hands down in such a contest."

"That's insulting."

"Sorry. You've been very provoking and I've had a very bad day."

Kobe calmed down. He said, "If you expect me to send police to protect your property, you will have to stop your efforts to pin the Tanaka murder on assorted other people. And that means stopping that young fool Arihito also."

Outraged, Akitada got to his feet. "I would have thought that your position required you to protect all those who live in the capital and to arrest arsonists. Apparently I've been mistaken. There's no more to be said."

Kobe had turned quite white. 'Very well." With a nod, he walked out. Akitada did not bother to accompany him. He sank back down and sat stunned for a considerable while. The breach with Kobe was complete. And Kobe had been right that he, Akitada, had allowed himself to be persuaded by his wife, by his sister, and by Arihito, a young man who was so besotted with a woman that he could not think straight. All three had overruled what his own mind told him, namely that Tanaka had been the killer. Nothing they had uncovered so far had proved otherwise.

And yet.

Masako's mother claimed Tanaka had been innocent.

But could he believe her? She was set on seeing the young people get married. And surely getting Arihito for her daughter would be a monumental achievement. She could hardly be blamed for lying under the circumstances.

He had become involved in the first place because he had wanted to please Yukiko. It was this that had brought about the present disaster. His weakness now shamed him. A man should never be ruled by his wife. His objections had been overruled not only by Yukiko, but also by his sister, and by a silly youth, himself in thrall to a female. "A single hair from a woman's head can tie up an elephant," Seimei would have said. Or "A woman's will breaks even a rock."

Seimei's favorite source of wisdom, Kung-fu-tse, had considered women to be difficult to live with. Intimacy with women, he had asserted, caused them to disrespect you, and keeping them at a distance made them resentful. Certainly, Akitada's relationship with Yukiko had proved the truth of this.

He realized somewhat belatedly that he had not checked on his wife. The fire, the loss of Raiden, and Kobe's visit had driven her from his mind until late the night before. And then he had decided to sleep in his study. He did not look forward to seeing her. With a sigh, he rose to walk across to her pavilion, hoping his resolve was sufficiently strengthened by the combined wisdom of Seimei and the ancient master.

Yukiko sat with her maid. Actually the maid was one of Kosehira's servants, borrowed for their short stay in the capital. But their stay was lengthening, and the understaffing of the residence was clearly no longer possible.

The maid, being well trained, rose immediately to leave husband and wife alone. Akitada eyed his pretty wife. She smiled at him.

It is said, " More dangerous than a tiger is a woman's scarlet undergown."

Akitada firmly suppressed a desire to explore the pleasures of scarlet undergowns in their present privacy. "Are you all right?" he asked. "I hope the fire didn't upset you?"

"No. Fires happen. It's Raiden's death that upset me most." She got up and came to him. "Oh, Akitada," she said, touching his cheek with a small perfumed hand,

"I'm so very sad for you. I know you loved that horse. And to lose him like this. Horrible!"

He stepped away from her touch. "We have to talk."

She looked surprised. "Please tell me what's on your mind."

He started to pace the floor as he told her. "This concerns your expectation that I prove Tanaka innocent. Every effort has been made by now, and nothing supports that Tanaka was not Atsutada's killer. The case against him is absolutely incontrovertible. You'll have to accept it. Both you and Arihito."

"No," she cried, stepping in his path. "You cannot give up. Arihito thinks the son did it. And Masako's mother swears it wasn't Tanaka. You cannot let such an injustice stand."

"Yukiko, this case has brought nothing but trouble. I have lost Kobe's friendship. The stable has been destroyed, and Raiden is dead. This cannot go on. I will not have it."

"This is not like you. The man I fell in love with would let nothing stand in his way. And if Kobe cannot tell justice from injustice he should not be superintendent. Or your friend."

So. She set herself against him, refusing to obey his wishes after he had explained his reasons. He said coldly, "Your opinions do not matter in the least. I've lost my patience. And by the way, I'm fully aware that you kept the news of your pregnancy from me because you wished to come to the capital and knew I would not have allowed you take such a risk. Now you are here, and we must make the best of it. If you'll excuse me, I must go and make arrangements for your safety in this house."

He heard her indrawn breath as he stalked out of the door.

21

More Complaints

Akitada's anger was directed at himself rather than at Yukiko and the others who had manipulated him into pursuing a hopeless case. He had known from the start that it would be unwise to pursue the matter, but he had done so anyway—to please a young wife who had ensnared his eyes with her beauty, his body with her youth, and his mind with her wiles. He had been a weak fool from the start, and now he had no option but to live with his choice.

But he need not remain a fool.

He stood on the veranda in front of his house where the black and stinking ruin of the stables reminded him of his stupidity and carelessness in not protecting his property and people.

The boy was sweeping up debris. To his regret, Akitada did not know his name.

"You there," he called out.

The boy looked up.

"Come here a moment."

The boy looked around as if for a hiding place, then dropped his broom, wiped his hands on his shirt, and trotted over. At the bottom of the veranda steps, he fell to his knees.

Akitada said in a gentler voice. "Get up. What's your name?"

"Yasaburo, Master."

"Well, then, Yasaburo, where's Genba?"

"Gone to see about taking away the horse, Master."

"Very good. When he returns, ask him to come to me, please."

"Yes, Master."

Yasaburo, Akitada thought. He must remember the name.

When he was in his study, he took out the roster of servants and retainers. Yes, there he was, this Yasaburo. The handwriting was Genba's, and the boy had been hired by Genba a year ago. He regretted that he did not know what was going on here while he served in Mikawa. Clearly the residence was understaffed. And under the present circumstances this was a serious business. He had fallen into parsimonious ways in the many years of his poverty, and his people had grown equally careful about spending money. The time had come to make some changes.

He looked briefly at the accounts Genba had kept of moneys set aside for the maintenance of the Sugawara residence. The necessary gold was kept in the smaller of two iron-reinforced trunks with elaborate locks. Normally Genba kept the key, but Akitada had taken it back for his stay in the capital. He now opened the trunk to check available funds. All was correct, but they were woefully inadequate for the present needs. Then he took another key for the larger trunk and opened it. Here was their entire wealth. He frowned at the gold and silver bars, and finally lifted out two heavy bags containing coins. These he transferred to the smaller trunk, then relocked the large one. He would have to spend some large sums of money, and not just on the bills Yukiko had run up at various shops. He needed to hire people. Money was required not only to pay them, but also for their rice and clothing.

He sat back down and thought about the threats they were likely to face.

Genba came in almost shyly. "You wanted me, sir?"

"Yes, Genba. Sit down. Some wine?"

"No, thanks." Genba relaxed visibly. "Raiden's been taken away. He'll be cremated. Do you want the ashes?"

"No. But when the stable's been rebuilt, we'll hang a scroll or plaque with his name. He was a faithful horse."

"That's what it should say on it, sir."

Akitada said, "Yes. You'll see to it?"

Genba nodded.

"I've left things far too long on your faithful shoulders, Genba. They are broad enough, but we need more people."

Genba brightened. "It would help at present, sir. The boy and I cannot keep watch day and night."

"I know. You need additional hands, and the house could do with more servants. Saburo's mother will like commanding a staff of many."

They both chuckled.

Akitada went on, "Meanwhile there is the immediate threat. That requires armed men. I recall that once before I needed armed protection for my home, and Tora found you and Hitomaro."

Genba smiled. "Hitomaro! I just thought of him this morning. What a fighter he was! And what a good man!"

"Yes, a true hero. I cannot expect you to find another like him, but will you look for some likely men? Fighters, ex-soldiers, men who have fallen on hard times and won't mind some guard duty?"

Genba nodded. "I will, sir, but times have changed. There aren't many who can use a sword who haven't found employment. The great lords are all setting up small armies on their estates to protect their property. They ask few questions and take anyone who can fight and kill."

Akitada sighed. Do the best you can, but don't leave until there are more servants. With more people here, it will be harder for this madman to do more mischief."

"Should I punish the boy, sir? He should've known better than to let the villain in, even if he claimed he was a clerk and you hired him."

"No just impress on him that we expect trouble and he needs to keep his eyes open. That's all for now. I'm going to talk to Lord Kosehira to see if he can spare some men."

∞

As it turned out, there was no need to walk to Kosehira's residence. Kosehira arrived himself, accompanied by Arihito. They stared at the destruction, expressed their sympathy on the death of the stallion, and then went inside to visit Yukiko.

Akitada would have preferred to meet in his study, but he could not very well forbid them to see their daughter or sister. Kosehira was naturally concerned about her in her present condition. Reassured, they settled down in Yukiko's pavilion, and Akitada reluctantly joined them. Yukiko avoided looking at her husband.

Kosehira made short work of the need for servants by telling Akitada that he would send over five of his men, all capable of defending the house and its inhabitants. He approved of Akitada's idea of hiring some armed men to guard the outside.

Then the conversation turned to the likely culprit.

"But can't you ask Kobe to arrest the man?" Kosehira asked. "He's clearly mad and dangerous."

"At the moment, Kobe and I aren't speaking."

Kosehira's eyes widened. "But why? What did you do?"

Arihito said, "Father, I think it's because of me."

"Oh." Kosehira frowned. "Really, the man ought to rise above such personal concerns."

"Kobe is holding on to a very uncertain position, Akitada said. "He has enemies who are only waiting to find something they can use against him. A miscarriage of justice of the size of the Atsutada murder would serve them eminently well. Besides, I'm afraid our asking questions is already stirring up complaints." He looked at Arihito, who flushed.

Kosehira caught Akitada's glance. "Does this have something to do with Arihito's going to see Minamoto Yukihiro?"

"Yes. The man went to Kobe to complain."

Arihito said, "I didn't use my name."

"Kobe knew I was behind it. Nobody else has been stirring up trouble over this old case."

Yukiko cried, "It's not stirring up trouble to right an old wrong."

But the men knew better. Arihito hung his head and murmured, "Sorry," and Kosehira said to her, "It is in this case, and it may all be for nothing. There is no evidence. Akitada has checked everything. You must give up this wild scheme. Already someone has set fire to his house and his favorite horse is dead."

Yukiko, solemn-faced, said, "I will do as my husband wishes."

Kosehira and his son took their leave in an atmosphere of gloom. Akitada walked out with them. They arrived in the entrance courtyard just as the boy admitted another caller at the gate. The caller was Minamoto Yukihiro.

Akitada's heart sank. "Go back inside," he hissed to Arihito, but it was already too late. Yukihiro looked toward the house and saw them.

He came forward quickly, smiling, until he recognized Arihito. Then he stopped and the smile turned into a scowl. "So," he cried, and hurried up the steps to them. "There he is! The scoundrel who invaded my house for heaven knows what criminal reasons. What is he doing here?"

Akitada made him a slight bow. "Welcome to my home, Lord Yukihiro," he said with cold courtesy.

Yukihiro ignored him. He made for Arihito, who had turned pale and then flushed in rapid succession, and stabbed an accusatory finger toward him.

Koschira stepped into his way. "I don't believe we've met. I'm Fujiwara Koschira," he said.

Yukihiro stopped. He stared at Koschira. Akitada thought he could almost see the quick thoughts passing through the man's mind. He would have recognized Koschira's name as well as his high rank.

In the end, he bowed. "My apologies, my lord. I had no idea we would meet under such regrettable circumstances. It so happens, I came to speak to Lord Sugawara about this matter. I was surprised to find the subject of my complaint in his very house. I am bringing charges against this person." He stabbed his finger again in the direction of Arihito.

Koschira said, "Allow me to introduce my eldest son, Arihito."

Yukihiro's jaw dropped. "Y-your son? Er, your Excellency."

Kosehira, looking grim, nodded.

Akitada found the scene more amusing than embarrassing. True, Arihito had behaved badly, but Minamoto Yukihiro had also overstepped the bounds of courtesy. He was curious how he would handle it now that he knew the offender was the son of one of the most powerful men in the government.

But it was Arihito who found his voice first. "I used a small subterfuge to get some information you would have denied me," he said firmly. "I regret that I had to use such means, but that was really your own fault."

Yukihiro blinked. "My fault? How could it be my fault? And what information? What do you want from me?"

"We wanted to know whether you might have had a hand in your father's murder," Arihito said bluntly. "It's clear you benefitted greatly by coming into your inheritance, and it turns out that you were at your father's house just before he died."

"What?" Yukihiro almost squealed in his outrage. "How dare you? You're accusing me of killing my own father? It's all nonsense anyway. My father and I made up our differences that day and I left. There are witnesses that he was alive and well."

"We have only your word that you had an amicable meeting. I think you quarreled again. You left all right, but you came back that night and killed him."

"You are mad!"

"Not at all. And I shall go to lay my accusation before Superintendent Kobe this very day."

Koschira found his voice at last. "Arihito," he said, "that's enough. Lord Yukihiro, you must excuse us. We must go." Taking his son's arm in a painful grip, he led him down the stairs and toward the gate.

Akitada and Yukihiro remained looking after them.

Yukihiro muttered, "He must be mad. I'm sure he's a great trial to his father."

Akitada did not comment on this.

"You surely don't believe this nonsense?" Yukihiro asked.

"It's an interesting theory, but the young man has no real evidence against you. It was rather wishful thinking because he wants to marry Tanaka's daughter."

The other man relaxed visibly. "Oh. I see. And his father approves of such a marriage? How very odd."

"His father has an open mind about Tanaka's guilt."

Yukihiro asked anxiously, "In other words, he also thinks I might have killed my father?"

"Not necessarily. There's another possibility. The woman Maruko. She expected that her son would inherit. She claims he is your father's child."

Yukihiro looked angry. "Yes, she tried that on me," he said. "It's an insult to my father and it didn't work. My father explained the relationship to me. He took her in because she'd been reduced to begging to feed her baby. She acted as his housekeeper in exchange for shelter and food. My father gave up women along with other pleasures when he retired. He was a devout disciple of the Buddha."

"But you continued to support both of them after his death. Why did you do that when you believed that she had lied?"

Lord Yukihiro shuffled his feet. "I didn't have the heart to throw them out," he muttered.

Akitada raised his brows in disbelief. "It's been fifteen years."

With some more shuffling, the other man said, "I grant you, they are a trial to me. Especially Hideyo. But it wouldn't do my reputation good. I've let it be known that I was obeying my father's wishes."

"Yes. I see. Do you know of any reason why Maruko might have done the murder?"

"No. None. The police were very thorough and had a solid case against Tanaka."

"Yes. It appears that way." Akitada paused. "Forgive me, but did you have a purpose for coming to see me?"

"Oh." Yukihiro flushed. "It was about the visit of that young man. I meant to ask you if you knew anything about it."

"Ah."

"Well, I trust that I have satisfied your suspicions," Yukihiro said, a little tartly. "I regret that I have no wish to be accused of murder so Lord Kosehira's son can marry this young woman."

Akitada nodded and smiled. "I don't blame you at all."

They bowed to each other, and Lord Yukihiro departed.

22

A Death in the City

After they had all left, Akitada wondered where he stood. Kosehira had looked angry enough—at least to Akitada's eyes because he knew his friend very well indeed—to disown Arihito all over again. Arihito had been oblivious to his father's temper; he had left still glaring at Lord Yukihiro. Kosehira had also been angry with Yukihiro—and possibly even with Akitada. Something was bound to happen, but Akitada would have no hand in it.

With a sigh, he returned to his home and walked through to Yukiko's pavilion. She was in the garden outside, which suited him well. What he had to say need not fall on the ears of the borrowed maid.

225

She turned when he stepped down on the gravel. "What have you decided?" she asked, searching his face. Apparently his grim expression did not bode well, for she added, "Is something wrong?"

"A foolish question," he snapped, "given the circumstances. Everything is wrong. We should never have come."

She flushed. "I'm sorry about the question, but I'm not sorry we came. I love my brother and shall always hurry to his side."

"Then you clearly place his needs above mine." His voice had been harsh and he saw that he had frightened her. Remembering that she carried his child, he said more calmly, "This cannot go on, Yukiko. You'll have to be guided by me or more disasters will strike."

"I'm very sorry about the stable and your horse," she said, raising her chin, "but it seems to me that those things were due to something *you* did. I cannot be held responsible for your actions."

He flushed with anger. She was right, of course, but no husband wants to be spoken to in this manner by his wife. He steeled himself to control his anger. "I came to tell you that Minamoto Yukihiro arrived just as your father and Arihito were leaving. He recognized Arihito immediately and a very ugly scene ensued. I believe your father will forbid Arihito to pursue this matter further. I doubt he will countenance the marriage, and he may really disinherit his son. He was very angry."

"Oh!" she cried, appalled.

"So you see: nothing has come of your mad endeavor to prove someone else was the murderer. If anything, matters are much worse now, both for your brother and for me. I have instructed Genba to hire servants and armed men to protect this house and its people. We shall have to live as if we were under attack."

"But surely the police—"

He interrupted her, "Perhaps the worst thing that has happened due to your harebrained scheme is that my friend Kobe no longer speaks to me. You can forget about police protection."

She stared at him, her eyes wide. He could not tell what she was thinking. Most wives, when confronted with the righteous anger of their husbands would be on their knees begging his forgiveness. Not so Yukiko.

After a moment, she asked in a steady voice, "What do you want me to do?"

"Nothing! Stop meddling in matters that are none of your concern. In the future, do nothing without my permission."

He saw her face and knew it had gone wrong. Their relationship would never be the same again. And suddenly his loneliness was back, that dreadful black despair he had lived with after Tamako's death. Shaking his head, he turned and left.

His second marriage had disintegrated before his eyes. To be sure, they had had occasional squabbles in the past, but nothing like this had ever come between them. From the way Yukiko had looked at him just now, he was sure she had no affectionate feelings left for him.

And there was a child on the way.

He clenched his hands.

That night, he sat for a long time staring into space. There was no escape from this marriage for him. Already he was deeply obligated to Kosehira. If the relationship between himself and Yukiko continued in its present mood, he was sure to lose Kosehira's friendship just as he had lost Kobe's. Divorce was out of the question. And if Yukiko lost all faith in him and returned to her family (presumably with his child), he would suffer in his career, and ultimately his other children would have to pay for that.

No, he could not let this happen. He must try to keep peace between himself and Yukiko. Perhaps it was not too late. As soon as Kosehira had dealt with Arihito's problem, he would try to patch things up with Yukiko.

Quickly—because he would have to return to Mikawa as soon as possible. Alone. Another wave of loneliness washed over him.

Eventually, his thoughts led him back to the silk merchant and the present he had ordered for his wife. Perhaps it would mollify her a little with that. He decided to check on its progress.

∞

But when he reached the silk shop the next morning, it was closed. The chanting he heard from within told him that the silk merchant had died. He regretted the death, though the merchant's illness should have prepared him. Thinking back to his visit, he was again troubled by what he had observed that day. His instincts told him that all was not well. The wife had spoken of puffer fish, and certainly Nakai's symptoms implied poisoning of some sort.

As he stood there, he saw a youngster coming through the small gate that led to the back of the merchant's house. He wore a rough hemp jacket and wiped his eyes. He was going to pass Akitada without a word, but Akitada stopped him.

"Has Mr. Nakai died?"

The boy stopped, looked at him with bleary eyes, and nodded. "The master died last night," he said thickly. "He was terribly ill. I helped, but he died in the morning."

Akitada had a vision of what that must have been like: the dying man, wracked by bouts of vomiting and perhaps bloody dysentery, and the boy being made to clean up. Akitada had little faith in the man's elegant wife dirtying her fingers. He put a hand on the lad's shoulder. "You must have been fond of him. I'm very sorry."

The boy sniffled and nodded. He seemed grateful for Akitada's interest. "He was a good master," he confided. "My father brought me to him before he left for the North Country. Master Nakai was like an uncle to me. Always making sure I got my share of food. He told his wife that I was a growing boy and must be fed properly."

The youngster was as skinny as a young bamboo, as boys his age often are when they are growing fast. From his words it was also clear that Mrs. Nakai had not been as kind. Her husband had had to intercede on the boy's behalf.

"What is your name?"

"Ichiro."

"Well, Ichiro, you must be brave to honor your master's memory. Will you stay on and work for his widow or did he have another heir?"

"I don't know, sir. I mean, I don't know if I'm staying." The look on his face suggested that he did not want to. "I think it's Mrs. Nakai who'll keep the business. Her and Mr. Ujinobu."

Aha! So Akitada had been right about the improper relationship between the merchant's wife and his assistant. And here was a motive for murder. He hesitated for quite a while. His own troubles were of a magnitude that should discourage him from paying attention to other people's lives.

Ichiro looked at him and shuffled his feet. Finally, he said, "Well, I'd better hurry. The mistress has sent me to the market for a nice bream." He made a face again.

"I won't keep you. Do you happen to know which temple your master's doctor belonged to? I saw him visit Mr. Nakai."

"Oh, the Reverend Ingen is from the Hoju-ji temple. The master was the one sent for him."

"Thank you, Ichiro." Akitada took a small silver coin from his sash and gave it to the boy. "My name is Sugawara. Perhaps I may want to speak to you again sometime after the funeral."

Ichiro smiled for the first time, and thanked Akitada with a very deep bow, then trotted off on his errand.

It was clear that grief had not affected the widow's appetite. A fresh sea bream was by no means inexpensive. One could not help thinking of a celebration, a very tasteless act. Surely the boy had thought the same when he had grimaced.

His suspicions thoroughly aroused, Akitada decided to visit the Hoju-ji temple.

The temple was south-east of the city and a long journey for the monk Ingen. Akitada wondered at it. He went home and sent Yasaburo for a horse, then took the nearest bridge over the Kamo River and turned southward.

His mood had darkened further at the thought that this horse was not Raiden, and that he would never ride him again. Clouds moved in, and as he crossed the bridge, the first drops began to fall. The weather suited his mood and he ignored the fact that he would be getting wet.

The temple was small and new. The previous, much larger, compound had been destroyed by a disastrous fire the year before, but temples tended to be rebuilt quickly.

Akitada left his horse with the gatekeeper and requested to see Ingen. A young monk was assigned as his guide. They traversed the large courtyard to the sounds of hammering and sawing coming from a new hall being built.

The monks' quarters were also partially new. They found Ingen in one of the original sections, busily mixing medicines by the light of an oil lamp, since very little daylight penetrated through the high windows on this dreary day. He looked surprised seeing Akitada, but welcomed him in. Clearly he did not recall their meeting in Nakai's shop.

Akitada smiled and said he hoped he was well, then explained his visit. "I happened to see you the day you looked in on Nakai, the silk dealer. His illness has caused me some . . . concerns, and I thought I'd talk to you."

"How is he?" the monk asked.

"Alas, he has died. You treated him for a stomach ailment, I think?"

Ingen frowned. "Yes. I'm sorry to hear it, but I think he had his mind set on passing into a better world."

This startled Akitada. "Surely not. He had a young and pretty wife and a very successful business. Are you saying you think he committed suicide?"

"Men kill themselves in many ways. Women, too." Ingen peered at him with wise eyes. "They don't always know it."

"Please explain. I spoke briefly to Nakai and found him cheerful enough, given the fact he was sick. His wife said he had eaten poisoned puffer fish."

"If he ate poisoned fish he knew about it and didn't care."

Akitada was out of his depth. "What did he tell you?"

"Nothing much. I went to him several times. After the first visit, he thought I was wasting my time. I doubt he took my medicine, though he said he did."

"What did you treat him for?"

"I made up a potion of seven herbs to soothe his belly. Do you know about medicine?"

"Alas, I know too little. Both my late wife and my faithful old servant knew much more than I."

Ingen studied him. "It is our lot to miss those we were once close to. I do not think Nakai's wife will miss him."

"I agree. That's partly why I came." He decided to be blunt. "Could she have poisoned him?"

"If you mean, has she given him poison, I do not know. But certainly there are other ways a woman may poison a man."

Buddhist monks frequently hated women on principle. Their faith prescribed an attitude of distrust and disdain toward women. But in this case, Akitada thought Ingen probably knew something or had observed what Akitada had seen. He nodded. "I was struck by the fact that Mrs. Nakai behaved in a very familiar manner toward their Assistant Ujinobu, a handsome younger man. Is that what you mean?"

Ingen made a face. "No. If you say so, I believe you, but the marriage was poisoned by the fact that she did not love her husband while he loved her too much."

"Ah. But clearly that might give her cause to wish her husband dead."

"Again, I don't know that she did."\

"Well, it seems a reasonable assumption that a young wife would prefer a young man to her aged husband."

Ingen gave him a sharp glance. "It is best not to make such assumptions. They may be quite wrong."

Akitada gave up. This monk knew things that he was not divulging. Instead he made Akitada feel like a vindictive busy-body who had no faith in his fellow human beings. "So you believe that Nakai was tired of living and gave up his life because he had a belly ache?"

Ingen laughed. "Who knows the ways of Buddha? Who knows the ways of men? Or women?"

"In that case, why did you bother to bring medicines to the sick man?"

"The boy asked me to come."

"The boy? You mean Ichiro?"

Ingen nodded. "That boy has a lot of love in him. I could not deny him."

Akitada thought about their meeting earlier and nodded. "He grieves. He may the only one."

Ingen smiled his enigmatic smile again. "You see? That is why I went."

"Are you willing to let his widow and her lover enjoy the benefits of murder?" Akitada asked, his frown deepening.

"The ways of Buddha are not the ways of man. I'm content to leave revenge to him."

"This is not a matter of revenge," Akitada snapped, now thoroughly angry. "This is a matter of protecting the innocent from their evil fellow humans. I may be too late for poor Mr. Nakai, but if I'm right about this poisoning, then there are two people still alive who are so ruthless that they may murder again, thinking themselves safe and free to do as they wish. I have the distinct feeling that Buddha will not protect their next victims."

Ingen's smile widened. "Do not underestimate Buddha. For here you are, bent on stopping evil-doers. Now you must forgive me. I have to make up some medicine for one of the monks."

Akitada departed. His anger soon dissipated, leaving him bemused and at a loss.

23

Keeping Devils Away

The death of the silk merchant was not really his concern. Nobody had asked him to intercede. Since the funeral arrangements would take another day, there was no point in a visit to the shop to ask about the progress of his order.

He grimaced. Yukiko would not be appeased with a new train, no matter how beautiful and thoughtful his gift was. There lay too much between them to return to their earlier carefree love-making.

Yukiko had grown up quickly. She no longer looked up to him but had instead set herself against him. No doubt this had a great deal to do with her birth. A Fujiwara woman was independent and took her life and that of her children into her own hands. This was surely not a bad thing when such a young woman was matched with a young emperor or one of the great men in government. Her husband expected only children from her.

He rode glumly homeward in the rain. He had chosen Yukiko and could hardly blame her for the fact that he had wanted someone more like Tamako, a quiet, intelligent, supportive wife in whom he could find refuge.

When he got home, he saw with surprise that several policemen stood outside it. He stopped beside one of them and asked what they were doing there.

The man eyed him askance and snapped. "Orders, sir. We're investigating a case of arson."

The man had not recognized him. Akitada said mildly, "It's my house. Are there more of you inside?"

The constable snapped to attention and saluted. "Sorry, sir. Yes, sir."

Akitada nodded and rode in.

The rain somehow made both sight and smell of the ruin more shocking.

Genba stood beside another policeman, this one a sergeant by his headdress, gesticulating as he explained something. They turned when they heard Akitada's horse and Genba came quickly.

He said, "Sir, I alerted the police. I told them as little as possible, since you weren't here."

The sergeant had followed, looking suspicious. "Are you Lord Sugawara?"

"I am." Akitada dismounted, giving the reins to Genba. "Just tie him up somewhere until he can be returned. You did well." Then he turned to the sergeant. "Would you like to come inside out of this rain? I'm sure you're wondering what happened."

The man relaxed somewhat and they went to Akitada's study where Akitada offered wine, which was gratefully accepted. "Very dry work, poking around burnt buildings." The sergeant chuckled. "Even when it rains."

Akitada said, "I suspect mischief. A few days ago someone scrawled threats on my gate. Now this."

The sergeant emptied his cup and sighed appreciatively. Akitada refilled it.

"Do you have someone in mind?" he asked after sipping again.

"I can't be sure, but there's a young man called Hideyo who seems to have developed a hatred for me. He is unstable, according to his mother, a woman called Maruko. They live in Prince Atsutada's villa in the eastern foothills. Do you know where it is?"

The sergeant frowned. "Isn't that where the prince was murdered some years ago?"

"Yes. You have a good memory."

"I was a young recruit then and was told to keep an eye on the murderer while he was in jail awaiting trial."

Akitada regarded him with sudden interest. "You don't say. What did you think of him?"

The sergeant shook his head. "I was very young. He scared me and I was ashamed of that. I watched him all the time, expecting him to turn into a ravenous tiger, I suppose." He chuckled a little. "Mind you, he was mean-looking and much bigger than me. He also rattled the door, shouting curses. Once, when I asked him what was wrong, he spat at me and called me a name. I was very glad when they found him guilty and even gladder when I heard he'd died."

This image of Tanaka seemed to fit his reputation as a violent man. It was just another instance of the hopelessness of their efforts to establish him as the innocent victim of some plot. If there had indeed been a plot, Tanaka had been the tool.

"Did anyone try to help him after he was jailed?"

"I doubt it. Nobody ever came to see him, except the captain. He's the superintendent now but was plain Captain Kobe back in those days."

"Yes. I knew him then." Sadness returned that their long association and friendship should have come to an end. Akitada sighed. "Mind you," he said, "I have no proof that this Hideyo set the fire. The boy who works for me described the intruder, and it sounded like him."

The sergeant nodded. "Yes. I talked to the boy. He seems bright enough, though it was pretty stupid to let him in in the first place, since the boy says he'd never seen him before. Is that correct?"

"I think so. The boy is young and assumed Genba had hired him for some purpose. Hideyo asked to be shown to the stable."

In retrospect, the whole business had been childishly simple and conceived with a childlike simplicity. With all the straw and hay in the stable, all Hideyo had needed to do was to pour some lamp oil and strike a spark. But it was surprising that it had worked. Akitada realized again how woefully understaffed his residence had been.

The sergeant declared himself satisfied, declined a third cup of wine, and departed.

A short time later, Genba came in. "Sir, I've sent for carpenters. They'll begin cleaning up and rebuilding. Also, some of the neighbors have sent their people to help. The police have stationed two men outside the gate. If you think it's all right, I thought I'd go into the city to look for some armed men. I'll say it's a temporary job. We can decide later if they suit us."

There was a new sound of authority in Genba's voice and he seemed to stand a little taller. Akitada smiled. "Excellent. Just what I had in mind. But please tell me who sent people to help us so I can thank them."

Genba recited several names. Akitada was moved by this token of their kindness when they had no obligations to share their servants. A more cynical thought suggested that this might have something to do with his new status and prosperity, but he put it from his mind as unworthy. He wrote the requisite letters expressing his gratitude, then went in search of the boy to deliver them.

He had just placed the letters into Yasaburo's hands with precise instructions, when there was a shout at the gate. Yasaburo hurried off to answer it while Akitada waited to see who it was.

The gate opened to a palanquin with bearers and a burly servant by its side. From the palanquin emerged his sister Akiko, dressed to go calling. No doubt in Yukiko's company.

He waited to greet her as she hurried out of the rain and up the steps to the veranda.

She stopped to stare at the burnt-out ruin of the stable. "What happened?"

"A vengeful lout set fire to it."

"Oh? Really, Akitada, must you always create such dramatic scenes? I take it you managed to irritate someone while looking for Atsutada's killer."

"Indeed. And I'd like a few words with you before you see Yukiko."

She raised her brows but followed him to his study without protest.

"Sit down. This may take a while."

She complied but muttered, "Must you be so commanding? I happen to be used to your ways, but I cannot think it a good way in which to deal with your wife."

"And that is precisely what I wish to discuss with you. You have filled my wife's head with all sorts of ideas that are causing trouble between us." He raised a hand. "No, don't interrupt. I've long been aware of the fact that Toshikage is the kind of husband who allows his wife excessive liberties, both in spending his money and in having her own way in all things. I do not approve, but this is between you and him and none of my business. However, you have now convinced Yukiko that she should have the same sort of marriage, and she is setting her mind against mine. You have encouraged her in this latest harebrained effort to pin a murder on anyone other than the true killer. I regret having acceded to those foolish demands. As a result, I have lost Kobe's friendship and my favorite horse, and now my home is no longer safe. And nothing, absolutely nothing has come to light to suggest that Tanaka was not the killer. You will therefore stop urging her to continue with this. And in general, you will stop destroying the peace of my marriage by encouraging her to defy my wishes. If you disobey me in this, I shall have to curtail your visits to my house."

He saw with great satisfaction that Akiko's jaw had gone slack and she was gaping at him speechlessly. Taking a breath, he continued.

"In the beginning, it was just a matter of your accompanying her on some shopping excursions. These have become costly, but Yukiko is used to liberal allowances and besides she controls her own money. I had no desire to interfere. Then you began a round of visits to the wives and daughters of high-ranking families. I disapprove of so much socializing, but in this instance, I could see that a small amount of it would allow her to make some friends. Naturally you yourself were quite eager to use Yukiko to gain invitations to houses you had not yet been to. In particular, you have both now gained entrance to the inner apartments of the palace."

Akiko finally found her voice. "How dare you?" she cried. "I have always enjoyed very close relations with the great families and visited the imperial palace long before you married Yukiko. Have you forgotten how I helped you in the past when you knew no one of any

consequence? It would seem to me that you'd be grateful we women are doing our best to promote your interests at court. Really, Akitada! This is outrageous! You
are an ungrateful beast. And if you talk this way to your
wife, then you may wave goodbye to your marriage *and*
your career."

Akitada slammed his fist on his desk. "I'll not have
you interfere between myself and my wife. Do you understand me?"

Akiko paled a little. "I have done no such thing. You
have neglected her the way you neglected Tamako. She
needs friends. I'm warning you, Akitada, if you don't
change your ways, you'll lose Yukiko. She comes from
a different background than Tamako, who had no family to return to. Yukiko will leave you if you don't give
her some freedom."

He was shocked to hear her say he had neglected
Tamako. Except for one short period, theirs had been a
perfect marriage. His voice shaking, he said, "I never
neglected Tamako. You know very little about my marriage and I resent the fact that you say such things when
you know how I grieve over her death."

Akiko sighed. "Very well, Akitada. I shall obey your
wishes, but do not blame me if Yukiko becomes bored.
On the whole, it is good that she is staying here while
she awaits the birth of your child. Taking her back to a
provincial backwater like Mikawa would have made her
miserable again. But, Akitada, if you value your marriage, don't speak to her the way you just talked to me."
She rose. "Now may I go see your wife?"

He nodded, too shocked by her comment about Tamako to think of ways to reinforce his argument, and Akiko made him a slight bow and left.

His sister's accusation was surprisingly painful. But she had not known their private life and the many moments of intense closeness between them. Tamako had been like a part of himself. In honesty, he admitted that he had never—or not yet—found that sense of contentment with Yukiko. Perhaps he did not love his young wife enough. Perhaps the age difference separated them. He did not know. But he knew that his marriage to Tamako had been good. Had he neglected her? Perhaps. But if so, it had been due to his work. And so he must neglect Yukiko also.

It was a man's lot.

He sighed and got up to look out at his small garden. The trees were heavy with moisture and rain drops danced on the surface of the fish pond. The acrid smell of burned and wet wood still hung in the air. He thought of Raiden, the gray stallion. He had loved him, and the horse had returned the affection. Life was made up of many losses, small ones and large ones. It seemed to him the disappointments and bereavements had been easier to bear in the past.

But his present unhappiness was due to devilment. It was as if he were plagued by any number of *oni*, those invisible, hidden evil spirits that plagued men in life and death. They served King Emma-O, the judge, in the underworld where they punished souls condemned to hell.

I. J. PARKER

People thought they also inhabited living creatures
from time to time. Perhaps this Hideyo had such a devil
in him who chose to plague Akitada and his family. *Oni*
were said to attack from the north-east, and Atsutada's
house was north-east of the capital and of Akitada's
home. It was the tiger-ox direction of the Chinese cal-
endar, which was why *oni* were depicted with fangs and
horns.

He felt bedeviled by many things: The breach with
Kobe. His troubled marriage. His sister's interference.
He wondered if the annual custom of cleansing his
house of *oni* had been conducted in his absence. Perhaps neglecting the ritual accounted for the many unpleasant and disastrous events he had encountered
since returning.

But these were idle fancies and he really did not believe in such nonsense. Alas, a formal ceremony would
not solve his problems. He must deal with matters himself. He had made a start with his lectures to Yukiko
and his sister. He must now settle the matter of the
Tanaka investigation.

He wandered about his room as he thought. He had
come to accept the proof of Tanaka's guilt offered by
Kobe and by his own investigation into the matter, but
there was still the one glaring fact that Tanaka's wife
insisted on his innocence. That did not square with the
evidence which included the abuse he had inflicted on
her. Yet Mrs. Tanaka, widow, wife, and Buddhist nun,
had never changed her mind about this.

Perhaps she was so adamant about Tanaka's innocence because she wished her daughter to marry

Kosehira's son, but Akitada had the feeling that she had a more profound reason for it. Speaking to her again would likely not produce any facts, so where could he go to learn more about Tanaka?

It suddenly struck him that he had never asked any questions about the sort of man Tanaka had been before his marriage. Perhaps an answer lay in his past, in his early life.

One last effort should be made. Tanaka, member of a poor but respected family, had served in the imperial guard. The imperial guard kept excellent records of its members because such records were regularly consulted for promotions and the assignment of government positions. Tanaka, however, had clearly come down in the world when he had ended up as a mere *betto* to Prince Atsutada.

The man to help in this matter was Nakatoshi, and Nakatoshi was the very person who could make him feel less of a failure and lift his spirits.

24

The Frog in the Well

A kiko had obeyed her brother within the letter of his prohibitions when she spoke with Yukiko. She did not encourage her to disobey him but rather warned her.

"You must know that Akitada doesn't bend once he has made up his mind. He's convinced that we have been wrong to pursue this matter of Prince Atsutada's murder. It will therefore be best to give up the idea."

Yukiko bit her lip. "He's angry, but he had no right to speak to me the way he did. I did nothing wrong. He is the one who angered that woman's son. It isn't fair to make Arihito suffer for what he himself has caused. I'm afraid it means that he no longer cares for me." She gulped. "Maybe he never did. Maybe I've been a fool."

"Nonsense!" Akiko said briskly. "His bad humor will pass. However, I think we'd better cancel our visits today. He doesn't much like you running around so much with me. He thinks I'm a bad influence."

"Oh, this is too much to bear!" Yukiko wailed. There was a moment's silence, then Yukiko said in a small voice, "I had no idea he could be so hard. It's a great disappointment."

Akiko patted her arm. "Don't let it distress you. Akitada is always fair, though he has his moods. I suppose the fact that he holds some fairly outmoded ideas has something to do with it. Keep in mind, he's your father's age."

Yukiko sighed. "He never seemed old to me. I thought he was a man who worked miracles and faced all odds in his battle to protect the country from villains. I thought he was wonderful!"

"Well," said Akiko, suppressing a smile, "he is that, too. Which makes him hard to live with. Never mind, my girl. You'll learn to adapt. Besides, he'll have to go back to Mikawa, and you and I will have time to visit and shop."

∞

The two women parted soon after and Yukiko decided to visit her parents. In order to appease Akitada, she sent the maid to ask his permission. This having been given, she climbed into a palanquin with her maid and went to her father's house.

The Assassin's Daughter

She found Arihito with him. When they saw her face, they asked what was wrong.

"Akitada spoke to me very harshly this morning," she said bitterly. "He accused me of having caused all his troubles. He thinks I'm to blame for the fact that Superintendent Kobe is angry with him and that the horrible Hideyo set fire to his stable and killed his horse." Her anger at such unfairness dissolved into self-pity, and she burst into tears.

Kosehira said nothing, but his mouth tightened.

Arihito cried, "How could he? And just when we're very nearly there."

Yukiko sobbed. "I can't do anything right. He finds fault with everything. He told Akiko that I'm going about too much. He wants me to stay locked up at home like his other wife. I can't bear it."

Kosehira snapped, "Daughter!"

Yukiko looked at him tearfully. "Yes?"

"You wanted this marriage. I regret that I helped you because you have shamed me. If your husband found it necessary to speak to you the way he did, it can only mean that you have disappointed him. And if you disappoint him, you disappoint me. I shall make allowance for the fact that you are with child, but I expect you to behave in such a way in the future that he has no complaint. Do you hear me?"

Yukiko gulped and nodded.

Arihito, looking shocked, cleared his throat. "I fear this is all my fault, Father. Yukiko was only helping me. Please don't blame her."

Kosehira glowered at him. "Yes, some of this is your fault. And I have also had enough of your persistence in the matter. We have all tried to prove that your young woman's father couldn't have been the killer. Akitada has probably tried harder than anyone. Nothing has come of it. Give it up. Neither you nor your sister know anything about the case. You've been like the frog in the well, thinking he knows all about the ocean."

"Will you allow the marriage, Father?" Yukiko asked after a moment.

"No!" Kosehira snapped. "Nothing has changed. The young woman is unfit as a ranking spouse. If your brother wants to take her secretly as a concubine, I suppose I could live with that. But you must both see that we cannot be associated with the family of such a notorious killer."

Arihito's head drooped. "I'm sorry, Father," he said tonelessly. "I think it will be best if I give up Masako. I'll not insult her by making her my concubine. For that matter, she has made it clear that she will not marry me if you are opposed to it."

Silence fell. Kosehira regarded his children with a stern expression. After a while, he said, "Yukiko, you may go to your mother now, but don't forget what I told you."

She rose, bowed, and left.

There was another silence.

Arihito sighed. "I'm very sorry, Father," he said eventually. "I was wrong and it was very good of you to try to help me. I see that now. I shall put my future into your hands."

Kosehira grunted.

"May I be allowed to tell Masako of our decision?"

His father frowned. "Not yet. We shall inform Superintendent Kobe first and make our apologies."

Arihito's head came up. "Apologies? The superintendent was as unhelpful as he could be. I don't call this proper behavior in a policeman. Especially when you outrank him and could make his life difficult."

"I hope I never hear you speak like that again," his father thundered, turning red with anger. "Superintendent Kobe has informed us courteously that we did not have a case. He was right and you were wrong. Furthermore, never threaten an official who is carrying out his duty." Kosehira blew out his cheeks in frustration. "Pah! This is a day I never hoped to see, a day when I had to be ashamed for two of my children."

Arihito knelt before his father, his forehead touching the boards. "Forgive me, Father. I was wrong."

"Come," said Kosehira, rising. "You can make your apologies yourself."

∞

Kobe received them quickly and with a reserved courtesy. When they were seated, he asked, "How may I help?"

Kosehira glanced at his son and said, "We have come to tender our apologies. This mad attempt at pinning the Atsutada murder on someone else has clearly failed signally. My son and I are aware that we have put you in a difficult position, not to mention the fact that we have doubted your investigation fifteen years ago."

He had spoken plainly, avoiding any of the courtly language he usually employed when meeting officials. He saw that it had been the right tone.

Kobe smiled a little at both of them and said, "No apologies necessary. I, too, know what it's like to be in love. Young men forget everything else in their devotion. I only regret that Lord Arihito had to face the facts eventually. Disappointment is painful, but it is a common part of life. Fifteen years ago, I was a young police officer still learning my business. It is reasonable to assume I could have been wrong."

Kosehira nodded slowly. "That excuses Arihito somewhat but not myself. I should not have used my position to support my son's endeavor."

"Surely it is a father's way to show his love for a child?"

"You are very kind and understanding." Kosehira regarded Kobe with new-found respect. "But this has damaged others also. I'm told my friend and son-in-law Akitada has lost your friendship. He also lost his favorite horse, but that doesn't signify by comparison. And as he has gained a violent enemy, he has put his life and the lives of his family in jeopardy. I regret this very deeply."

Arihito finally spoke. "My sister expects a child and . . . and all of this . . . has deeply upset her. I shall never forgive myself."

Kobe had become serious. "I didn't know. Perhaps it will be best if I go to express my felicitation and offer protection?"

Koschira nodded. "That would be a most generous gesture. I'm sure Akitada would be very happy to see you. He has grieved a good deal over this breach."

"I take it then that nothing new has turned up in your search?" Kobe asked Arihito.

"Well . . ." Arihito hesitated and shot a glance at his father. Koschira offered no help.

"Speak up."

"We did wonder about Minamoto Yukihiro, sir. It seemed so convenient for him to visit his estranged father the very day the prince was murdered. He claimed they made up their quarrel, but there's no proof of that. He could just as easily have quarreled again and returned that night. And . . . umm . . . he needed money badly."

Kobe's lip twitched. "That last point, I think, you discovered by interrogating his servants while pretending to be a harmless student working on a paper commemorating the prince?"

Arihito flushed and nodded.

Kobe heaved a sigh. "Well, I can lay that suspicion to rest anyway. Lord Yukihiro couldn't have gone back to his father's house that particular night because he was elsewhere."

Arihito blurted out, "It's easy enough to get a friend to say so, sir. If you'll forgive me."

"It wasn't a friend who was his witness."

"So you did check on him?"

"No. We did not. It wasn't necessary."

"I don't understand. You just took his word for it?"

Kosehira moved. "Arihito!" he said in a warning tone.

"Sorry, sir," his son muttered.

Kobe sighed again. "Lord Yukihiro was seen by me that night. He was at some distance from his father's house, and I know he had no opportunity to go there later."

Arihito gaped at him. "*You* saw him?"

"Yes." Kobe compressed his lips.

Arihito flushed again. "In that case no more need be said. I think we have said enough. Thank you for your time, sir." His voice was flat, and his expression suggested that all sorts of new suspicions had arisen in his mind.

Kobe growled, "Not so fast. I don't like discussing cases with outsiders, especially not when facts can be distorted into ugly gossip, but in this case I seem to have no choice. It's clear you don't believe me. So here's what happened. We were called out to a disturbance in the amusement quarter. A fight had broken out in a sleazy brothel that caters to men with odd tastes. The fight was over, but we ended up arresting several men who had engaged in the rape of a nine-year-old boy. The boy objected to the violent way they had used him. Yukihiro was one of those men. They all spent the night in jail. Now are you satisfied?"

Arihito looked shocked. "Oh! Oh, I see. Please forgive me for doubting. I would never have thought . . ."

His voice trailed off.

Kobe's lip twitched again. "You would never have expected such a man to be a pervert, but you thought murdering his own father was quite within reason?"

"No. Yes. Something like that. I'm very sorry."

"Well, keep the story to yourself."

"Yes, sir."

Kosehira rose. "Thank you, Superintendent. Your patience with my son has been exemplary. I apologize again for any uneasiness we may have caused you."

They bowed and departed.

25

The Pharmacist

As he had done so many times in the past, Akitada sought out Nakatoshi in his place of work, the Ministry of Ceremonial. As the senior official, Nakatoshi enjoyed a pleasant room in the back where he could look out at a small courtyard with neatly raked gravel and some potted trees.

He was happy to see Akitada, who had felt a pang of guilt that he was forever coming to his friend for help with some case. Their very pleasant dinner at Nakatoshi's home had brought this finally to his mind, and he resolved again to have a more personal friendship with Nakatoshi.

But for today he needed information about Tanaka that Nakatoshi could provide. To make up for this selfish purpose, he began by explaining what had been happening recently. Nakatoshi's eyes grew wide with concern and commiseration. Akitada ended with, "So you will understand why I have again come to you. I want to lay this case to rest and never think of it again. I have tried all reasonable possibilities of clearing Tanaka's name but one. I have not looked into his background. Mind you, I have no great hopes, but there is the one incontrovertible point that the man's wife has never wavered in claiming his innocence. So I'd like to know what happened to Tanaka before the murder and even before his marriage. He comes from a decent but obscure family and served in the imperial guard. Something happened to make him change that career. I want to know what it was, because it must have been drastic. In that event may lie some clue to the murder."

Nakatoshi nodded eagerly. "Yes. That's quite easy. Since the ministry of ceremonial deals with rank issues we will have some information here. And then, when we know under whom he served, we can get more answers from those who served with him or were his superiors. Were you thinking that he may have made friends who involved him in the murder plot?"

"A friend or an enemy. An enemy who wouldn't mind shifting suspicion on him."

"Ah! Allow me." Nakatoshi clapped his hands, and a servant appeared. "Get my assistant, please," he told him.

The assistant was young and bright-eyed. He looked at Akitada with great attention as Nakatoshi explained that they wanted a look at rank records for several years preceding the death of Prince Atsutada in the year of Kannin.

Nakatoshi asked Akitada. "How long before do you think?"

"I believe his daughter was four, so the marriage would have been about five years before. Perhaps we should start there."

Nakatoshi nodded. "The second year of Ten'ei, then, Hiroshi, and the next six years."

Hiroshi disappeared and they returned to a discussion of the Tanaka case.

"What will you do about this Hideyo?" Nakatoshi asked.

"What can I do? At least some of the police showed up to investigate the fire. We gave them what information we had. Mostly what a twelve-year old boy who helps in the stables remembers about a man who claimed we had sent for him. His description fits Hideyo, though the boy thought him much older. Since Kobe and I are barely speaking and he's opposed to listening to anything that involves the Tanaka case, I don't think much will be done." He chuckled. "I confess I've taken to glancing over my shoulder."

"I can't say I blame you."

"I feel foolish and cowardly, actually. But there is something very disturbing about that young man. It's in the way he looks at me and the way he keeps clenching and unclenching his hands all the time. I felt as if he would lash out at any moment."

"Very angry, in other words?"

"Not just angry. He seemed . . . possessed." There is was out. Akitada had seen cases of possession and had always believed them to be faked. Sometimes people wanted to attract attention or donations; sometimes it was a matter of the possessed, usually a woman, doing it in order to please the priest or shaman. Hideyo was different, and because Akitada could not account for his behavior, he was uneasy.

He said as much to Nakatoshi, and Nakatoshi related some incidents he had observed. But Hiroshi and a servant returned at that point, bearing stacks of dusty document boxes.

"Dear gods." Akitada was appalled. "I had no idea you kept such detailed records."

"Oh, yes. Nothing more important than rank and promotion," Nakatoshi said with a laugh. "Not even laws. But it won't be too difficult. The guards' records are separate in each of the boxes."

But even though Nakatoshi involved his assistant in the search, it took them several hours to find what they were looking for. The story they pieced together was not pretty. Though assigned to one of the most respected regiments of the imperial guards as a young man of twenty, Tanaka soon began accumulating reprimands. He served for five years without promotion. In his sixth year he was arrested for a brutal beating that cost a prostitute her life. The case was apparently particularly serious because he had also involved the young son of a ranking court noble. The result was dismissal from the guards.

"That explains a lot," commented Nakatoshi.

Akitada said glumly, "It may explain everything. The man must have been a brute without a conscience. Now I wonder why Atsutada gave him a position of trust as his *betto*."

"Didn't you say Atsutada took pity on his family?"

"Yes. I suppose that could have been enough reason for him. Especially if he was inclined to help a man so very drastically come down in the world. I expect Tanaka's story was widely known among the good people at the time."

"I suppose so, but I don't recall. I was still at the university and Tanaka never went there apparently."

"The other thing that puzzles me is why a university professor would give his daughter to a man with such a bad reputation."

"I'm afraid you have to search elsewhere for that. You won't find the answer in any of the archives. I assume the professor is dead?"

"Yes, I believe so." Akitada sat lost in thought as Nakatoshi watched. Finally Akitada heaved a sigh and said, "Well, I no longer have much doubt that Tanaka was the killer. For whatever reason. It doesn't matter if he killed his master for the gold found later in his house, or if he acted in hopes of gaining rewards because he got rid of a man who was a thorn in the side of Michinaga and his friends."

Nakatoshi nodded. He directed his assistant and the servant to take away the documents. Then the two friends sat together for a little while longer, chatting about other matters.

∞

Since life at home had few attractions at the moment, Akitada walked into the city. It was another pleasant day, and the sun dappled the street whenever he walked under trees. At the canals, children sailed small boats made of wood scraps and servants and housewives washed clothes. The cherry trees had lost their blooms, but the pink petals still lay on the ground, looking strangely like snow. And everywhere, the willows wore their brilliant golden first leaves. His city was beautiful.

He had a vague idea of checking on Yukiko's silks, though it was unlikely that the shop was open after the funeral.

Merchants could not afford to take the same amount of time to mourn their loved ones as the officials did, but surely a respected shop like Nakai's would honor the death of its owner by remaining closed for, say, a week. It was inconvenient. Akitada hoped to have left for Mikawa long before.

He found the street filled with busy shoppers, but Nakai's shop was shuttered and the usual markers warning of a recent death were attached to its entrance. As Akitada paused to look at it, someone plucked at his sleeve. It was Nakai's youngest employee. He looked better today, but there was still a sadness in his face.

"Do you remember me, your honor?" he asked. "You asked about my master." He nodded toward the shuttered shop.

"I remember. I liked your master and liked that you mourned his passing. I'm very sorry he died."

"Yes. He was a good master. I was lucky. But it's all over now."

"Well, a nice, hardworking youngster like you will surely be useful in the shop."

He shook his head. "The mistress runs the shop now. Her and Master Ujinobu. They told me to leave." He scraped at the dirt with one sandaled foot. Without looking at Akitada he asked, "Could I come work for you?"

"Alas, I already have a boy."

He nodded and hung his head. "Thought so."

They stood side by side in silence, looking at the shuttered shop. In the end, Akitada asked, "Did Mrs. Nakai tell you why they aren't keeping you on?"

"No. But I know why. I told the master about Ujinobu."

Akitada looked at the boy more sharply.. "You told him what?"

"Ujinobu's been selling our silk to another shop. For a long time. I didn't say anything at first because I thought the master had told him to do it. But one day, the master looked for a particular piece and couldn't find it. I waited for Ujinobu to remind him, but he never did. Later that night I told the master about it. He got upset."

"Ah. I expect Ujinobu had misunderstood something. Or perhaps Mr. Nakai had simply forgotten."

"That's what the mistress said, but the master wasn't forgetful. He told me many times that I must remember things because in a business you can't afford to forget."

"How long ago was it that you told Mr. Nakai about Ujinobu taking the silk to another dealer?"

The boy thought. "It was the day before he died." He frowned. "You don't think it made him worse? He and the mistress quarreled. Mind you, he'd been sick for some weeks. Off and on. Only that night he got worse. Amida, I hope it wasn't me!"

"It wasn't you," Akitada said, hoping against hope that that Nakai's death had had nothing to do with Ujinobu's malfeasance. "As you say, he was sick before. Did he tell you what was the matter with him?"

The boy shook his head. "I'd better go look for a job. Maybe I can sweep someone's shop for a penny. My mother's nursing the baby and we don't have much money."

Akitada reached into his sash and gave him a piece of silver. "Here, buy something for dinner tonight, and if you don't have another job by the end of the week, come to the Sugawara house and ask for Genba. Tell him I sent you. I'm Lord Sugawara."

The boy's eyes grew round. He bowed quite deeply, muttering his thanks. Akitada smiled and walked away.

He decided to go home, but at the street corner, he passed the sign for a pharmacy. On an impulse he walked in. The shop was dimly lit, but the smells were overpoweringly strong. Herbal medicines mostly, Akitada thought, but he knew that pharmacists also dealt in exotic animal parts and minerals. Herbs were plentiful in their country, and shark fins and ground oyster shells were also easily come by, but many of the most efficacious remedies tended to be foreign, rare, and very expensive.

When his eyes had adjusted, he looked around. The walls were lined with shelves and many small drawers made of dark wood. On the shelves stood rows of identical jars. The jars and drawers had labels with the names of the contents. Two large picture scrolls of craggy mountain landscapes painted in ink were hanging on the back walls. Each bore an inscription, a poem perhaps, but Akitada could not make out the writing. The raised floors on either side of the stone walkway where he stood were also dark. At the edge of the platform lay thick grass mats for people to sit on. On one of the platforms stood a low desk with a mortar and pestle and a set of small scales, as well as a tidy stack of white rice paper to wrap the medicine in. Otherwise the place was quite empty.

It seemed strange to leave the shop open to thieves like this. Akitada called out, "Anybody here?"

Nothing happened.

He peered again at the two ink paintings. They were very good. The pharmacist must be a man of taste. But then pharmacists were held in greater regard than physicians, with the possible exception of the court physicians. He turned to leave the shop and was nearly at the entrance, when a deep voice asked, "What is it you need?"

Akitada jumped a little. When he turned, he saw that a tall, slender man in a gray robe and with a long black beard had appeared behind him. He must have walked without making a sound, and Akitada's eyes flew to his feet. He wore black slippers.

"I'm sorry I startled you." The pharmacist waited.

Akitada made him a slight bow and said, "I saw your shop and decided to look in. You have some very fine paintings.

It was difficult to tell if the pharmacist smiled at this. He said, "You did not come for the paintings, I think."

"Call it idle curiosity. It's been a long time since I have visited a pharmacist."

"Ah! Well, what can I tell you?"

Akitada slipped off his shoes. "Could you show me some of your treasures?" He stepped up on the raised section and approached the long lines of small drawers and neatly labeled jars.

The pharmacist followed. "Well," he said gesturing, "the drawers contain dry materials and the jars wet ones."

"Wet?"

"Tinctures and salves. Ointments and plasters. That sort of thing."

"And you keep the herbal medicines in the drawers?"

"Actually the herbal materials are on the other side. I keep my treasures on this one. Rare things that come from far away. Would you like to see?"

"Very much."

The pharmacist proceeded to open and close drawers while he explained. "This is antelope's horn, and these are bear's testicles. These are gall stones from an elephant, and there you see scorpions and tiger bones. Most of these will be ground up, of course. Here are galls stones from a cow and I have quite a few pieces of rare tortoise shell. And that is a dried hornets' nest."

Akitada shuddered. "I find it hard to believe people swallow such things willingly, though I know it is so. I assume, being rare, they are expensive."

"Yes. A very small dose of the elephant's gall stone is five pieces of gold. When people suffer they are willing to pay and swallow anything. Of course, most of my trade consists of herbal tonics, especially the 'precious formula' of six herbs. And there is always a demand for medicines that promote a man's powers and those that prolong life."

"Yes, I can see that." Akitada glanced around, trying to think how to introduce his question.

The pharmacist offered helpfully, "Perhaps the gentleman wishes to enhance his performance in the bedchamber? I have the very thing for that."

Akitada snapped, "Certainly not."

"I beg your pardon. It is a frequent failing in more mature gentlemen."

Akitada had had enough. "It's certainly not why I came," he said. "My visit has nothing to do with me. My name is Sugawara. I wondered if you know the Nakai family. Mr. Nakai died recently. He owns the silk shop farther down this street."

The pharmacist nodded. "I knew him."

Had the man's eyes narrowed? The problem with men who wore beards was that one could not read their faces as well as those of clean-shaven people.

"It occurred to me that you might have supplied medications during his illness?"

Somehow, the atmosphere turned positively chilly. "Mr. Nakai was a customer, yes. But I know nothing of the family or of the cause of his death."

"Did he consult you about a specific complaint?"

"I do not discuss my clients' complaints with others. Surely a man of your learning must know that."

There was no longer any doubt that this pharmacist would not be cooperative. Akitada blamed himself for not having used a better approach. As it was, he apologized, bowed, quickly retrieved his shoes, and left the shop.

On his way home, he went over the conversation in his mind. In retrospect, he thought, the pharmacist's hostility had started before he had suggested that he had supplied the medicine that might have caused Nakai's death. It had started the moment Akitada had introduced himself and mentioned Nakai's death.

And that was very interesting indeed.

26

The Arrest

By the time Akitada reached his house, the matter of the pharmacist and the silk merchant had receded among his problems, and his domestic dilemma had taken its place. He felt in retrospect that he had been too harsh with Yukiko. He should not have blamed her for showing her love for her brother—they were after all the children of the same mother and had grown up together—or for her youthful enthusiasm and her wish to be a part of the social life in the capital. Yukiko was still very young and her upbringing had been very different from that of Tamako, who had been the only child of a widowed university professor.

That reminded him of Mrs. Tanaka who had also been the only daughter of a professor, though there the similarities ended. He must really look into her background and perhaps speak to her again.

The gate was opened by Genba who said, "Oh, good. The police sergeant has just arrived. He wants to speak with you, sir."

The sergeant was talking to the boy.

His name was Yasaburo, Akitada reminded himself guiltily, and thought of the other boy, so suddenly dismissed. Was there room in his household for two boys? The extra expense to keep a poor boy was surely more beneficial than the purchase of expensive silks.

The sergeant saw him and came quickly. He saluted. "I came to tell you, sir, we've arrested the fellow who set fire to your stable."

Surprised, Akitada asked, "You mean Hideyo? The son of the woman who lives in the house of the late Prince Atsutada?"

"The same." The sergeant grinned widely. "You should've been there, sir. He started for us with an axe, but his mother got after him before he could do any damage. She moves faster than I thought possible, and she had a broom. She laid into this Hideyo with its handle, hitting him about the head until he cried out and dropped the axe."

"Really? I thought she doted on him."

"Well, once he sat there, chained and whimpering, she tried to get us to let him loose again. Claimed he was really harmless and only acted up when someone threatened him. Said he'd be all right now." He laughed out loud and cheerfully described Maruko's tirades to convince them of her son's innocence.

"She tried to tell me he was with her all day. I asked her what day. She said 'the day of the fire'." The sergeant laughed again. "And all the time her son's looking daggers at her and muttering curses."

Akitada shook his head. "It sounds as though he's turned his fury on her. I would not have believed it."

The sergeant chuckled. "I doubt it. He's a mama's boy, that one. As we were leaving, he was crying out to her. She ran after us halfway through the village. What a woman!"

"And was he with her that day?"

"No idea. We didn't take her word for it and took him with us." The sergeant grinned again. "He was trotting along behind our horses. Fell a few times. I'm afraid he isn't very pretty at the moment."

Akitada grimaced. He hated brutality. But he bit his lip. "Thank you for coming to tell me, Sergeant. Did the boy Yasaburo prove helpful?"

"Yes, sir. With your permission, I'd like to take him back so he can identify Hideyo as the one who burned your stable."

"Yes, of course."

"And Superintendent Kobe sends his compliments and asks if you'd like to be present when he questions the fellow in the morning."

This was a surprise that Akitada accepted eagerly.

∞

Shortly after sunrise the next day he walked to police headquarters.

Kobe received him with considerable reserve, and Akitada thanked him immediately for arresting Hideyo and sending the sergeant to inspect the stable.

"My job," Kobe said curtly.

After a moment's hesitation, Akitada said, "I owe you an apology. In the matter of Tanaka I had no right to question the thoroughness of your investigation. As it is, I merely found more corroboration."

Kobe looked mildly interested. "Yes?"

"Yes. Not only was there no evidence against any of our suspects, but it appears that Tanaka was the type of character who would indeed murder a man for a hand-ful of gold coins."

Kobe grimaced. "Not that a handful of gold coins isn't a nice amount of money. Most of the common folk would consider it wealth."

"Yes, of course. But to take a man's life for such an amount? I admit I wondered about Tanaka. He was reasonably well-born and served in the guards before he became a *betto*. And even a *betto* surely isn't desperate enough to kill for such an amount."

"There was a quarrel. The gold was coincidental."

"Yes. But that requires a personality that is easily led to violent anger. And I found that Tanaka had been arrested as a young man."

Kobe smiled for the first time. "Yes. Quite right. That was before my time, but we found it recorded in the archives. A very ugly case of a group of young guardsmen getting drunk in one of the brothels. The next morning, one of the women was found dead. She'd been beaten and strangled. The matter was suppressed and some money was paid to the brothel owner for the loss of one of his women."

"I was told that Tanaka was the one who killed her, and that another young man there was a member of a leading family. Tanaka was subsequently dismissed by the guards."

"Perhaps that may have been the case. He certainly was dismissed. But the documents only named him and two others as being present. Neither name suggested any connection to someone in power."

Akitada grimaced. "I don't like it when those in power pull strings to protect their own."

"I know, but it's human nature to protect your children."

It was true. Kosehira had certainly tried to use his influence to help Arihito. Or for that matter, Yukiko. Akitada sighed.

"Well, do you want to come along when I talk to this Hideyo?"

Akitada came out of his reflections with a start. "Yes. Very much."

They walked across to the jail, where a guard led the way to Hideyo's cell.

"He's safe enough with the chains," the man said, "but don't get too close. He bit Kenji when he brought him his gruel."

"Like a wild animal," Kobe muttered as the man slid back the bolt and opened the cell door.

Hideyo cowered on the straw like a chained dog, and like a dog, he growled and showed his teeth. There was very little about him that was human. His hair stood up in angry spikes and he glared at them from his deep-set eyes. Some bloody scrapes and bruises marred his face. His whole body began to tremble with fury, and a string of vile curses came from his lips. He spat at them.

Kobe snapped, "Stop that! Do you want a whipping?"

Evidently not, for the spitting and cursing stopped. Hideyo still glowered, however, particularly at Akitada.

"Do you want to tell Lord Sugawara why you set fire to his stable?"

Hideyo did not answer. His eyes still on Akitada, he slowly grinned. He had a tooth missing and a cut lip, evidently the result of resisting arrest. Akitada reflected how quickly his respectable appearance had changed into that of someone people would shy away from.

"Tell me," he said, "what happened to you the night Prince Atsutada was murdered? You went out that night, didn't you? You went to the garden house. What did you see?"

Hideyo's face crumpled. "I don't want to talk about it," he wailed in a high voice. "I won't tell! I'll never tell." He cowered away from them. "Don't hurt me! Don't hurt me! Mother! I want my mother." The rest was one single loud wail.

Akitada and Kobe looked at each other. Kobe said to Hideyo, "Nobody is hurting you. Did someone hurt you when you were a little boy?"

The cowering figure sniveled and nodded its head.

"Was it Tanaka?" Akitada asked.

"I won't tell. I'll never tell. They can't make me. I promised."

Kobe sighed. "I doubt we'll get anything useful out of him. Do you want to go on?"

"No. Let's go back."

They knocked at the cell door, and the guard let them out.

"He's mad," Kobe said as they were leaving the jail. "One moment, he's a vicious brute, and the next a squalling child. We are pushing the trial forward, by the way."

"Why?"

"The imperial consort is ill. And since she's expecting a child, there may be an amnesty. You know what that means."

Akitada knew. Amnesty meant that all the city jails would be emptied and the prisoners set free.

"But rushing the trial won't keep Hideyo locked up, will it?"

"If he's found guilty, he'll be moved to a jail outside the capital."

"Oh."

They paused outside the headquarters building. Akitada said awkwardly, "Thank you. I don't mind telling you that I was very uneasy about Yukiko's safety."

Kobe smiled. "May all be well and you be a new father again. I look forward to seeing you with a babe in your arms."

Akitada laughed. "Perhaps you, too?"

Kobe shook his head. "I doubt it; I'm too old for fatherhood." His face saddened. " I would have liked to dandle grandchildren, but I doubt that will ever happen."

Akitada said quickly, "You don't know that. Your children may think again when they have lived a little longer. The young are selfish, but life teaches them that we need others."

"Perhaps. I will hope so."

They looked at each other, old friends and sometime enemies, and found pleasure in their relationship. Encouraged by this, Akitada said, "Speaking of others, there was a silk merchant in the city who died recently. His name was Nakai."

Kobe's eyebrows rose. "Nakai died? Now that's a pity. He was a fine man."

"Yes, I thought so, too. I happened to visit the shop some days ago to order something for my wife. He was already ill then. A monk called Ingen stopped by. I wondered at the behavior of his much younger wife with his assistant Ujinobu. It struck me as improper."

Kobe smiled. "I see. And so you decided they did away with old Nakai?"

Akitada laughed. "I know it sounds foolish if you put it like that, but . . ."

"Well, I'll have someone ask some questions. That Ingen might have the answer."

"I tried that. Ingen retreats into Buddhist platitudes. But the pharmacist down the street acted very strangely when I asked him if Nakai had been a customer. You may get something from him."

"I see. As you've already followed all the leads, there won't be much left for the police to investigate."

Akitada kept a straight face. "Perhaps not. I just thought I'd mention it."

"Well, a few questions might be in order. I'll let you know what comes of it."

They nodded to each other and parted, Kobe to go back inside, and Akitada to return home.

27

Domestic Matters

Greatly relieved that he had made peace with Kobe and that Hideyo was safely jailed, Akitada set about making peace with his wife. It seemed to him now that he had been unduly harsh with her, especially given her condition. In fact, his lecture, though justified, might be considered unnecessarily brutal.

The closing of Nakai's shop gave him an excuse to speak to Yukiko.

She was not alone. Her brother sat with her. Their faces were glum, and they looked up at him with little pleasure.

Arihito, always well-brought up, rose to his feet and bowed. "Akitada. Forgive me. When I didn't find you home I came to talk to Yukiko."

Had they talked about him? If so, it had not been good. Akitada had taken note that Arihito had not offered him the embrace customary between brothers. He glanced at his wife's face. It was expressionless.

With an inward sigh, he said, "Welcome, Brother. No need to explain. I'm sorry I wasn't here to greet you. May I join you?"

They nodded. He could not make out if they were surprised or irritated.

Turning to Yukiko, he said, "I hope I find you well? I didn't have time this morning to look in."

"Thank you. I'm well."

"I came to tell you about the man who set fire to stable. He is behind bars and we are safe again. You may make plans to go out, if you like."

"Thank you. That is a relief."

"The other item of news concerns your order of silks. I'm afraid, the owner of the shop, a Mr. Nakai, has died. The shop is closed at present. I'm sorry that this will delay things."

Her eyes widened with concern. "I'm sorry, too. Not about the silk. I liked Mr. Nakai. What happened?"

Akitada was blunt. "From what I've learned so far, I suspect his wife poisoned him. But there is no proof. Neither his doctor nor his pharmacist will talk."

Yukiko was clearly shocked. "Oh, how terrible! Was she having an affair with that very handsome assistant?"

"You noticed?" Akitada asked, surprised.

"Yes. He was much too familiar with her when Mr. Nakai wasn't there. If you're right, what truly evil people! You must try to look into it."

Akitada grimaced. "I'm afraid you're putting too much faith in my abilities again. Besides, I need to get back to Mikawa and mind my own business."

He was disappointed that she did not protest against his leaving. She merely nodded and murmured, "Poor Mr. Nakai."

A brief silence fell. Akitada saw their glum faces and decided to ask. "Has anything happened that has cast you both into such unhappiness?"

Arihito said, "I went to see Masako." He swallowed and shook his head.

Since he seemed unable to continue, Akitada looked to Yukiko, who explained. "Since my father has withdrawn his approval, Arihito went to tell Masako that he would give up his inheritance if she would agree to be the wife of a penniless man."

Akitada said dryly, "A generous offer, but I assume you would have had enough to support a family, Arihito."

His brother-in-law did not look up. "I have some property of my own. Left to me by my mother's father."

The noble families generally had enough farms scattered across the country to bestow gifts on children and grandchildren. Masako, on the other hand, had nothing and lived on the charity of that crazy old woman, Lady Otomo.

"What happened?" Akitada asked Arihito.

"She will not marry me without my father's approval." He finally raised his head to look at Akitada bleakly. "She will never marry me."

Yukiko said with a touch of anger, "I suppose it shows an honorable spirit, but it is really too stupid of her."

Akitada sighed. "I'm very sorry, Arihito." He wanted to add some encouraging remark about getting over it and finding another young woman to love but bit his lip just in time. The young knew nothing but the present. They knew neither hope nor regret and lived in the moment only.

He had meant to make his peace with his wife and perhaps make love to her also, but this was not the time. So he claimed urgent business with repairs and other household matters and left the siblings together. Perhaps Yukiko would find the right words to console her brother.

∞

The following morning Akitada inspected the work of rebuilding the stable. To his surprise, he found the boy from Nakai's shop waiting for him. His own boy, Yasaburo, hung about nearby eyeing the visitor with a scowl. When he saw Akitada, he came running.

"Sir, sir!" he called out. " This boy won't go away. I think he's a thief and up to no good. I've been watching him."

"Thank you, Yasaburo. I know him. He's no thief, just a youngster who needs a job."

Yasaburo's face revealed shock and displeasure. "You won't hire him, sir? He's scrawny. I bet he can't work and eats for two."

Akitada eyed Nakai's boy with a smile. He was hanging back, looking very worried. Yes, the child needed feeding up, and he was small. Akitada realized he did not know his age. He said to the sturdy, well-fed Yasaburo, "I happen to know he's a good worker and very loyal."

Yasaburo was near tears. "Are you sending me away because I let in that man?" he asked with a trembling voice.

"No, not if you are more careful in the future and help the new boy. His name is Ichiro."

Yasaburo was reassured but not altogether mollified. "Will I have to share my bed with him?"

"I doubt it, but we'll leave arrangements to Genba. I expect you to be nice to him." Akitada accompanied this with a frown, and the boy nodded.

Walking across to the newcomer, Akitada said, "Welcome, Ichiro. Have you come for work?"

Ichiro knelt and touched his head to the gravel. "Yes, sir."

"Get up. You came sooner than I expected."

Ichiro stood, brushing dirt off his clothes. It occurred to Akitada that he would find conditions a good deal rougher and dirtier than in a shop.

"I'm sorry, sir," the boy said," but I couldn't get any work and last night there was no food at home. I hoped you might let me do something until you decide."

"I suppose you've talked to Genba? Genba runs the stables."

"Only to say you'd told me to come, sir."

"You'll need other clothes to work here," Akitada said. "I'll speak to Genba."

Ichiro's face lit up. "I can stay?"

When Akitada nodded, he fell to his knees again and bowed many times. "Thank you, Master! Thank you."

Feeling a good deal better about things, Akitada went in search of Genba.

Genba was getting the carpenters organized. Akitada was pleased with the way the quiet, humble Genba had grown into his role as *betto*, for that was what he had become in Akitada's absence. Unaware of his master's arrival, he spoke with authority to the men, giving his instructions in a clipped tone new to Akitada's ears. Akitada stood by, smiling, content, and somewhat self-satisfied that he had found good men to serve him, men he held close and depended on.

Mrs. Kuruda, nominally in charge of the household staff, was a different matter. She still managed to irritate all that worked under her as well as Akitada. But perhaps in time she might become bearable. In any case, her employment was for Saburo's sake and not because she had shown any great talents.

Genba eventually caught sight of Akitada and hurried over. He apologized for not having found any armed men yet.

"What was available, sir, couldn't be trusted. Every one of them was a deserter."

"Never mind, Genba. Superintendent Kobe has the villain under lock and key. We should be safe enough." He explained about the boy Ichiro, and Genba promised to look after him.

Akitada returned to his study to worry about the funds needed to pay for materials and workmen. A short while later, Genba showed in a soberly dressed woman from the silk shop. She had brought the silks and the train he had ordered for his wife. He paid what he owed and worried some more about expenses. After the woman left, he called Mrs. Kuruda and had her take everything to Yukiko. He ate his midday rice in his study, hoping Yukiko would come to thank him for the gift. She did not, but perhaps her brother was still with her.

In the afternoon, Kosehira arrived. He looked unusually severe and wasted no time explaining his arrival. "I've spoken to Kobe and have come to make apologies to you also," he said, sitting down.

Akitada's raised his brows. "What in the world for, Brother?"

"For allowing my children to cause so much grief."

"Never mind, Kosehira. They didn't intend the outcomes. How did Kobe take your apology?"

"Very well. Arihito was with me. Kobe was kind enough to excuse it by blaming it on young love. Alas, I cannot claim such an excuse for my daughter. However, I have spoken to her. In fact I spoke to both of them. Arihito was properly chastened, but Yukiko is another matter. I'm afraid she has a mind of her own." He shot Akitada an uneasy glance and sighed heavily. "I used to love that about her. I trust you find it in your heart to forgive her."

Akitada did not know how to respond. Then he said, "I wish you hadn't done this. Yukiko is my responsibility. She is my wife. You may claim youth and love as an excuse for Arihito, but Yukiko has been a married woman for more than two years now. The fault therefore lies with me. I, too, have spoken to her. It was long overdue and has grieved me to remind her of her duty. I'm afraid she did not take it well."

Kosehira looked shocked. "Oh, Akitada, I cannot tell you how sorry I am. Do you mean she set herself against you?"

"Not quite that, but I think I've managed to disenchant her with her married state. Please don't mention this to her. I'm trying to mend matters in the short time that's left."

"So you will go back Mikawa?"

Akitada nodded.

Kosehira said, "I'm glad. That was another reason I wanted to speak to you. I'm afraid the prime minister will send for you. It seems someone has complained that you are not at your post."

Akitada sat up. "The prime minister? That's not good. I suppose I should have expected it. I've been here for more than a week. I've had several reports from Saburo that all is quiet in Mikawa, but clearly I should have gone back days ago." He bit his lip. This was all he needed on top of the other disasters. A reprimand for neglect of duty would mean no more governorships and no more promotions for some time.

Kosehira had become glum again. "I tried to smooth things over, but you still have enemies close to the prime minister. I'm sorry, Akitada. It's all due to Arihito's foolishness. At least he's gone to tell the young woman that the marriage is off."

Akitada knew that the fault lay not with Arihito but with his own besotted tolerance of his wife's notions. He said, "I'm sorry for him. That must have been very difficult."

"Well, she had already withdrawn her consent. Something about not wishing to go against my wishes. I suspect Arihito offered to marry her without my consent. A generous offer when you consider what the young fool was giving up. She would have none of it."

"She sounds like a young woman with strong principles." Akitada could not help comparing Masako to his wife, who had so far shown little respect for the wishes of father or husband.

"It just could not be. You must see that." Kosehira sounded defensive.

Akitada nodded, but it troubled him that Tanaka's daughter seemed in every way her father's opposite. Where every action and every tale had proved Tanaka to be selfish, greedy, violent, and murderous, Masako had never at any time acted the way one would have expected his daughter to act. On the contrary, she had rejected an offer of marriage into one of the great families in the land.

They sat together a while longer. Before he left, Kosehira appealed once more for patience toward Yukiko, and Akitada reassured him.

"She will give you a son or daughter," Kosehira said. "The child will fill her life and bring you two together. Yukiko is deeply in love with you. I know, because she would not rest until I agreed to help her."

This information did nothing to reassure Akitada who simply felt again he had been manipulated by Kosehira and Yukiko. His wife, who had been charming, lively, intelligent, and affectionate when they courted, now seemed merely willful and temperamental. He noted with some resentment that she had not bothered to thank him for the silks. But he said nothing of this.

"I'm grateful if you and your good lady will look after her while I'm gone," Akitada said. "Nothing must happen to her or the child."

"Don't worry. Yukiko is young and healthy. And we'll have some sutra readings to make sure all will be well."

Tamako had been neither young nor healthy, and Akitada had been on assignment in Kyushu. Both she and the child had died. There had been no sutra readings and she had had no family to look after her. He would never be rid of the guilt and grief for those deaths.

Kosehira left with an embrace and more encouraging words, but Akitada's mood had further slipped toward black despair.

28

The Widow

Contrary to all expectations, it was Mrs. Kuruda who managed to cheer him up. She arrived in his study the next morning, all smiles and bows, to thank him for hiring Ichiro to lighten her burdens. Akitada did not disabuse her about his reasons and accepted the thanks with a modest smile.

"Of course," she said, adjusting what must seem to her excessive gratitude, "you know what boys are. More trouble than they're worth. This one won't be any different, I think."

"From what I know, Ichiro is honest and hardworking. I feel certain he'll be a big help to you."

"Hmm. He'll need training, I suppose. Well, I know all about that. I've raised a boy myself, and he was a handful, I can tell you. Saburo managed to give me gray hairs before my time."

"You surprise me."

"Oh, well, he's grown now. Very different! In fact, I'm sure he's the best assistant you've ever had, if I do say so myself. I'm proud of how I raised him. Always with a firm but loving hand."

"Saburo is indeed a credit to you, Mrs. Kuruda."

"Yes, and now he writes he's taking a wife. I hope she proves to be a biddable daughter-in-law and fertile. I may look forward to grandchildren after all. I don't mind telling you, sir, I'd almost given up hope. He seemed to take no interest in women at all. I even blamed myself for that." She shook her head at the thought and chuckled.

Interested, Akitada asked, "How so?"

"Why, by sending him off to the monks, of course. I thought he'd learned some of their habits. You know what I'm talking about, I'm sure. Those monks positively hate women and won't have anything to do with them. To my mind, that's unnatural. Saburo was a very pretty boy and I imagined he'd become a favorite playmate of the abbot, or whoever. Thank heavens, he came to his senses at last."

Akitada thought this hilarious, especially since he knew quite well that Saburo had always had a very strong interest in women of dubious habits. His romantic exploits had only been curtailed by his shyness about his appearance. With a smile, he said, "I'm sure you needn't have worried."

"Worrying is what a mother does. But about the boy: I'll take him in hand and make sure he does his work properly."

She departed briskly and Akitada felt a little sorry for Ichiro. But his mood had lifted and he decided to look for the boy and prepare him a little for Mrs. Kuruda.

The rain had finally stopped, but the day was overcast, and the wooden roofs and walls of his home were black with moisture. The pile of burned rubble had disappeared. Instead men were unloading timbers and boards from ox-drawn carts.

Genba was supervising, and Akitada went to ask him about Ichiro.

"Him? Oh, he's working with Mrs. Kuruda, poor tyke." Genba chuckled. "Yasaburo always knows when she wants something and goes into hiding."

Akitada found the boy in the kitchen, sweeping the floor.

"There you are, Ichiro. I came to see how you're getting along."

Ichiro grinned. "Very well, Master. Mrs. Kuruda will be pleased to see how clean her pots are."

"Did Genba assign you to the kitchen?"

"No, Master. Yasaburo and I decided that he'd work outside and in the stables and I'm to work in the kitchen and the house."

Akitada raised his brows. "And are you content with this division of duties?"

"Yes, Master." The grin widened. "Yasaburo's afraid of Mrs. Kuruda. I like her. She's a very important lady and I will learn much from her."

"And Genba agreed?"

"Mr. Genba was very glad we worked it out." The boy suddenly looked uneasy. "You don't mind, Master, do you?"

"No, Ichiro. Not at all. But I will have to leave soon for my post in Mikawa. I want you to be sure to talk to Genba if anything troubles you."

"I will. Thank you, Master."

Satisfied that he had made most of the preparations to leave his home in good hands, Akitada was still faced with the nagging thought of the silk merchant's death. He perched on a barrel and regarded Ichiro thoughtfully. "What sort of work did you do for Mr. Nakai?" he asked.

Sadness returned to the boy's features. "I did a little of everything, Master, mostly cleaning and running to the market for his wife."

"No deliveries?"

"No. Mr. Ujinobu took care of those." He grimaced.

"You didn't like him?"

"No, Master. He was a thief."

The statement had been blunt and made Akitada blink. "A thief?"

"Yes, Master. He took our silks and sold them in the market."

"How do you know?"

"I saw him. I was buying vegetables and saw him talking to a woman. She gave him money and he gave her three pieces of silk."

"But that could have been a delivery to a customer."

"It wasn't. I know her. She's an official's wife. I later asked the master if they were customers and he said no. After that I tried to follow Ujinobu whenever I could. He did it again. He carries regular deliveries in packages. The silk he sells is tucked inside his robe."

"You're very observant." Akitada eyed the boy with satisfaction. He had the makings of being useful in the future. "Did you mention the matter to your master?"

The boy hung his head. "I waited a while to be sure. When I did, he said not to tell anyone. He'd take care of it. But the next day he got so terribly ill and then he died."

Here was a second motive. Not only was Ujinobu sleeping with his employer's wife, probably in hopes of marrying her and taking over the business, but his theft had been found out and he was about to be arrested. So was he the killer, or Nakai's wife? Akitada thought they were in it together. In fact, he suspected that Nakai had been poisoned for a long time prior to his final, fatal dose.

But proving it was another matter.

He said nothing to Ichiro as he thought about the problem. The boy watched him uneasily, then he said timidly, "I didn't like them. You won't send me back, will you?"

"No, Ichiro. You did the right thing. I'm just thinking how we're going to catch them."

Ichiro looked anxious. "I'd rather not tell the police, Master. They might not let me go home to look after my mother."

"You go home every evening?"

"Yes, Master. You don't mind? Mr. Genba wasn't happy about it. And Mrs. Kuruda is bound to want me to wash up after dinner. Only, my mother has nobody and she's not well."

Akitada tousled his hair. "I don't mind. I'll talk to Genba and Mrs. Kuruda. Just make sure you work hard during the day."

"I will, Master."

∞

Akitada expected the summons from the prime minister to arrive any moment. Under the circumstances, he decided to use the time to make one more attempt to bring justice to Mr. Nakai. He set out on foot for the silk shop, but called first on the pharmacist who had behaved in such an evasive manner two days earlier.

The man recognized him immediately, and this time Akitada saw he was afraid. Not wasting any time, he said, "I talked to you a few days ago about the medicine you provided to Mr. Nakai."

"I did nothing wrong," cried the pharmacist, waving his hands and backing away. "Mr. Nakai himself bought the medicine. It is good medicine. Works very well. Many of my customers swear by it. I told him to be careful. I always stress the need to be moderate. Moderation is everything in such a case. He understood and promised. I cannot be held responsible if he did not heed my warnings."

Akitada raised a hand. "Slow down. What was the nature of the complaint that you prescribed the medicine for?"

The pharmacist flushed. "I'm not sure . . ."

"In the name of the gods," Akitada snapped, "the man died. He has no more secrets."

"Mr. Nakai married late in life. He was concerned about losing his . . . life force. Once a man is over forty, he should not engage more often than once every three or four days. It appears that Mrs. Nakai made certain demands that exhausted his semen. He found it impossible to complete the act. At the same time, he wished to bring her to joyfulness. It's a common dilemma for older husbands with eager young wives." He faltered again.

Akitada found nothing to like in these explanations about old husbands with young wives, but he bit his lip and said, "Ah. You provided an aphrodisiac. And it must be taken in small doses?"

"Yes. I told him so. But he wanted more and more and in the end he sent his wife."

"He sent his wife? And you gave her more of the medicine?"

"Yes, she said her husband was busy in the shop. I saw nothing wrong with it when he'd been buying it all along."

"Was the time his wife came to you the last time you made up the concoction?"

"Yes. He died soon after. But it wasn't my fault."

Akitada had heard enough. "Perhaps not," he said, "but you should not carelessly issue poisonous substances to people's wives."

The pharmacist's jaw dropped, and Akitada left. His lips compressed grimly, he walked to the silk shop which he found open for business again.

Ujinobu seemed in charge of the shop this time. Like the woman who had delivered the silks, he wore dark clothing and a mournful expression. He recognized Akitada immediately and came to greet him.

"I hope nothing was wrong with the order?" he asked after having bowed deeply.

"Nothing. Thank you. I wish to have a word with Mrs. Nakai."

"I'm afraid she's seeing no one because of her husband's recent death. We hesitated to open the shop. There's the taboo, you know, but our customers tend to take the old religion somewhat lightly. Still, it would not have been right for a recent widow to appear in public."

"I'm aware of Mr. Nakai's death. In fact, the boy, Ichiro, has come to work for me and has told me all about it."

Ujinobu blanched. "Ichiro? B-but how did he come to you?"

"It seemed he was afraid to remain here."

A brief silence fell. Ujinobu goggled at him. "A-afraid? Oh, the boy makes up things. He's a terrible liar. I don't think you'll want to keep him on."

Akitada stared back at the man and noted that he was sweating. "I found him quite truthful. Now I wish to see Mrs. Nakai."

Ujinobu was practically writhing with nervousness. "Mrs. Nakai is indisposed. Her husband's death has made her quite ill. It's out of the question."

"In that case, perhaps she will see the police."

Ujinobu's resistance collapsed. "Excuse me," he gasped and rushed off to the back of the business. Akitada followed more slowly. He could hear raised voices. Ujinobu's sounded nearly hysterical, the woman's merely angry. The voices were coming from behind a door. When Akitada reached it, it flew open and a pale Ujinobu nearly collided with him. Not bothering to apologize, the man hurried past Akitada, leaving the door open.

Mrs. Nakai, in sober black silk stood inside, looking at him. He walked in and closed the door behind him. Black suited her. She was a remarkably beautiful woman with creamy skin and large eyes.

"I think you know why I'm here," he said. "Your lover has warned you."

She made a show of being shocked. "There must be some mistake. If you mean Mr. Ujinobu, he is not my lover." She sighed and raised moist eyes to his. "I just lost my beloved husband, sir. How can you speak to me this way? From you I would have expected kindness and concern."

Akitada snapped, "Don't play with me. Your husband died from poison, and the pharmacist told me that you bought it from him."

She gasped and started trembling. It was hard to tell, and the light was not good since the shutters to the outside had been closed. "Please have pity, sir. You are mistaken. I loved my husband. He ordered me to get him that medicine. I only picked it up for him because he was too ill to go himself. Everybody will testify to that. The pharmacist knows it's true. If he says otherwise he lies. Truly, sir, I'm innocent."

It was very convincing, and she was very beautiful in her pretended distress. Akitada had once before met another beautiful woman who had murdered her elderly husband. She had attempted to seduce him. When he had rejected her, she had screamed for help and laid charges against him for attempted rape. He had been very young and naïve in those days and the situation had almost ended badly.

He said coldly, "The medicine is a dangerous aphrodisiac and must be taken in very small doses. You knew this. According to the pharmacist, it was you who urged your husband to try it in the first place. No doubt Mr. Nakai's desire to satisfy a much younger wife and his diminishing powers in the bedchamber made it all too easy."

She turned away. "Such things are private between a husband and his wife. The pharmacist had no right to talk about it to strangers. I was in all things a good wife to my husband. No one can prove otherwise."

"I doubt that. Even your shop boy knows that you betrayed your husband with his assistant. Soon the police will also know."

"The boy lies," she cried. She suddenly came to him, her hands extended beseechingly. "It's all lies." She fell to her knees before him, sobbing. "Have pity, sir! I'm all alone. Think of your own lady, so young and lovely. Would you want to see her accused of being faithless, of betraying you with other men? For her sake, have mercy on a woman whose only fault was marrying a man older than she."

This comparison of herself to Yukiko and of her marriage to theirs, nauseated Akitada. "How dare you!" he snapped. " My wife has nothing to do with your evil plot." He stepped away from her.

She prostrated herself. "Please," she pleaded, "don't do this to me. If you spare me the police with their whips, I'll do anything. I'll be your slave. Oh, gods! My husband loved me too much. That's why he took the medicine. Please have pity."

Akitada knew better now than to fall for another seduction. He turned on his heel, saying, "You have just shown me the face of a faithless and murderous woman," and left quickly for the front of the store.

But she came running after him, screaming, "Out!" and then, "You cursed officials are all alike. You think you can do whatever you want to a poor woman. I'm a respectable businesswoman, and my beloved husband isn't even dead two days, and you come here to threaten me so I'll do what you want."

Ujinobu was not in the shop, but two saleswomen and several customers stared wide-eyed as Mrs. Nakai sobbed. "Oh, is there no one to protect helpless women? What do you want? Money? I'll pay it to buy my peace. Silk? Take what you want, only don't ask me to betray the memory of my husband by being your whore."

Akitada took one look at the gaping faces and fled.

29

Amnesty

It did not help that he knew instantly how badly he had mishandled the scene. He should have gone to Kobe first with his facts and returned with the police. Now he had alerted these two villains who would do their best to escape the law. Ujinobu probably had already taken to his heels before Akitada had confronted the widow. Under the circumstances, all he couIld do now was to inform the police as quickly as possible and hope for the best.

Kobe listened to him, his face lengthening. When Akitada paused, he said, "Did they look likely to run?"

"Ujinobu may be gone already," Akitada said regretfully. "But the woman is greedy and a fighter. I think she'll try to bluff her way out of the charge."

"Without Ujinobu to implicate her, she may well do it."

"The pharmacist and the boy Ichiro will testify, but I doubt Ingen will add anything useful. He seems to believe being murdered was part of the man's karma. I'm sorry, Kobe. I mishandled it. So much has happened lately that I cannot seem to think straight. And now I also expect to be called in by the prime minister with a reprimand for leaving my post."

Kobe sighed. "I'm afraid I'm going to add to your worries. They've declared the amnesty I feared. The order came this morning. We've just turned loose all of our prisoners."

"What?" Akitada was on his feet. "I must go home. I'm sorry to leave you with the Nakai case, but I think you'll be able to get a confession. And Ujinobu hasn't had time to plan his escape. Hideyo, on the other hand, is mad. He'll make for my house sooner or later."

He did not wait for Kobe's comment but dashed out and practically ran all the way home.

There he was initially relieved to learn that all was well. He instructed Genba to send the carpenters home and close the gates. Then the boys were told to watch the two gates. Next Akitada went to his room to get his sword. Buckling it on, he walked to Yukiko's pavilion to warn her. There another very unpleasant surprise awaited him.

The pavilion was empty.

He returned to the gallery and shouted for servants. Mrs., Kuruda appeared from the direction of the kitchen.

"What's the matter?" she called on a note of irritation.

"Where's my wife?" Akitada shouted back.

"Gone out with your sister!"

There was no time to correct the woman for her disrespectful speech. Akitada went toward her, momentarily frightening her when she saw his hand on his sword. He had merely steadied it against his thigh, but Mrs. Kuruda shrieked, turned, and ran awkwardly back toward the kitchen.

"Wait!" Akitada shouted, of course without stopping her.

He finally slowed down. "Mrs. Kuruda, please come back here!"

She paused, took a few more steps, and paused again, glancing back over her shoulder. Seeing him standing, she turned.

He said, "I'm sorry. I didn't mean to frighten you, but I must know where they went. That madman is loose again."

"Madman?" She glanced toward the kitchen again.

Akitada could not imagine why she associated the kitchen with safety. Perhaps she kept some long, well-sharpened knives there. "I must find them and make sure no harm comes to them, so please tell me where they are."

"But I don't know, sir. I don't ask impertinent questions."

That was laughable. But Akitada had no time to waste. He hardly knew where to start.

Genba, of course.

But Genba, though he had seen Lady Akiko's palanquin arrive and Lady Yukiko join her in it, knew nothing else. They had departed, no one knew where to.

Akitada explained his worry and saw the concern on Genba's face. "Do you want me to come with you?" Genba asked hopefully.

"No. You must stay in case she returns. I'll go speak to my brother-in-law. He may know where they went."

But Toshikage also knew nothing of his wife's plans. "She never tells me," he said. "Very independent spirit, your sister."

That was true enough but not at all helpful at the moment.

Toshikage realized belatedly that the danger Akitada feared might also affect his wife. "You don't think this creature would harm Akiko?" he asked.

Toshikage's priorities were clear: he doted on his wife and all others receded into the background where she was concerned. Akitada gave him a distracted look and said, "Probably not. I must go."

On his way out, Toshikage called after him, "What should I do?" but Akitada did not bother to answer.

He went back home, hoping the women had returned. They had not, but Kobe had sent two constables to stand outside Akitada's gate. It was something, if they frightened Hideyo away, but he might decide to slip in from the back. Once, years ago, when they had expected an attack, they had all taken turns watching and patrolling the grounds, but this time they were too few.

In the end, Akitada decided to check with Hideyo's mother. Perhaps he had gone home to her. And if not, then she might at least know what he was likely to do. In any case, it was better than doing nothing.

He sent Yasaburo for his horse, still stabled at the neighbor's, and took to the road. On this occasion, he was not in the mood to enjoy the green and thriving fields or even note that all the cherry trees had lost their blooms and now melted into the overall greenness with their new leaves. It was already very warm, a sign that summer was coming. Horse and rider soon perspired in Akitada's hurry to reach Prince Atsutada's villa.

They clattered through the village and up the mountain road without pausing. When Akitada reached the house, he found everything quiet. He slid off the horse and tied the animal to the gate post. The gate stood open on an empty courtyard. The pile of wood that Hideyo had been splitting still lay nearby.

He called out, keeping his hand on the hilt of his sword and letting his eyes roam, expecting Hideyo to rush at him any moment. But nothing happened, and Hideyo's mother did not appear either. He climbed the steps to house slowly and pushed open the door. A smell of dirty bodies and refuse hit his nose. He called out again, this time, "Maruko?" But all remained silent.

The silence began to get on his nerves. Where was she? She had never struck him as the sort of woman who would walk far from her comfort. She was too heavy for much effort. He recalled vividly how she had panted when they had climbed to the summer house where the prince had died. He glanced up at the thick growth of trees that hid the summer house and felt a cold shiver.

Taking the first steps into the dim interior took a good deal of courage. His chances of survival were much poorer if he encountered Hideyo somewhere in this warren of unfamiliar rooms with strange dark shapes in every corner. The house was not only incredibly untidy, but Maruko had apparently collected and hoarded all sorts of discarded furnishings, most of them now nearly hidden under mounds of clothes and quilts. A man might hide anywhere, and Akitada recalled that on that earlier occasion the constables had dragged Hideyo out of some hiding place in this house.

He moved cautiously, stopping to listen from time to time, and searching every room thoroughly before moving on to the next. Once he heard a scrabbling noise and something brushed against his legs and made him jump. His sword was half out of its scabbard when he realized he had disturbed a cat.

In the end the house proved to be empty. He emerged from its back and looked across the overgrown garden and called out again for Maruko. There was no answer and no sign of anyone.

Later he would wonder what made him go into the garden and follow the path to the garden house. The afternoon heat brooded under the trees and more sweat trickled down his back. He walked slowly, stopping from time to time to listen. The silence was unsettling. Not even a bird sang. When he crossed the little bridge he encountered a cloud of gnats and swatted at them. The garden house looked unchanged from where he was. He felt foolish for having come this way, but then he heard a faint sound and the hairs on the back of his head bristled.

His hand on the sword once more, he approached the garden house, this time without calling out.

The doorway stood empty, but the sound was much louder now, an angry buzzing.

And then he knew.

He walked forward and stepped up the short stair.

She lay inside, looking at first glance like a large mound of discarded bedding. But there was the buzz of a black cloud of fat flies and there was the unmistakable smell of death. And then he saw her hair and one fat hand, bloody and speckled with flies.

He went closer, holding his breath, and looked down.

She was unrecognizable except by her size. Her face no longer existed. Something sharp and powerful enough to cut through skull and facial bones had delivered blows to it, leaving a mass of blood, bone splinters, and brain. And thick masses of greedy flies. No one could survive such an attack, and Maruko had died quickly. Her blood was already congealing, and the flies had gathered for the feast.

They had risen in a sluggish, irritated swarm when he had come closer and now gradually settled back to their repulsive work.

There were other places on her body where they congregated, separate puddles of blood from other wounds. Akitada's eyes automatically searched the space around her and found the weapon: an axe. Probably the same axe that Hideyo had used to split the wood and which he had raised to attack Akitada not long ago.

And now the fear was back and Akitada turned quickly to scan his surroundings, expecting the monster to lie in wait among the trees. But there was nothing, just silence, and heat, and a buzz when a fly changed position. It was clear to him that Hideyo had murdered his own mother, the one person who had protected him. The murder of one's parent was the most terrible crime known to man, and Akitada shuddered. This was truly a madman's work, though perhaps there had been hints that Maruko had not always been kind to her son. If Hideyo could do this to his mother, what would he do to Akitada or his family?

And suddenly he was seized by a sense of urgency. He must find Yukiko and his sister, even if he had to knock on every palace gate in the city. He must take them home and guard them until Hideyo was back in jail.

30

The Summons

He hurried back to the house to get on his horse and rode into the village to report the murder. The village warden merely gaped, and Akitada shouted at him. Eventually he made himself understood and left, driving his horse hard to reach home.

There, all looked quiet. His gates were closed, and when he pounded on them, Genba's suspicious face appeared at the tiny window.

"Oh, it's you sir," he said, disappearing to open the gate.

"Her ladyships? Akitada asked as he dismounted

"Not back yet, sir. All's been quiet."

311

"He's loose. I just found his mother. He butchered her. Dear heaven, where are they?"

Genba said soothingly, "He won't dare attack a palanquin, sir. Lady Akiko's servants wouldn't allow it."

Akitada said nothing. Lady Akiko's servants were in no condition to fight off a madman while carrying the palanquin.

Genba said, "There was a messenger here. He left this." He produced a folded letter. It was sealed and bore the purple ribbon of the highest office.

The prime minister's summons.

Distracted by his worries for the women, Akitada ignored protocol and tore the letter open where he stood. He scanned it quickly. It was as he had feared: an order to appear immediately before the *Dajodaijin* and the three ministers under him. He glanced up at the sun. It was late afternoon.

"When did this arrive?"

"About an hour ago." Genba looked anxious.

He would be late. No doubt a prime minister and three ministers were not gathered to wait an hour or more for a mere governor to report. A governor moreover who was in deep trouble for deserting his post. No time to change into court costume. Akitada shoved the letter inside his robe and got back on the tired horse.

"I've been summoned," he said to Genba, knowing he would understand. At the gate he paused. "Send out the two boys and anyone else you can spare to ask at the gates of the great families and at the palace if my wife and sister are there."

"Already done, sir. Yasaburo's back. They stopped earlier at the house of Fujiwara Yorimichi but left again. Nobody knew where they went afterward. Ichiro isn't back yet."

Akitada wanted to question Yasaburo, but there was no time. He hurried off.

Later he was to come to think of it as the day when time ran out on so many levels. He had ignored the fact that he should never have stayed away from his post for more than a very brief visit. He had allowed Yukiko to do as she wished for too long so that when he finally corrected her, he had managed to turn his marriage into a disaster. He had meddled in the Prince Atsutada case until Hideyo, already unstable and violent, had murdered his mother and was even now somewhere in this big city, searching for him and his family.

And now he could not even protect them because the desertion of his post had finally produced the crisis he should have foreseen.

He arrived at the *Dajokan-jo*, the office of the Great Council of State, tense and sweating. When he gave his name at the gate, he was directed inside with many shocked glances at his improper appearance and late arrival. But no one said anything beyond demanding his sword before he saw the prime minister. He was passed on from official to official until he was ushered into the great man's office.

The prime minister was not alone, though two of the ministers had left. The prime minister's brother, the minister of the left was in charge of popular affairs and hence governors. He had remained along with a secretary. All three regarded Akitada with serious expressions. Without bothering to acknowledge Akitada's obeisance, the prime minister dismissed the secretary, and Akitada was left alone with the two highest-ranking Fujiwara officials in the government.

"You have been absent from your post, I've been told," the prime minister said.

"For a short while only, Excellency."

His brother frowned. "I don't recall sending for you."

"No, Excellency. Things were rather quiet and I thought— "

"You thought?" interrupted the minister. He turned to his brother. "He *thought*, Prime Minister."

It was strange and rather silly that the brothers should address each other by title, and Akitada, already overwrought, hid an involuntary laugh with a cough. "I'm sorry, Excellency. It was meant to be a very brief trip, but then things got complicated and I . . ." He faltered, wondering how much to tell them of his ill-fated investigation into an old murder.

The prime minister cleared his throat. "Sugawara, the fact remains that you absented yourself from your post without being ordered to do so or requesting permission. I must say I didn't expect it from you. That is a very serious offense and cannot simply be overlooked."

"Not at all," said his brother, nodding emphatically. "We cannot have officials who simply do whatever they want whenever they want. Where would the government be?"

Akitada opened his mouth and closed it again. There was nothing he could say in his defense. He was afraid they were about to take away his governorship completely. In that case he was unlikely to get another appointment for years and probably never another governor's post. But what did that matter if something happened to his wife and unborn child. He gulped and said, "I'm afraid I'm rather distracted. I cannot find my wife, you see, and there is—"

"Your wife?" cried the prime minister. "What nonsense is this? I saw her myself just this morning. She and Toshikage's wife called on my first lady. Lovely woman, your wife, and looking perfectly healthy to my old eyes."

"You saw her?" Akitada asked quickly. "Did she mention where she was going afterward?"

Both men stared at him. The minister said, "Have you lost your mind, Sugawara? This isn't about your wife. It's about your serious dereliction of duty."

"Yes, Excellency, but I have reason to fear for my wife's safety."

They looked at each other. The prime minister said, "Are you telling us that you've been chasing your wife all the way from Mikawa without catching up to her?"

Akitada flushed with embarrassment. "No, Excellency. We came up together." An idea presented itself at the last moment. "My wife is with child. I brought her because she wanted to be with her family at this time. I fully intended to return immediately."

The minister frowned again. "My felicitations, Sugawara. Your lady is Kosehira's daughter, isn't she?"

The prime minister nodded. "Yes, she is. Well, perhaps this explains your journey, but you didn't return to your post after delivering her here."

It was not going to be so easy, but at least they were no longer quite so angry with him, proof once again that his marriage to Kosehira's daughter was protecting him. He did not like the idea and braced himself for more trouble. "My wife is very fond of her brother Arihito," he said, "and they asked me to look into the antecedents of a young woman Arihito wishes to marry. I'm afraid that effort has delayed me and caused a madman to threaten my family. I just learned that he has been released from prison. Hence my worry about my wife's safety."

There it was out. Let them do whatever they wished to him.

The prime minister seemed speechless, but his brother suddenly got curious. "Yes, it's the amnesty. It's one of your clever investigations, then? How fascinating! What happened?"

Akitada searched for words, but the prime minister snapped, "Don't bother to answer! You had no business letting yourself be distracted from your duty and you had no permission to stay. Your brazen effort to confuse us with some silly tale about madmen running about because they wish to attack your wife isn't going to work. I must say I'm shocked. I thought better of you. In any case, you will return to Mikawa at daybreak tomorrow."

Akitada opened his mouth, but the prime minister raised his hand. "Enough! This is an order. You are dismissed."

∞

Akitada was so upset by what had just happened that he almost forgot his sword. One of the officials ran after him with it. He thanked the man, pushed it through his belt, got his horse, and hurried off.

It had been his first reprimand from the prime minister himself. There had been other times when he had managed to offend, but those had generally involved the censors or his immediate superior. In a way, today marked a mile stone in his rise up the bureaucratic ladder. He did not find much amusement in the thought.

He remembered to stop at the imperial palace to enquire if his wife and Akiko had paid a visit. They had, but they had left again a short while ago. The gate guards did not know where they were going but thought they'd turned east.

It was the way home, and Akitada hurried that way. He hoped they had reached his home safely. Already, his thoughts went to the preparations ahead so he could leave for Mikawa in the morning. There was too little time. So many things would be left undone, among them making his peace with Yukiko.

He left the *Daidairi* by the Ikuno Gate and crossed Omiya Avenue to Oimikado. This was the shortest way home, but traffic slowed him down. To the right and left stood the palaces and mansions of the great families or imperial family members. His own home lay nearer the outskirts of the city and was far more modest than these. The fact that these streets were wide and well-travelled was reassuring. If the women had taken the same way, they should have reached home safely. He slowed his tired horse a little more to organize his thoughts.

Genba must receive funds and instructions and he must visit Kosehira to apprise him of his departure and to put Yukiko's affairs into his hands. He hoped that Arihito's disappointment would not lead to more stubborn efforts on Yukiko's part to stir up trouble. And finally he must speak to Yukiko. He resolved to be as gentle as possible and not to lecture her again. This resolution would require a good deal of effort when he was so worried about her.

He became aware of some vague noise as he was getting close to the side street that would take him to his own compound. Someone was shouting in the distance. After a moment's puzzlement, Akitada kicked his horse into a gallop, dimly aware that servants from adjoining properties were craning their necks in the direction of the noise. He felt fear turning to panic when the shouting was punctuated by the screams of women.

Bursting around the final corner, his sword in his hand, he saw the full disaster ahead. He pulled back on the reins and slid out of the saddle before the horse had stopped.

31

The Sorrow
of the World

The palanquin was on its side in the middle of the street. Near it, one of the bearers lay still, his white shirt covered with blood. Another bearer cowered on the ground, both hands covering his face as blood oozed out between his fingers. The other two bearers must have run, but Akitada had no time to look for them. His horrified eyes had moved past the palanquin to where Hideyo stood, an arm about Yukiko and a long, bloody knife at her throat. Akiko was on her knees before him, begging him to let Yukiko go. Beyond them, Genba came running from the house, then stopping as he took in the scene. Hideyo shouted something at him, and Genba dropped his sword.

Akitada also slid to a stop. Hideyo half turned toward him. He bared his teeth in a mockery of a smile. Akitada saw Yukiko's eyes meeting his own, and the sudden hope in them. His heart almost failed him.

She wanted him to be the hero she had fallen in love with, and Akitada despaired.

"Welcome, Sugawara," Hideyo shouted. "You're just in time. I'm about to cut your daughter's throat. I'll start with her and then you can watch me do the same to your wife." He jerked his head toward Akiko.

He was clearly confused by their ages, Akitada thought. "Put that knife down, Hideyo," he called, his voice a strange croak. "You don't want to do this. The women have done nothing to you. You want me. Let them go. I'll take their place."

Hideyo laughed. "Why not? Throw away your sword first."

Akitada hesitated.

Yukiko screamed, "No, Akitada, don't do it. Kill him! Kill him now!" She kicked back wildly at Hideyo who gasped and loosened his grip.

For a moment it looked as though she would escape; when his arms slipped, she ducked to get away, but he snatched at the back of her gown. She twisted to get loose, falling on one knee.

Akitada's heart stood still and the blood roared in his ears. Hideyo still had that knife, that long wicked blade, in his free hand. He could plunge it into her back, and there was nothing anyone could do. He started forward, knowing he would be too late.

"Stop or she dies," Hideyo bellowed. His knife was at Yukiko's back.

Akitada stopped.

"Toss your sword over here!"

Akitada did as he was told. His eyes were on Yukiko. "Don't move, Yukiko," he called to her. "Be still!"

Hideyo laughed triumphantly and jerked her backward by her gown so that she fell on her back, her pretty silk gowns billowing about her slender figure. "You want to see me rape your daughter?" he called out to Akitada. "Look at her! She's opened her legs for me!" He leaned down and used the knife to raise her skirts.

Yukiko stared up at him and spat in his face. Then she scrambled to get away from him.

Hideyo exploded in fury. He roared, "You bitch!" Then he started kicking her. Yukiko rolled onto her side, and he kicked her in the stomach. When she rolled again, he kicked her back, her hips, any part of her body he could reach. Yukiko rolled, twisted, screamed once, then curled up and lay still.

At Hideyo's furious onslaught on his wife, Akitada charged, diving for his sword, and rushing Hideyo. Hideyo, caught up in his frenzied kicking and cursing, reacted too slowly, and Akitada buried his sword in his belly. The kicking finally stopped and Hideyo stood screaming on the dusty road.

At that moment, Genba reached them also. With one clean swipe he cut off Hideyo's head. Head and body tumbled onto the road.

Akitada was on his knees beside his wife. "Yukiko? Yukiko, open your eyes! It's over." He brushed the hair away from her cheek. She felt warm to his touch and her cheek was rosy, and he thought that she must be all right, that she had only fainted.

Behind him, Genba muttered, "Oh, Amida! What a thing!"

Akiko joined her brother. "Akitada!" she said urgently, shaking his shoulder, "We must take her inside and send for a doctor." Her voice was tight with fear.

"I'll go," Genba said, hurrying away.

Akitada saw no blood. "No, she's not hurt. She just fainted. She'll be fine."

Akiko snapped, "She's hurt. And she's with child. Don't let her die in the street like some tramp."

He stared at his sister. Then he bent obediently and lifted Yukiko as gently as he could. His sister held Yukiko's skirts and her train.

It was the new train, he noticed inconsequently; the cherry blossoms and birds had become dirty from being dragged on the street.

He carried her inside the compound and then up the stairs to the main house. There, he placed her on the dais in the reception room. Yukiko was not heavy, but she was a dead weight and the court robe and train added considerable weight. Akitada had staggered on the stairs where his legs somehow lost their strength. He could go no farther than the dais in the reception hall. Collapsing beside her, he took her limp hand in his, his eyes searching her face. She was still unconscious.

Alerted by Akiko, maids and Mrs. Kuruda came running, the maids silent and wide-eyed with shock, Mrs. Kuruda voluble.

"What happened? Did she fall? Dear gods, she's bleeding! She's losing the child! Someone get the midwife! Mrs. Konishi will do. Quick!"

Akiko said, "Genba went for the doctor! She's hurt badly."

Akitada now saw the blood staining Yukiko's skirts. And he remembered how Hideyo had kicked her. Sickness rose and he staggered to his feet to vomit.

Mrs. Kuruda shouted at him, "Go away, sir! This is no place for you. We'll look after her." Then Akiko came and pushed him out of the door.

He stood outside in the dim corridor for a little, swallowing down the bile in his throat. Not again, he thought. Not again, I cannot face it again.

Inside the room, voices murmured. In the end, he went to his study and sat down behind his desk to wait.

How could it all have gone so wrong?

Not just what had happened today. It seemed to him that it had started long ago. Long before he had ever thought of death and dying. Before he had fallen in love with Tamako. Karma, they called it. He had been predestined to love and lose what he loved.

It was easy enough to blame disaster on something outside himself, but he had helped it along. He had been careless, neglectful, distracted by his career, and so he had lost what he had not deserved. Yori. And then Tamako. And now Yukiko.

He buried his face in his hands.

Kosehira found him like this. He came in with dragging steps, his face a mask of sadness.

Akitada stood. "Yukiko?" he asked. "Is she . . . did she . . . oh, dear gods, tell me!"

Kosehira sighed deeply and sat down. "They wouldn't let me see her. Her mother is with her now. The child . . . I'm afraid she lost the child. I'm very sorry, Akitada."

"The child? Never mind the child. What about Yukiko?"

"That monster hurt her, but the doctor is encouraging. She lost the child, but the bleeding has stopped. She's in pain, but he's given her medicine."

Relief washed over Akitada. "Where is she?"

"They've taken her to her room."

"I must see her."

"No, Akitada. She's not herself. Let her rest and heal."

But Akitada was already at the door.

Kosehira cried after him, "Wait, Akitada. Maybe later!"

Akitada hurried down the corridor and to the gallery that led to his wife's pavilion. The door of the pavilion opened and his sister emerged. She came to meet him.

He asked, "How is she?"

Akiko was pale and her hair and dress were disordered. "She's resting. Did her father tell you?"

"Yes. She lost the child, but how is she? I must see her."

"No, Akitada. She doesn't want to see you. You'll simply make her worse."

He had been about to move his sister out of his way but now let his arms drop. "Why? How? She's my wife."

Akiko shook her head. "She's not herself. Can you expect it after what that beast did to her? After losing her child?"

"I should be with her," he said helplessly and looked past her to the door. "What can I do?"

"Go back and give her time. Her mother and her maid are looking after her now. The midwife is also still here. Someone will let you know when she will see you." She turned and went back inside.

It seemed all wrong, but he no longer knew what he should do. He stood for a moment longer looking at the closed door, then turned and went back.

Kosehira was still in his study. "Poor fellow!" he said heavily. "I know how you must feel."

Akitada did not think so, but he said nothing. He walked onto his veranda and stared sightlessly at the garden. She had lost the child, but she lived. That was all that mattered. In time, they would patch up their broken bond. But it galled him that he had been excluded during this crisis. Not even the doctor had bothered to report to him. All he had was Akiko's assurance that she was alive and healing.

Kosehira came to stand beside him, putting his arm around his shoulder. "There will be other children."

"She won't see me."

"Oh, this is women's work, Akitada. Surely you of all men would know that about women giving birth."

"She's hurt. The child doesn't matter." He turned to Koschira. "Don't you care about your daughter more than a child that wasn't real yet? That was only a vague promise?"

"Oh. I see. But Akitada, one must care about the unborn. My daughter cares. It will make it very hard for her, knowing there will be no child to hold close, to play with, to nurture, to raise. You don't care about the child? You surprise me. I thought I knew you better. I love all my children and grieved for the unborn I lost."

Akitada stared at him, made a sound of exasperation, and left the room.

Walking to the courtyard, he found Genba supervising repairs to Akiko's palanquin. Memory returned, and Akitada went to ask, "The wounded bearers? How are they?"

"One's been taken home on a litter with a bad stab wound in the upper chest. The other's over there."

Akitada glanced where Genba pointed. The bearer sat against the wall of the gatehouse. He wore a blood-stained bandage around one side of his face but seemed all right.

Genba asked, "How is your lady, sir?"

"She lost the child, but I'm told she will heal."

"I'm so very sorry, sir. I know how you must have wanted the little one. And she also, poor young lady."

"Thank you. I'm glad it wasn't worse."

After a brief silence, Genba said, "It's bad enough, but he might have killed her."

"Yes."

Kosehira had followed him out. He muttered, "Terrible! What's the world coming to when we're no longer safe in our streets?"

It was ironic that this was not the first time Yukiko had encountered a madman, but last time Akitada had been quicker and no harm had come to her. Would she blame him? Yukiko had always made the mistake of thinking him some superhuman hero. Alas, she was finding out he was merely an ordinary husband.

Another memory surfaced, recent yet seemingly from another time. He turned to Kosehira and said, "I've been ordered to return to my post at daybreak. The prime minister will not forgive another delay."

Kosehira frowned. "Inconvenient, but tragedies tend to be. Leave it to me. I'll make explanations and get you a delay of a day or two. He's not inhuman, you know."

Someone was pounding on the gate, and when Genba opened it. Superintendent Kobe walked in, followed by several police officers. Behind them came Toshikage.

Toshikage saw him and rushed past Kobe and the others. "Akiko? How is she? Is she safe?"

"Yes, Brother," said Akitada, feeling suddenly very tired. "She's with my wife."

Kobe said, "We saw the body," He searched Akitada's face. "Your work?"

"Mine and Genba's. He attacked my wife."

"Is she all right?"

"He was brutal. She lost the child, but I'm told she'll survive."

"Amida be thanked for that anyway. He must have lain in wait, watching for you. We checked your street several times today without luck."

They went to Akitada's study. where Akitada sent for Akiko and then poured wine. He hated the fact that there was nothing he could do but wait. Serving wine to his guests seemed wildly inadequate.

Akiko arrived quickly and was fussed over by her husband.

"I'm not hurt," she told him impatiently, "but two of our bearers were attacked. The others ran."

Toshikage glowered. "They can find other work. I'll not have cowards guarding you."

Kobe said, "It's not often that knife-wielding maniacs attack sedan chairs."

Toshikage snapped, "They ran and left my wife at the madman's mercy."

They had also left Yukiko who had lost their child and might still die, but Akitada knew that sedan bearers could hardly be expected to fight off attackers. He asked Akiko, "How is she?"

"Sleeping. Don't disturb her. She needs the rest." She turned to Toshikage. "I'm ready to go home." She brushed at the dust and stains on her clothes. "Akitada, remember not to upset her. I'll come back tomorrow."

Toshikage and Akiko departed. Kosehira heaved a sigh and said, "I'll have a word with her mother and then run along also. There's the matter of the prime minister to attend to."

Akitada muttered his thanks and saw him out.

When he returned to Kobe, the superintendent said, "I don't have much time either, considering the problems caused by the amnesty. And you have too much to deal with. I've been told about Hideyo murdering his mother. The report said he used an axe?"

With an effort, Akitada recalled the earlier horror: Maruko in the summer house, practically chopped to pieces. Perhaps he should be grateful that her son had left the axe behind when he went looking for him. He said, "Yes. It was the same axe he had been using to chop wood. I was surprised at the fury of those blows. He must really have hated her."

Kobe snorted. "Why look for a reason? He was mad."

Akitada frowned. "No, I think there was something else. Do you recall Minamoto Yukihiro's arrest the night of Tanaka's murder?"

"Yes. Some brawl in a low dive."

"It involved a raped child, you said. A boy."

"Yes, very nasty, but what's your point?"

"Yukihiro is one of those who prefer boys."

Kobe's eyes widened and he whistled. "You mean Hideyo? It would make sense. So that's how his mother got him to feed and shelter them all those years?"

"Yes. Her claim that Hideyo was Atsutada's son never convinced really anybody. She sold him to Yukihiro, and later she blackmailed him. Hideyo had his reasons for how he acted."

Kobe considered this and nodded. "Well, it's done now. No point in going after Yukihiro." He sighed. "But there's something else I wanted to tell you about.

We've brought in the pharmacist. He decided to talk. He says that old Nakai came to him for that medicine after he married his second wife. It seems he was anxious to satisfy her, but at his age he was unable to. The pharmacist warned him about the dangers of taking too much, and all went well for months. Old Nakai was hugely pleased. Then, quite suddenly, Nakai complained of a bellyache and nausea. The pharmacist warned him again. Shortly before Nakai's death, Mrs. Nakai came to purchase the medicine, saying her husband was too busy in the shop. The pharmacist gave her the same lecture on its dangers. And then Nakai died."

"So she poisoned him with the aphrodisiac?"

"Yes, but probably slowly at first. And he cooperated to please her."

"The boy told Nakai that Ujinobu had been selling Nakai's silks to other shops. It was after this that he got much worse."

"Ah, yes. Ujinobu has fled, but we shall get him. He'll testify against her. And so will your boy and the pharmacist. I'm on my way now to arrest the woman. And that settles matters nicely. I assume you'll return to your post as soon as your lady can travel?"

Akitada merely said, "I'm to leave shortly."

Kobe seemed quite pleased with what he probably saw as two solved cases and a return to normalcy, but Akitada knew the price had been too dear and he dreaded taking Yukiko back to Mikawa.

32

The Nun's Tale

He tried to visit Yukiko, was again told to be patient, and ate his evening rice alone and with little appetite. Afterward he spent some hours preparing for his journey back to Mikawa, then spread his bedding on the floor and lay down. His thoughts were with Yukiko. It was beginning to strike him as strange that he had been prevented from seeing her. His imagination painted all sorts of terrible things, and when the watchman in the street outside called the hour of the rat, he got up, threw his house robe over his undergown, and walked to Yukiko's pavilion.

The house was silent. The scent of flowers came from the garden as he passed along the gallery. He paused before Yukiko's door and listened. All was quiet inside also.

He opened the door and walked in softly on bare feet. A lamp flickered in the breeze caused by the opening of the door. By its light, he saw two women lying near each other in the center of the room and another in the far corner. The maid, he guessed. All seemed asleep.

He approached the bedding in the center. Quilts covered both sleepers, and both had long, dark hair. For a moment, he did not know which was Yukiko, but then he saw her hand, curled up next to her head. Her face was half hidden by her hair. He sat down quietly beside her and leaned forward to peer at her. She seemed to breathe well, and her color was normal.

It was the curled hand that nearly brought him to tears. It was childlike in its innocence. Just so his children always slept, and their defenselessness and trust in being protected always choked him up and filled him with fear for them. His heart melted for his young wife who had been brutalized before his eyes. Pain and shame filled him that he had been unable to protect her.

He stretched out his hand to caress her, but there was a gasp, and the figure beside her suddenly sat up to stare at him with frightened eyes. Yukiko's mother. He put a finger to his lips and smiled. After a moment, she lay back down.

He sat for a long time beside his young wife, but her mother did not go back to sleep, and eventually he felt guilty for disturbing her and rose to return to his own bed.

∞

The next morning brought both reassuring and disturbing news. He was sitting on his veranda, eating his morning gruel when he heard someone clearing her throat in the room behind him. He turned to look, and Yukiko's mother stood there.

He jumped up to ask anxiously, "Is she all right? Has something happened?"

Her mother gave him a smile. "No, Akitada. She is feeling better. Please, may we sit down and speak frankly?"

"Yes, of course."

Lady Hatsuko had taken time to dress and twist her hair into a bun at the back of her head. He remembered that it had been loose the night before and she had looked as young as her daughter. For that matter, he thought, Lady Hatsuko was probably his own age. Even in daylight, she still looked very attractive. But she had stopped smiling, and this made him uneasy.

She knelt and sat back on her heels, folding her hands inside their full sleeves on her lap, and sighed. "I wish this hadn't happened."

He was nervous about what was to come and said irritably, "Surely you don't think I wanted it."

Her eyes flew to his. "Oh, no. I have made you angry. I'm sorry."

Tears rose to her eyes, and he felt like a brute. "Forgive me. I didn't mean to snap at you. But please tell me what's wrong."

She looked down again. "I've never seen Yukiko like this. She's afraid. She is most afraid that you will take her back with you to Mikawa. Somehow she's convinced herself that something else will happen and that she will never be able to bring a healthy child into this world."

As her mother had suggested, Yukiko had never been given to such wild fancies about looming disasters. But Akitada was more troubled by something else. If she felt this way, she had decided that the danger to her and any children she might have came from him, or if not directly from him, then from the work he did. After a long pause, he begged, "Please tell me what to do. It doesn't sound as if my wife wishes to be my wife any longer."

She shook her head and cried, "Oh, no. You mustn't think that. Dear Akitada, please be patient with her. She's had a very hard time. Can you not allow her some time? Kosehira told me that you have orders to return to Mikawa. She cannot travel yet. Will you allow her to stay with us until she is well enough?"

He felt a great relief. "Yes, of course. I did not expect her to come with me so soon. But can she not remain in my house? It is her home now. Between us we can surely make her comfortable."

Lady Hatsuko looked doubtful. "Her mind is uneasy. I . . . I'm afraid she might get worse if she's by herself."

"Dear gods," Akitada muttered, trying to digest this. Yukiko had never struck him as being the type to become deranged. He recalled suddenly that Kosehira had feared that Arihito might harm himself. Apparently his mother-in-law thought her daughter's state of mind was due to the fact that she feared her husband. He felt his face set and said, "Then I must trust that you and Kosehira will look after my wife while I'm gone."

"Oh, I'm so glad you understand, Akitada. When she's better, she'll join you again. Or, since you have only one more year in Mikawa, you will be together when you return."

He looked at her bleakly, wondering if she knew how deeply she had hurt him. After a moment, she bowed, rose, and left his room. He remained, staring at the door, wondering how he would bear this abandonment.

∞

Kosehira arrived eventually. He looked distracted and asked first how his daughter was.

Akitada told him that Lady Hatsuko had thought she was doing well. He did not mention Yukiko's state of mind or that her mother wanted her to stay in the capital.

Kosehira brightened a little. He said, "I've just come from the prime minister. He sends his condolences and insists that you take time to make sure Yukiko is well enough to travel." He dabbed some perspiration from his brow. "I thought he might not believe me. The story sounded so outrageous."

"No doubt."

Kosehira frowned. "You should be relieved. It wasn't easy. The man has taken against you. He seems to think you create trouble wherever you go."

"He is right, I think."

"Come now! Don't let it get you down. There will be another child. Several, in fact if I know you and my daughter."

"Then you have misjudged either or both. It seems Yukiko doesn't want to return to Mikawa with me."

"What? I'll speak to her." He was already on his feet.

Akitada said sharply, "No! I will not have her coerced. She's been through a terrible ordeal. I've told your lady that I would be obliged if her parents looked after her until she is fully recovered."

Kosehira sank back down. "Well, if you're sure. It's probably for the best. When the time comes, we may bring her to you. I have a mind to visit your Mikawa." He smiled. "Yes, I think that will do very well. That Hatsuko, she always knows what's best. Remarkable woman! Wise!"

Akitada did not agree. All he knew was that this would be another obstacle separating him from his wife, one that pretty much destroyed any hopes he had had of making peace between them.

Kosehira left to see his wife and daughter, and Akitada wondered what he was to do with the time he had been allowed by the prime minister. He wanted to talk to Yukiko, but that had been discouraged. Perhaps he might try later. There was a great deal to be discussed if he was to leave her and return to his duties. Once again he considered that there was a great difference between a wife who had been an orphan without any family and a highborn young woman whose parents doted on her. But he had made up his mind that he would never again play the ogre in hopes of controlling Yukiko.

The memory of courting Tamako all those years ago came to him. She had lost her father and refused Akitada's offer of marriage as merely a gesture of charity. But in the end, he had won, perhaps because they had become very close during the years when her father had been Akitada's professor at the university. He wondered again about Masako's mother marrying Tanaka, the young guardsman. Had she had no better suitors from among the students who must have frequented her father's house? Perhaps she had been attracted to a soldier rather than an educated man.

As he sat in his own misery, he was tempted to think about other unhappy couples. The path of love and marriage was anything but smooth. Masako's mother had also lost her father. It was after this that she had married Tanaka even though he already had a very poor reputation. Perhaps she had been desperate.

And suddenly he felt a vague idea stirring in the back of his mind. It was far-fetched, but if it were true, then it would explain so many puzzling aspects of the case. Yes, it would explain even the biggest puzzle of all, the unwavering insistence of Masako's mother that her father had not killed Prince Atsutada.

He would get to the bottom of this once and for all, and afterward he would speak to his wife and then return to Mikawa. Perhaps, if he had guessed correctly, he would not have to remember this trip as his complete failure at both his marriage and his work.

∞

The Koryu temple was as peaceful among its towering pines as he remembered from his last visit. He hoped he would not be turned away this time. A different gate-keeper nun admitted him, giving him a cheerful smile. He took this as a good omen. As last time, he was taken to the abbess, and again he asked to speak to Nyodai.

But this time the abbess shook her head firmly. "I told you, my lord, that I would not let you trouble her again. She was very upset last time. She is in my charge and I shall protect her."

"For all that she is a nun now, she is still a mother. From what she told me during my last visit, she cares very deeply for her daughter. Her love for her child seemed to me to outweigh everything else. It is on behalf of her daughter's happiness that I am here."

The abbess drew herself up and regarded him coldly. "Nyodai's life is no longer that of the world. Her first love is not for her daughter but for Buddha."

Akitada said, "Then she has changed profoundly in the meantime."

The abbess compressed her lips.

"I insist that you allow me to speak to her. I believe that she will not be able to give her full devotion to Buddha until she gives this final gift of a mother's love to her daughter. She has a secret that weighs heavily on her mind."

"If you refer to her former husband's murder of Prince Atsutada, then you have asked her that question and she has answered it. I see no point in upsetting her again."

"This has nothing to do with the murder and everything to do with her daughter's father."

The abbess opened her mouth to object, then closed it again. She suddenly looked thoughtful. "I see," she said after a moment. "I hope you know what you're talking about." She rang a small bell. When a nun appeared, she sent her for Nyodai.

They sat together in silence. Akitada felt great admiration for the abbess who had understood his purpose but did not ask questions. When Nyodai entered the room, the abbess surprised him again. She rose and said, "Nyodai, Lord Sugawara has another question. I hope you find it in your heart to answer him. I shall leave you in privacy." And with that, she walked out of the room, closing the door behind her.

Nyodai's face was expressionless. She looked older, frailer than last time. She knelt and sat on her heels, her head bowed, her hands moving the beads of her rosary in her lap.

"Forgive me for troubling you again, Mrs. Mori," Akitada said. If he had hoped to get a reaction, nothing happened, though the beads seemed to move more quickly. "I address you as Mrs. Mori because I believe that you have yet to put away the past. Until you do that you cannot hope to find the salvation you seek here."

The beads stopped moving, but still she said nothing. Akitada thought her a perfect image of misery and inner pain. What had made her keep her secret all those years when doing so had been agonizing?

After waiting for some response that did not come, he said, "You told me several times that Masako's father was a good man and that he was innocent of murdering the prince. I didn't believe you. Everything pointed to Tanaka being the killer. And yet you insisted. I'm here today because I have realized that you told the truth."

The hands holding the prayer beads started shaking and the beads clicked together. Her head sank a little lower.

"It's time for the rest of the truth, Mrs. Mori, the whole truth. You will finally be rid of the great burden and Masako can be happy."

Tears fell on the trembling hands, but still she did not speak.

"You told the truth because Tanaka was not Masako's father. Am I right?"

She said nothing.

"I think you fell in love with a young man who used to come to your father's house. You became lovers and you conceived a child. But the smallpox epidemic struck, and your father became ill. You tended to your father, and then your lover also contracted the disease. When first your father and then your lover died, you were desperate and accepted Tanaka's offer of marriage. Masako was born and raised as Tanaka's daughter. Tell me, did Tanaka know she was not his?"

She raised her face. It was wet with tears. "He guessed. I denied it, but he beat me anyway. He beat me and he raped me. I thought the child inside me would die, so I swore she was his."

Akitada nodded. "I thought so. You must have suffered a great deal with that man. Why did you stay?"

"He was good to the child, and we had no place to go and no money."

"Then he finally believed she was his?"

"Yes. He was proud of her."

"Who is her father?"

She cried, "I cannot tell you. I will never tell. I'd rather die than tell." Her hands clenched around the beads.

He believed her. With a sigh, he said, "You needn't break your word. I think I know. And if I can manage it, I shall try to make your daughter happy. Perhaps then you, too, may find your peace here. Or perhaps you may find it with that good man who loves you."

He made her a bow, perhaps a little lower than was warranted by her rank, but he felt the utmost admiration for this woman who had suffered so much for so long and so silently.

He rose to call the abbess back. She came in, gave him a searching look, and then went to put her arm around the weeping nun.

"I think," said Akitada, "that all will be well now. In time, Mrs. Mori will tell you herself. The secret is hers. Thank you for your help." He bowed again and left.

33

The Otomo Dragon

It was still daytime when Akitada reached the Otomo mansion. The sun was cruel to the old place, showing its ruinous condition too harshly. He felt sorry for the old woman inside. Clearly she did not have the funds to maintain her ancestral home. The old trees at least were a healthy green and hid some of the worst parts of the compound. He knocked, and like last time, the gate creaked open after a long wait. The same old man stood there, blinking up at him as if his old eyes, like the house, could no longer bear the bright sunlight.

Akitada knew better than to make much conversation. He announced his name in a loud voice and stated

343

his wish to speak to Lady Otomo. The old man said nothing, but he turned to shuffle off toward the main house. As before, Akitada had to wait a long time. Finally the old servant reappeared. Instead of climbing down the stairs from the veranda, he coughed to catch the visitor's attention and waved him up.

The walk through the dim corridor with the Otomo armory ended again at Lady Otomo's door. The servant's lantern caused the gilded carvings to writhe like a pit of snakes. Akitada blinked and saw they were not snakes but two intertwined dragons. Dragons were the emblem of emperors, and the Otomo were descended from an early ruler. The past was more significant to them than the present.

The door stood partially open and the old man simply waved at it before turning around with an audible moan of pain. He was well past the age when he should be working. Akitada thanked him, feeling obscurely guilty for having caused him pain.

He pushed open the dragon door. The room was unchanged in its lack of light. If there were doors to the outside, they remained shuttered. The same oil lamp flickered, but the room appeared to be empty.

Akitada stepped in and called out, "Lady Otomo?"

There was a rustling from the curtained dais, and then the cracked voice commanded, "Approach!"

Akitada walked across the room, glancing into the dark corners. He saw no one. "Are you alone, Lady Otomo?"

"No. It seems you are here. What do you want this time?"

She had not improved her manners. It did not matter. He was beginning to have a perverse admiration for her stubborn attachment to a pride that had long since become pointless. Seating himself on the dais beside her curtained enclosure, he said, "I'm glad Masako isn't here. What I have to ask you might prove embarrassing."

"Not to me or her. There's nothing that can embarrass me, and Masako is made of sterner stuff than you realize."

Akitada chuckled. "I've had some suspicions. Did you take her into your confidence?"

There was a brief silence. "What are you talking about? Don't speak in riddles. It gets tedious at my age."

"Masako is your granddaughter, isn't she?"

He heard a choking sound from behind the faded silk curtains and rose, afraid that he had shocked her too cruelly. "Forgive me," he said and pulled the curtain aside.

He saw a tiny, shrunken figure inside the threadbare curtains. It did not match the strong, sharp voice that now shrieked, "How dare you! Get out! Get out! Yukio! Kintaro! Help!"

Her face was as shriveled as a dried fruit and the hands she waved at him mere claws. He thought she must be at least eighty years old, though the thin strands of hair that barely covered her skull were as black as in her youth. The hair was also long and seemed to gain in volume. He realized she had dyed and augmented it in a desperate effort to preserve her youth.

No one came. Perhaps it was not surprising, given the fact that Kintaro, presumably the servant who had admitted him, was deaf, and Yukio, the maid who had been here on his last visit, was likely out shopping or else cooking in a distant kitchen. Two servants were all the grand Lady Otomo could afford, and they were clearly not up to looking after her.

"Please listen to me!" Akitada said firmly and sat down again near her.

The old woman glowered but she stopped calling for help.

"As I said, I believe Masako is your granddaughter, your late son's child. Have you always known that she was his child?"

Her face crumpled, and tears filled her eyes. "No, but Tabito told me about her mother before he died."

"Tabito?"

That made her angry. "Tabito! Tabito, my son! He was my baby. The others died before him, but Tabito lived. He was strong and he was beautiful. He was the best of my children. He was kind and handsome and very intelligent. He was my hope! But they killed him! Between them, they seduced him and then they killed him!" Her voice had risen until she screamed the last sentence at him.

"I don't understand. Who killed him? I thought he died of smallpox."

"Don't be stupid! They gave the disease to Tabito. He kept going there for lessons in Chinese literature because she was there and had bewitched him. My son was only nineteen, and one day, he came home to me with the disease and he died in my arms. Now do you understand?"

Akitada sighed. He recalled his own son's death from the same disease and how Tamako had blamed him for his death. Lady Otomo had hated Masako's mother and grandfather. "I thought it was something like this," he said quietly. "Did you know that there would be a child?"

"No. She came to me later. She had a small child with her and begged me for help. I told her what I thought of her and father. I told her I would have them both arrested if she claimed the child was Tabito's. She went away."

"Ah! But later you changed your mind?"

"Yes. About the child. Not about the mother."

Akitada thought that the threat of the police had frightened Masako's mother enough not to reveal her daughter's parentage. Having lived through Tanaka's arrest and trial, she would have been terrified of them. When Mori offered her marriage and adopted Masako, she must have been immensely relieved. But apparently she had not even told Mori about the Otomo connection, perhaps to protect him and the peaceful life they had found with him. But her life had not been completely peaceful. In the end she had sought refuge from her memories in the Koryu temple.

"Why did you change your mind?" he asked the old woman curiously.

She moved impatiently. "I'm old. You get fanciful when you're old. I talk to my son every day. One day he asked me to look after his child. So I had her found and brought her here."

"And do you now believe she is your granddaughter?"

The old face smoothed as grief and anger left it. She almost smiled. "She is my granddaughter. She's like Tabito. She's his daughter. I don't need her mother's word for that. I can see it every time I look at her and hear it every time she speaks to me."

"Does she know?"

Again the impatient gesture. "No. If she knew, she would expect to be treated like my heiress and that would change everything." She pointed a finger at him. "I forbid you to tell her, or anyone."

He almost smiled. "I think you misjudge Masako. She has too much character for that. After all, she turned down an offer of marriage from Fujiwara Arihito who has a brilliant career ahead of him."

"Pah! A Fujiwara! That is nothing."

"Since she loves him, her only reason was that his father objected. Masako doesn't need wealth and rank." He paused, then added, "I think she must be very fond of you to come here every day."

She bristled. "What do you mean?"

"This house is a ruin and you have a sharp tongue. Why would a pretty young woman like Masako want to spend her days here unless she has a fondness for you."

To his surprise, her face softened again and she cackled. "A sharp tongue, you say? You're not much better, Sugawara. You think she's fond of me?" She leaned forward, "Do you really believe she's fond of me?"

Akitada nodded and smiled. "No doubt about it. It occurs to me that a marriage between your granddaughter and Kosehira's heir might be a very good thing. Two great families would be united."

She glared, "I cannot abide the Fujiwara. Newcomers, all of them. Greedy and soft! Not like the Otomo."

"Kosehira is a very good administrator. He loves his family as much as you love yours. For that matter, my family suffered from the rise of the Fujiwara for a very long time, but Kosehira has been my friend. I think a connection with the ruling family could mean the Otomo will rise again."

She stared at him. He could almost see the thoughts working in the way her features became first sly, then thoughtful, and finally uncertain.

He said quickly, before she could come up with another objection, "If Masako and Arihito have children together, the Otomo line will continue. No doubt you could adopt one of their sons, and this would resurrect the family name. And Tabito would live on in his grandchildren."

A short while later, Akitada walked homeward, smiling to himself and feeling almost happy.

34

The Mirror of the Heart

Whatever happiness lay in store for Arihito and Masako, or for old Lady Otomo, nothing of the sort awaited Akitada. As soon as he reached his home, he went to see Yukiko. His heart misgave him because he felt so guilty for what had happened to her. His young wife suffered doubly, both physically from the attack by Hideyo, and from her grief over having lost another child. He hoped he was bringing her some news that would cheer her.

He paused before her door and cleared his throat. After a moment, Lady Hatsuko opened the door and peered out. He said in a low voice, "If she's awake, I'd like to see my wife."

Lady Hatsuko hesitated, then opened the door wider. Turning toward her daughter, she said brightly, "I'll

351

return with some nourishing soup, my dear. You must eat. And here is Akitada to keep you company."

Yukiko cried, "Don't go. I'm not hungry."

Lady Hatsuko, that wise and kind lady, winked at Akitada and said, "I won't take long. You two have a nice chat." And then she slipped past Akitada and hurried away.

Akitada entered slowly and closed the door behind him. Approaching the bedding where Yukiko reclined against an armrest, he gave her a tentative smile and said, "How are you, my love?"

"There's no need for you to entertain me. I'm doing well enough," she muttered, turning her head away.

He sat down beside her and studied her face. She was very pale, her eyes red from weeping and set in dark circles. It was painful to see her this way. He reached for her hand. She withdrew it.

"You're angry with me. I don't blame you. I should have taken better care of you. I hope you'll forgive me."

She looked at him. "I used to love that about you, your passion for justice. But I see your passion does not extend to your family or the unborn."

"That's untrue, Yukiko. I care for you and my children more than for myself. Come, my love, let's not quarrel. I must soon leave to return to my post. Perhaps even tomorrow. Do you wish me to take your anger with me?"

She did not change her expression. He saw only coldness in her face. It seemed odd to him that such a young face, one that had not quite lost its childlike softness, could be so unforgiving. She said, "You care nothing for the child I lost. You cared little for the child I lost earlier. But I shall never forget. I tell you now: I shall not have any more children, for I cannot bear losing them."

Akitada blinked. It sounded as though she refused future marital relations with him. Perhaps she meant to divorce him. He said, "Yukiko, you're wrong. I care. I care about your pain. Don't say such things. Don't think them."

"Well, have you shed any tears for the little son who will never be?"

Son? The child had been a boy?

He said, "I only just found out a few days ago that you were with child. I haven't really had time to think about it much. How long have you known without telling me? But never mind that now. There can be other children. Living children. Not every conception ends in the premature death of the child."

She sat up, her eyes flashing, "There! I knew it. You don't care. You think there will be many more children, so why grieve over this one? You think a wife can be made to bear child after child, and if she's lucky and survives all those births, there will be plenty of heirs to your name even if half of them die. Well, Akitada, there won't be any more children. At least, I won't give them to you. So, you'd better look for another wife."

He sat stunned and said nothing. A part of him wanted to rush from the room. Another part wanted to shake her, to remind her of the joy they had shared. But he knew he must not aggravate her further. It would make her ill. If he could stay on in the capital, it might perhaps be possible to reassure her and to court her anew, though he would need patience he did not have. He bowed his head. "Yukiko, your words grieve me. I don't deserve them. How can I go on loving you if this is the loveless life you're asking me to lead?"

He got no answer. Her face was cold and set. He waited, but the silence stretched. In the end he sighed. "Well, never mind that now. Time will heal this grief. I came to bring you some good news."

"There is no good news. Please leave."

"Yukiko, I've found a way for Arehito and Masako to marry. You see, she's not the assassin's daughter after all."

She finally looked interested, and he poured out his story of Masako's true parentage and of Lady Otomo relenting about an Otomo marrying a Fujiwara. He expected a smile at that point, but Yukiko's face remained set.

When he was done, she just nodded, said, "Good," and turned her head away again.

Akitada got up quietly and left.

∞

He went to tell Kosehira next. Kosehira at least was amused and happy. He embraced Akitada and sent for Arihito.

"Arihito, my son," he greeted the young man when he came in, "we have good news. Prepare to become a married man!"

Arihito was taken aback by this and looked uncertainly from his father to Akitada and back. "I don't wish to take a wife, Father," he said. "At least not now. So forget whatever arrangements you've made."

Koschira laughed out loud and punched Akitada's arm. "He has no idea! Oh, this will be wonderful! Tell him."

Akitada wished he could recapture his smile at this turn of events, but he only managed to inform Arihito in a reasonable steady voice that there was no longer any obstacle to his marriage to Masako. Arihito's eyes grew wider and wider the further he got into his account of Lady Otomo's secret, and in the end he looked stunned.

"But did Masako know?" he asked.

"No. The old woman didn't want her to become greedy."

Arihito said angrily, "She doesn't know Masako very well."

Koschira laughed again. "Well, what do you say, son? Can we make plans for a wedding?"

Finally a slow smile appeared on Arihito's face. "If she agrees. Will you come with me, Father? She insists on your approval."

"I look forward to it," said Koschira and embraced his son.

It was good to see them happy and full of plans, but after a while, Akitada interrupted to excuse himself.

"I must get ready for my journey," he explained.

"Oh." Koschira apologized. "You brought such very good news, I forgot."

"Please look after Yukiko for me. I don't like leaving her in her present state, but I know she'll be in good hands. Genba and Mrs. Kuruda will look after her and the house, but if you think more servants are needed—"

"I have more than enough for both houses. They've been getting lazy."

Akitada nodded. It was easier than arguing. "I'd like to keep Yukiko's maid in Mikawa for my daughter, but Yukiko may wish to hire someone else."

"The woman who is with her now was her nurse. She cannot do better than that."

"You leave me nothing else to fret about," Akitada said with a nod.

∞

His next visit was to Kobe's office to tell him about Masako's parentage and to say goodbye.

Kobe was astonished to hear about old Lady Otomo. "I thought she was dead," he said. "But come to think of it, it was the year of the epidemic that the Tanaka woman's father died and she married Tanaka. To tell the truth, her father may have been an educated man but he was also a drunkard. No wonder he paid no attention to what his daughter got up to with his students."

"One student only," Akitada said mildly. "You are being very unfair to Masako's mother. And I would have thought you more of a romantic than to make such suggestions."

Kobe laughed. "It's my work that makes me suspicious. But I can't wait to tell Sachi. She'll love it." He paused. "So you're headed back to Mikawa?"

"Yes."

"You don't look very happy about it. No doubt, you will have been sorely missed. You'll have all sorts of mayhem waiting for you to straighten it out."

Akitada managed a smile. "I'm leaving Yukiko behind to give her time to recover. You will keep an eye on my people, won't you?"

"Of course!"

∞

When Akitada eventually returned home from having also made his farewells to Nakatoshi and Kaneie, he found Mr. Mori waiting for him.

The little clerk was smiling so widely that his face must hurt. Akitada found himself smiling back. "Mr. Mori," he said, "what a nice surprise! I'm being called back to my post and had no time to pay all my visits. You have saved me from regrets."

Mr. Mori chuckled. "As you're pressed for time, sir, I thought I'd just pay my respects and assure you of my deepest gratitude. You've made us all very happy." He paused, then said again, "So very happy!"

"I'm glad to hear it. Did you know of Masako's parentage?"

"I did, or rather, I knew something like it. My wife told me that she'd fallen in love with a student and of his death. She's suffered so much. As it was her secret, I did not mention it to anyone. But I can tell you now when Lady Otomo called at my house and demanded to see Masako but not her mother, I thought something was up. It seemed peculiar that a great lady like that should have heard of our Masako and taken such a dislike to her mother."

"What happened?" Akitada said, interested in spite of himself.

"When I offered to send for my wife, her ladyship got quite angry. No, she wanted to see the girl and no one else. Well, Masako came, and I could see Lady Otomo was very impressed. Of course, Masako is the most charming girl." He smiled with fatherly pride. "Anyway, Lady Otomo told her she needed a companion and would Masako come live with her. The money she offered was negligible, but I thought it might be a great thing for Masako to live in the Otomo house. And my wife thought so too when I told her."

"Masako's mother approved?"

"Oh, yes. She was happy about it." His face fell. "It was afterward that she left me for the nunnery. She said with Masako settled she was free at last."

"I'm sorry," said Akitada, thinking of the pain that must have caused this kind and generous man. And trying not to think of his own pain.

Mori smiled a little sadly. "I couldn't very well deny her that, could I?"

Akitada thought of Yukiko, who apparently also insisted on being free of him. He said, "She may yet change her mind." And afraid to give Mori—or himself—false hopes, he added quickly, "Your daughter will still be in your life, and you'll have the joy of grandchildren."

Mori's smile widened again. "They are so good to me, Arihito and Masako. Now that Masako knows who her real father was, they could have forgotten about poor Mori, but they both came to tell me the good news. And they called me 'Father'." He dabbed away a tear and added, "And all this happiness is due to you, sir."

There was little else for Akitada to do except bid his wife farewell. That last meeting, however, a meeting that he had dreaded but that was of the utmost importance to him, almost did not happen.

Kosehira breezed in as Akitada finished packing some papers and documents and sat down. Akitada poured him some wine and said, "You see me finally on the point of taking up my duties again. Please convey my thanks to the prime minister for his forbearance."

"Naturally. Well, Brother, you must write and I'll write to you. And perhaps we'll bring Yukiko to you after she's had a rest."

"Thank you."

"I brought the carriage to take her back with me. Hatsuko is helping her get ready."

Shocked, Akitada started to his feet. "She is leaving now?" he asked. "I thought . . . I haven't discussed things with Yukiko yet."

Kosehira looked surprised. "She told me you had spoken with her and that she wanted to come with us today. You are bound to leave at dawn, and I think she doesn't feel safe alone in the house. She's still not at all well."

Akitada, halfway to the door, turned. "Yes, yes, I see that, though . . . I just hadn't realized. I suppose I'd better see her off then, rather than the other way around." He hurried out.

But Yukiko was no longer in her pavilion. The only thing of hers that remained was the stained silk train with the swallows of good omen that Akitada had ordered from Nakai's. He turned and ran to the courtyard. There he saw the carriage, the oxen already in place, their driver ready with his whip. He shouted, "Wait!"

Yukiko was leaving him without a word of farewell. The magnitude of her resentment struck him an almost physical blow. It also made him very angry. Four years of marriage meant nothing to her in her rush to get away from him.

Lady Hatsuko raised the reed curtain and peered out at him from the carriage. "Did we forget something?" she asked cheerfully.

"Yes," he ground out. "My wife forgot her goodbyes."

His mother-in-law was taken aback and turned inside to ask. Akitada walked around to the other side and lifted the curtain. Yukiko looked back at him, her face pale and cold. Indifference, he thought, as cold as the fading moon at dawn.

"I thought you understood," she said in a faint voice. "I want to go home."

She did not look well. Perhaps she was truly ailing. Akitada asked, "Are you still in pain? Has the doctor been consulted and has he given his approval for you to be moved?"

Lady Hatsuko said, "She is doing well, Akitada. The doctor said she just needs rest and quiet. Do not worry. She will be looked after."

Akitada searched his wife's eyes. There was nothing there, neither sadness nor regret. They called the face the mirror of the heart. Yukiko's face was blank.

"Forgive me," he said sadly. "I would have done anything to prevent what has happened."

She nodded.

"Will you write?"

She nodded again.

He thought they both knew that nothing would ever be the same again. The fact that he had needed to ask the question proved that.

Akitada stepped away. The driver snapped his whip and the carriage departed. He stood looking after them until they disappeared through the gate.

"Well," Kosehira said, coming up beside him and startling him. "There they go and I must leave also. I wish you a safe journey tomorrow. You'll be back here before too long."

Akitada nodded. They embraced briefly, and Kosehira walked away. Genba closed the gate after him and came to join Akitada.

"You'll be alone in the house tonight," he said, giving his master an anxious look. "If you'd care to share our evening rice, Ohiro and I would be honored."

Akitada tore his thoughts from what had happened. The invitation was a kindness offered by a friend who felt his pain. Putting a hand on Genba's shoulder, he said, "Thank you and your wife, but I suddenly have a great longing to see the children again and Tora and Saburo. I think I'll leave today. Get the horses ready while I pack what I need."

Genba squinted at the sky. The sun was setting. "It's late," said doubtfully.

"It's summer and the days are long. I can easily make Otsu before night." Otsu, he thought, the town where he had fallen in love with Yukiko. Otsu, the place of meeting and parting. "I have nothing now to hold me here."

Historical Note

The time of this novel is 1033. Akitada is still governor of Mikawa but on a visit to the capital.

In the eleventh century, a central government in Heian-kyo (Kyoto) ruled Japan under a hereditary emperor and the court aristocracy. Power rested primarily in the hands of one branch of the large Fujiwara family, though some of the old clans, frequently descended from earlier emperors, persisted. But it was Fujiwara nobles who controlled the emperors via their marriage politics and they controlled the country by placing their relatives and friends in administrative posts.

Among such posts were those of the provincial governors. It had long been considered important to have provinces headed by court-appointed governors and controlled by court-appointed police chiefs. All other administrative positions in a province were filled either by the governor's own staff or by local men. Governors were appointed for four years and were expected to keep the peace and collect taxes to send to the central government. The provincial administration was to some extent a miniature of the central government. Apart from the all-important duty of collecting and transmitting tax goods, governors were expected to provide census information, maintain roads, post stations, temples and shrines, and deal with disasters ranging from droughts to epidemics. At the end of each tenure, a governor had to present a discharge accounting to prove that he left the provincial treasury and granaries in as good a condition as when he had found them. This had become necessary since governors traditionally used such appointments to enrich themselves.

While governors could bring their families and household staff with them, this was not only expensive and possibly dangerous, but their womenfolk resisted being banished to a dull provincial life among the illiterate and unwashed when the capital had so much more to offer. Thus, most governors served far from their loved ones.

In a noble family, marriage customs and the position of women depended on circumstances. Wealthy noblemen practiced polygamy while ordinary men generally had only one wife. The reason for having multiple wives was probably the high mortality of women and children; if a man could afford it, he took more than one wife to assure the survival of his family. The bonds of matrimony were not by any means particularly sacred. A husband could divorce a wife by simply telling her so. In addition to his original spouse, he could have several secondary spouses, and he could also keep concubines and establish lovers in separate dwellings. As a rule, the first marriage was carefully planned by both families to enhance their careers. The first wife therefore came from an influential family and took the rank of principal spouse. Subsequent wives might be chosen for any number of reasons, including love or the likelihood that she could produce strong children. A noble wife could divorce her husband, or she could leave him, but since she would lose her children, such cases were rare. She retained ownership of property that was hers by inheritance, though the marriage contract might tie this to her subsequent children. Both husbands and wives had affairs, though for wives this was more difficult since they spent their time in the women's quarters in the back of a large compound of buildings. Highborn women, however, often served as ladies-in-waiting at the imperial palace where anything might happen.

A newly-wed couple might live in several places. Some bridegrooms moved in with the bride's family, some brought the bride home to their own family home, or indeed to any other the husband might choose. Occasionally, a husband remained in his family compound and merely visited his wife at her father's house. Both families, the bride's and the groom's, hoped for advantages in social standing, rank, and income from the union. Secondary wives generally lived separate from the husband's main residence. Prince Genji's arrangements for his wives in Lady Murasaki's *Genji* apparently were unique.

The typical noble mansion in the capital would have been located in the north-eastern sector of the city. Heian-kyo, like preceding Japanese capitals, was laid out in a grid pattern with the imperial city, the *Daidairi*, occupying the northernmost center section. The *Daidairi* was the government center and contained not only the palaces of the emperor and crown prince but also all the ministries, storehouses, imperial guard barracks, and official reception halls. It was enclosed by walls and had numerous gates to surrounding streets. From its most important gate, the Vermillion Sparrow Gate, the wide Suzaku Avenue led straight south to Rashomon, the Rampart Gate, which was the main entrance to the capital.

The layout of a noble family's compound depended on whether they were wealthy or had come down in the world, but generally it also observed the lucky north-south orientation and was fenced or walled with one or more roofed gates, a central hall, and a number of separate wings or pavilions connected to the main house by galleries. The north wing or pavilion was usually the residence of the principal wife. Separate from the dwelling were service buildings like stables, store houses, kitchens, and quarters for retainers and servants. A garden was always included and often contained a small lake, footpaths, and small brooks.

The practice of healing in Heian Japan was shockingly unscientific by modern Western standards and was based on practices imported from China. In 982, Tamba Yasuyori compiled the *Ishinpo* ("Prescriptions from the Heart of Medicine"). It consists of quotations from Chinese texts and lists remedies that startle modern readers. Treatments tended to be based on herbal medicines and required specialized knowledge. This to some extent explains why pharmacists were treated with great respect in Japan. Both medically trained men and pharmacists could serve as coroners in legal situations. The more learned men were taught at the Imperial University and were most likely to treat the upper classes. For the rest of the population, there were monks, itinerant healers, peddlers, masseurs and acupuncturists. Frequently masseurs combined the skill of manipulating the body with acupuncture (the use of silver needles) and moxibustion (the burning of herbal medicines on the skin). Most widespread among all classes was healing by exorcism, a ritual commonly performed by a Shinto priest and a female medium.

Shinto is the native religion of Japan. Buddhism came to the country from China. Both coexisted peacefully, sometimes even sharing the same compounds. Shinto was the faith of the emperor and affected agriculture, hence survival. Buddhism was the overwhelming choice of the nobility who took enormous pleasure in its pomp and circumstance. Shinto abhorred death and birth as polluting; Buddhism invariably handled funerals and assisted with prayers at times of births and deaths. Neither was involved in marriages, which were family affairs.

As for law enforcement, this was firmly in the hands of a police force that investigated, arrested, interrogated (often with some torture), tried, and punished the guilty. Trials were conducted by judges and punishment was either prison or exile with hard labor. Small villages and some wards in a city additionally had wardens to keep the peace. The periodic amnesties by the emperors were notorious and guaranteed that the capital or countryside were never without crime. The rationale behind such amnesties was the belief that showing mercy to criminals would please the Buddha and the gods who would respond by lifting some affliction to an imperial person or to the country at large during epidemics and droughts.

About the Author

I. J. Parker was born and educated in Europe and turned to mystery writing after an academic career in the U.S. She has published her Akitada stories in *Alfred Hitchcock's Mystery Magazine,* winning the Shamus award in 2000. Several stories have also appeared in collections, such as *Fifty Years of Crime and Suspense* and *Shaken.* The award-winning "Akitada's First Case" is available as a podcast. Many of the stories have been collected in *Akitada and the Way of Justice.*

The Akitada series of crime novels features the same protagonist, an eleventh century Japanese nobleman/detective. *The Assassin's Daughter* is number fifteen. The books are available on Kindle, in print and in audio format, and have been translated into twelve languages.

Books by I. J. Parker

The Akitada series in chronological order
The Dragon Scroll
Rashomon Gate
Black Arrow
Island of Exiles
The Hell Screen
The Convict's Sword
The Masuda Affair
The Fires of the Gods
Death on an Autumn River
The Emperor's Woman
Death of a Doll Maker
The Crane Pavilion
The Old Men of Omi
The Shrine Virgin
The Assassin's Daughter

The collection of stories
Akitada and the Way of Justice

Other Historical Novels
The HOLLOW REED saga:
Dream of a Spring Night
Dust before the Wind
The Sword Master

The Left-Handed God

Please visit I.J.Parker's web site at www.ijparker.com
You may contact her via e-mail from her web site.
The novels can also be ordered in electronic versions.
Please do post Amazon reviews. They help sell books
and keep Akitada novels coming.

Thank you for your support.